★

"They're going to get the body," a man said.

The small boat held a few crew members. From what I could see, they all wore white.

"What's wrong? You need to get inside," a redheaded man called. He leaned toward me, grabbing my arms before I hit the floor.

"Why do I need to get inside?" I wanted to ask, but all that came from my mouth was a jumble of sounds made by the knocking of my teeth against each other. I trembled so hard from fear that I couldn't get my balance to stand straight.

"You need to get where it's warmer," the second man helping me said. They gripped my arms, walking me toward the elevators.

"No!" I got in the redhead's face. "I need to see him!" Both men backed down, possibly thinking I was a maniac.

I dashed toward the rail. People let me through.

Some men from the rescue boat knelt on the ice, checking the person lying on it. Was that person alive? I wanted to be down there to know for myself.

★

Previously published Worldwide Mystery title by
JUNE SHAW

RELATIVE DANGER

JUNE SHAW

DEADLY

REUNION

W⊕RLDWIDE®

TORONTO • NEW YORK • LONDON
AMSTERDAM • PARIS • SYDNEY • HAMBURG
STOCKHOLM • ATHENS • TOKYO • MILAN
MADRID • WARSAW • BUDAPEST • AUCKLAND

Recycling programs
for this product may
not exist in your area.

DEADLY REUNION

A Worldwide Mystery/November 2013

First published by Five Star Publishing.

ISBN-13: 978-0-373-26871-9

Copyright © 2011 by June Shaw

Printed in U.S.A.

Acknowledgments

My friends, family, and other loved ones, I can't thank you enough for giving me your unending support. Without your pleasure at seeing my written babies come to life, I would not feel such fulfillment by creating them.

Extra love and prayers for special loved ones who moved into your next lives after I started writing this book.

I would never have learned as much about writing novels without the outstanding members of SOLA (New Orleans chapter of Romance Writers of America), Guppies, Sisters-in-Crime, and Mystery Writers of America. My Red Hat group is a hoot and also great support.

Alice Duncan has been fantastic for championing and editing my work. Rosalind Greenberg and Tiffany Schofield can't be beat for helping their authors.

I especially thank the Thibodaux High School class of 19 (cough). Excuse me. During our class reunions, I've wondered what kind of lives all of you led since we graduated. I knew one day I'd write a novel about a reunion. Thank you all for being my friends.

Which leads me to say thanks so much to crewmembers and staff of the cruises I had to take to carry out my extensive research for this book. I won't mention names or cruise lines, but I have your names written on paper and in my heart. You were so generous with answers to so many questions I asked.

Any mistakes made or liberties taken about cruises are my own. Many thanks also to those of you who sent champagne to our staterooms. Loved it!

A huge thank-you goes out to my readers. I cannot tell you how much I appreciate you. I love to hear from you and hope you will contact me. You can reach me at www.juneshaw.com.

Thanks so much.

ONE

I STEPPED ONTO the cold Lido Deck.

"I see you got old and lost your figure," my former high school classmate said.

What a way to start a class reunion.

"I flew to Anchorage to hear insults?" I said.

"You know I was kidding, Cealie. Come here." Sue Ingstrom threw out her arms.

"And you—" I said, ready to give a sassy retort to this woman I hadn't seen in decades "—are gorgeous." To my dismay, she did look great. Her slinky dress revealed perky breasts thrust over a slim waist. Her hips were slender and legs shapely, accentuated by spiky heels. Her neck and face seemed so tight, my lipstick could bounce off them.

"I'm thrilled that you could join us." She grabbed me in a hug, her rigid breasts surely indenting mine. "You know I was joking, right?"

"I did put on a few pounds," I admitted. "And these wrinkles—"

"Can be taken away by a good plastic surgeon."

That was supposed to make me feel better? I shivered from the chilly air and imagined the ship rocking, although we couldn't leave shore until we completed this safety drill. "Have you seen the others? This is my first reunion." I glanced at the gathering crowd, wondering if I would recognize people I'd known so well, whose main concerns back then had been zits, passing exams, or next week's boyfriend. Now many of us were grandparents.

"I saw everybody, especially Miss Popular. She sure has problems."

"That's what convinced me to come. And getting to visit my son and his family. They live in Skagway. I can't wait to see them and the old gang."

"Not many of them showed up."

"Please close in spaces to let others move in," a petite female crew member said through a megaphone as I processed my disappointment about getting to see only a few friends. But I couldn't complain. I'd moved out of state and easily found excuses for not attending reunions. "We have passengers coming up from the main deck. Be careful. And make sure you have your life jacket," the crew member yelled.

Sue squeezed against me alongside the outdoor pool. Unable to make my wrinkles suddenly disappear, I sucked in my stomach, drew up my five-foot, two-inch frame, and still remained half a foot shorter than my striking classmate.

Scores of passengers wore their life jackets, while many of us gripped ours. What was it that enticed so many people to board ships when the journeys always began with crew members letting us know our ship might sink? Did we enjoy the possibility of flirting with death? Did we think that if faced with that terror, we could win?

Voices carried. Stomping feet echoed from outdoor steps.

I peered around. Would classmates still know me? What were they doing with their lives?

I stared at women. One had the round face and tiny eyes of someone I'd known in school. She didn't return my smile. But a bride did.

"A bride," I said, stepping to the young woman in a strapless wedding gown. "Are you getting married?"

"We did this morning on the ship."

"Congratulations." I spied the young man in a tux behind her. "And congratulations to you."

"Thanks," they said in unison.

They answered my questions about the ceremony and themselves, and I turned to make sure Sue saw them. She was no longer around. Figuring she had located our friends, I squeezed through other passengers until I found her.

She was leaning toward a man in a hot-pink knit shirt who appeared fifteen years younger than we were, her breasts stabbing his chest. They shared sensual smiles.

His skin looked as firm as hers and his body as trim. But nature probably gave him his youthful appearance. He might have been her adopted son, but their flirty looks and body language told me they weren't related. I knew about Sue's earlier life but had not heard much since our graduation.

"I'm glad I found you," I told Sue and grabbed the young man's hand. "Hello, I'm Cealie Gunther. You two know each other?"

He flung her a lewd smile. "We just met."

"Sue is actually my aunt. I only call her Sue because we're the same age." I lowered my head to make sure the skin on my neck drooped and a slight double chin formed. If this guy thought she was a youngster, I'd make sure he knew better. I almost wished I'd left in my gray roots. Sue's highlights ran to the base of her dyed brown hair. Anticipating a reunion with high school friends, I'd made extra preparations and figured the other *girls* would, too. I'd had my hair dyed and styled, gotten a manicure and pedicure and relaxing massage. A shopping trip and study of our yearbook rounded out preparations.

"Aunt and niece the same age—cool," he said.

Cool. We'd used that word to describe everything.

"Did you come on this trip alone?" I asked, not deterring the guy from casting a lusting scan over my classmate's figure.

His wanting to make out with her would not be a good

thing. This was my Aunt Sue. But before that, she had been my Uncle Stu.

Uncle Stu became Aunt Sue two years after we finished high school. Friends and I thought he might wait to become a she, but his parents allowed the surgery.

I never found out how much of him had been altered.

"I came alone," the man wearing pink told me.

"Your wife's not with you?" I asked, but no one paid attention. Our crew member with the megaphone ordered us to put on our life jackets. She gave instructions for hooking up the straps.

Our new friend helped Sue with hers, laughing flirtatiously as his hands grazed her man-made breasts. She returned his smile and leaned into him, speaking softly.

Not soon enough, our instructions ended. We should return to our cabins to replace life jackets and be careful walking, especially holding up the straps.

"My cabin's aft. Nice meeting you two," the man in pink said. He winked at me. "Make sure you don't trip on that strap."

"Isn't he cute?" Sue asked the moment he evaporated into the crowd, heading to the rear.

"And young."

"Sometimes those are the best."

Conversing became difficult as we squeezed with scores of others into the smaller area near the elevators and stairwell.

"What deck are you on?" Sue asked.

"Pacific."

"Me, too."

"Great." I faked a grin and hoped we didn't have adjoining cabins.

"We'll meet all the others at dinner."

"Good. I'll take the stairs now."

"Me, too."

We walked one deck down the wide crowded stairwell and then headed for the starboard hall. Announcements blared from speakers, but the buzz of people walking and talking drowned out the message.

"My cabin's right there." Sue pointed a few doors down. "I'll see you later at dinner."

Nodding, I watched her go. A man in the group walking behind her looked familiar. No...it couldn't be Randy. No men from our class were invited on this trip. I was only imagining how other people from my class looked now.

In my stateroom I unpacked, wishing I'd brought more clothes made of wrinkly fabric. I always traveled lightly, especially since I'd shed my life of so many *things*. Things took up space and held people back. After my husband died, I found so many items stuffed into cabinets and closets, I decided to lighten my life and my house. I'd since then shucked the house. Now I travel. I might need to purchase a few items in the on-board shops, I saw, counting the tops and dresses I'd brought and coming up short.

I'd worn comfortable shoes, knit slacks, and a light sweater for my flight here, planning to change into a nicer outfit to meet school friends. But until I could buy more items, I decided to keep on what I wore. Sure, first impressions were important, especially since I was about to face women I'd befriended and sometimes competed with. But that was long ago. I had come way beyond that petty thinking, I told myself.

And then I envisioned Sue.

I grabbed my sexy skirt, the leather one that stopped inches above my knees. Yanking it on, I pulled on a fluffy sweater and exchanged my sensible shoes for chunky heeled boots.

In the mirror covering the closet door, I found a more youthful Cealie. I grabbed my makeup kit and dabbed on more blush, swiped on another coat of mascara, and drenched my lips with coral lipstick.

The mirror's image made my shoulders slump. I stared at a middle-aged woman trying to look younger than her grandkids.

Tugging off boots and skirt, I replaced them with the comfortable clothes and wiped off the makeup. A light coat of liquid makeup hid a few wrinkles. A touch of pale pink lipstick and a pinch of mascara rounded out the work on my face. I wiggled my fingers through my waves and glanced out the door to my balcony at the crystalline blue water we rolled through.

I hadn't come on a cruise to remain in my room or sit on my balcony. While waiting for dinner, I would get around other people and maybe find some I knew. I trotted down the hall, snagged an elevator, and descended to the Grand Atrium.

Every inch of the room displayed opulence, from the glittering chandelier hanging from its domed ceiling three decks above, to the shiny gilt-trimmed glass elevators carrying guests, and the matching circular restraining walls above. Hundreds of voices competed with jazz from the grand piano played by a female pianist wearing a tux. Exquisite fawn-colored carpet and gold medallion wallpaper looked new. The scent of liquor drifted from passengers who were filling every spot near the bar. No face looked familiar.

I spied people gathering at one end of the deck above. The time for our dinner seating must be approaching. I walked up the circular marble stairwell, imagining I was Scarlett O'Hara, although my slight shortness of breath reminded me I was nowhere near her age.

One of numerous crew members in tuxes with our maître d' greeted me at the dining room door. The crew member checked the table number on my sailing card and guided me into the massive room with shiny china, crystal, and silver on white linen-topped tables. Two women sat with each other at a nearby table for six.

"Oh, my gosh! Cealie, it's you." Jane Easterly stood and squeezed me in a hug.

"Jane, I've missed you." I noticed her slight extra plump, which felt comforting, probably because of my own.

Tetter Hargroove sat with a tentative smile. "Hey, Cealie."

I bent down and hugged her. "It is so great to see you."

"You don't know how many times I wanted to call you," Jane said, "but I couldn't find your number until lately when I was looking for a ticket in a drawer."

"I'm so glad you did." I sat across from her. "I was afraid I might not recognize either of you, but y'all look fantastic."

"You, too," Jane said.

"You haven't changed," Tetter offered.

She lied, but I accepted the compliment. "I would have thought you two might look really different, but you don't."

"I haven't gotten any taller, just like you." Jane grinned. She was tiny, a pinch taller than I was. Her soft blue eyes flashed extra bright, and chestnut brown hair flipped at the ends. She wore a periwinkle dressy casual pant set.

Blond in school, Tetter now wore her white-blond hair in a sleek chin-length cut. Colored? Natural? I couldn't tell. An unusual paisley-printed pink-and-orange shirt looked great on her pale coloring. The tip of her nose kept that endearing upward tilt. Her eyes, though, lacked their former luster.

"Sue hasn't gotten here yet?" I asked. "She told me she saw all of you."

Tetter shook her head, her tight lips curved down at the edges. Of course she had that major problem we'd come to help her solve. I couldn't bluntly ask about it but was certain she would talk about it soon.

Jane leaned toward me. "You haven't found anyone else to marry?"

"I don't have any marriage plans." An ache tightened in

my chest. I had found someone but couldn't stay with him yet. "But you're still married?"

"Thirty-five happy years. Just like Tetter. She eloped exactly one month after our wedding."

Tetter nodded, no change in her expression.

Our tuxedo-clad table stewards arrived and introduced themselves, an exuberant young woman and an insecure-looking man, probably on his first voyage. They took our drink orders, opened mauve linen napkins on our laps, and handed us menus. While we made selections from the enticing fare, our male steward retrieved breads for us to select.

"I feel like a queen," Jane said once we turned in our orders. "This is only my second time to cruise."

"You'll love it. And Alaska is fantastic," I said. "Tetter, you've cruised before?"

"Yes." Eyes forlorn, she sipped from her water goblet. My gosh, she looked troubled.

A sommelier brought us wine. "To being together. And West-side High." Jane lifted her wineglass in a toast.

"Yay, W.H.S.," I said, Tetter and I clinking our glasses against hers. Our old friend, everybody's buddy, was staying too quiet. I hated to pry into her business so early but might need to.

"Are many others from our class coming?" I asked, noticing passengers filling tables around ours. None resembled former schoolmates.

Jane shook her head. "I was trying to get everyone from our gang. We were going to have a great little reunion of our closest friends."

"And you invited Stu—now Sue," I said. "Did y'all get close?"

"No, I just felt sorry for him. Her. Whatever," Jane said. "Especially after people started canceling. Angie's mother broke her hip. Suzanna's youngest grandson broke a leg while water-skiing. Jo Ann's husband needs a triple bypass."

"Poor things," I said. "I'll miss them, but I know family comes first."

Our entrées came. We raved about how good our exquisite dishes looked and tasted. We were finished with our breads, soups, salads, and entrées and studying the dessert menus when Sue showed up.

"I'm just in time for the good stuff." She took a chair and glanced at my menu. All of us ordered the Exotic Chocolate Explosion.

"Were you unpacking all that time or did you take a nap?" I asked.

"Getting a massage." Sue flashed a bright smile.

"I didn't think the spa opened until seven tonight," Jane said. Sue didn't respond. She peered in every direction around the dining room. "This place is wonderful. It's my maiden voyage." She grinned at us. "I feel like a virgin."

"A virgin cruiser." Tetter's tone lay flat. Normally, she would crack jokes about Sue's comment.

"Enjoy." Our waitress brought mountains of soft devil's food cake with chocolate sauce swirling down the sides, topped by dollops of whipped cream and a plump cherry.

My mouth watered. I set down my wineglass and grabbed my dessert fork.

"I can't eat this," Sue said. "My figure would be ruined."

Before anyone could respond, a woman's scream pierced the air, coming from outside our room.

People glanced at each other and the entrance. Everyone from our table darted from the room, along with lots of others. Some individuals were down in the stairwell.

"Get back! They're coming with a stretcher," a crew member yelled. "We need space. Please get back." More crew members joined him. The crowd shifted away.

A wrenchlike squeeze gripped my chest. I saw the unmoving man lying faceup. He wore a hot-pink shirt. I nudged Sue. "Isn't that the man you met on the Lido Deck?"

She stared down the stairs. "I'm not sure."

Uniformed men maneuvered a stretcher into the area. They slid the man onto it. His arms hung over the sides.

And my aunt who just arrived in the dining room might have spent the last hour and a half alone with him.

TWO

"WERE YOU JUST with him?" I asked Sue.

"Hush." She angled her head toward surrounding people who'd done as we had—rushed out of the dining room after a woman out here screamed. We stared down at the limp passenger on the stretcher.

My stomach clenched. I leaned to Sue. "He *is* the one we met at the safety drill."

"Let the doctor through," a crew member below urged. A man wearing all white rushed near and bent over the stretcher.

"Please return to the dining room," crew members told all of us.

"I don't feel like eating anymore," I said. People around repeated the same sentiment. Many crowded around the bank of elevators. I had the same idea, but the area was too jammed. I returned to our table.

No-longer-appealing chocolate mountains sat untouched at our four places.

"Did you see Tetter and Jane?" Sue asked, sitting with me.

"Not since we ran from the table," I realized. "I wonder if they're coming back."

"It seems like they'd say something before leaving us."

I craned my neck, searching for them. A small section of wall near the entrance separated us from the other side. Possibly our friends forgot the location of our table, although any waiter could direct them here. "Maybe they went to the restroom." I scanned the dining room. Chandeliers glittered. Mauve candles in sconces flickered on walls. Fresh flowers centered each linen-topped table. People of many nationalities wore tuxes and waited on tables with elegant settings. All looked prepared to treat royalty, not the ailing victim of an accident.

"Let's get out of here." Sue sounded apprehensive, exactly as I felt. We strode to the polished, open exit doors. "Let's go to the medical center to find out how Jonathan is."

"His name's Jonathan?"

Her cheeks flushed. She kept her eyes lowered. "Jonathan Mill."

"I'd certainly like to find out if he's okay," I said.

From her purse Sue pulled out a small folded sheet with the ship's deck plan. "The medical center is on deck three."

We took the first elevator we could board. I was about to ask Sue if she'd spent the hour or so with Jonathan before his fall, but a grinning family of five stared at us. "Are y'all having fun?" the young wife with a Southern drawl asked. "We sure are. We've never done this before, and we all love it."

"We do, too," I said. Except for meeting a man and then seeing him unconscious.

Soon after the family got off, we arrived on deck three. In contrast to the exquisite setting of the rest of the ship, this area could have belonged on a battleship. Gray metal. With the gangway on one end, it looked functional and smelled of oil and wet rope. Thick opaque plastic sheets cut into two-inch-wide strips shut off an opening marked Crew Members Only. Wooden counters stood on either side of an entrance— the stations where security members checked IDs before letting people inside.

A door to the left was labeled Medical Center.

A stern-faced security guard met us right inside the room. "I'm sorry. Unless you have an emergency, you'll need to come back later."

I peered beyond him toward the empty rear hall. The doctor and nurses must be back there, trying to help the man who'd fallen down the stairs.

Sue stood chest to chest with the guard. "A man fell and seemed badly hurt. His name is Jonathan Mill. I need to know how he's doing."

The guard's eyes softened. "What is your relationship to Mr. Mill?"

Sue glanced at me and then met the guard's gaze. "We're friends."

He shook his head.

"Intimate friends," I blurted. I'd barely met the downed man but cared about him. I cared about everyone, particularly a person who'd gotten hurt.

"I'm sorry. Only immediate family members or a traveling partner can get that information at this time."

"Have you seen him?" Sue asked.

"Yes, ma'am." The guard hesitated a moment, then seemed to decide. "I'm sorry, but I'll have to ask you to leave."

We stomped to the elevator.

"What floor?" Sue asked, stepping inside.

"Let's go to a bar."

She checked her deck plan. "They have plenty on different floors. We'll go to the promenade deck, okay?"

I nodded. "I sure hope Jonathan is okay," I said, a truth that might get her to offer feedback.

She stared at numbers lighting above the door as though their movement were most important. The door pinged open.

People fingered items for sale around gift shops. Shirts and jackets with the ship's logo hung in the hall. I glanced around, searching for the classmates we'd found and then lost from the dining room.

"Here's a bar. No, it's too full and too bright. Let's check another one," Sue said, stepping ahead, not slowing to look for anyone.

The Ginger Bar was subtly lit with brown-leather seating areas. Some tables. Many booths. A man in a far corner played a quiet song from the '70s on a piano. We took a table and ordered margaritas.

"Sue, you didn't know him before? You just met him on the Lido Deck, right?"

She hesitated a long minute. "Right." She exhaled. "I'm sure he'll be okay."

"Me, too. He seemed young to have had a heart attack. Maybe he tripped. He told *me* to be careful," I said and waited for a response.

She licked salt off the rim of her frosty margarita on the rocks.

"Sue, were you with him?"

"I told you where I was. Getting massaged." She took two quick swallows of her drink and turned away.

She obviously wouldn't say more about Jonathan now or probably would lie if I pushed her. "Do you know what Tetter's problem is?" I asked, realizing that sounded callous. "When Jane invited me to come, she said Tetter had a major problem we would help her solve. You know everyone loves Tetter, and we sure want to help her."

"I haven't kept up much with classmates. Jane told me the same thing she told you."

Okay, I'd work on getting her interest elsewhere, then maybe redirect some questions. "My son Tommy and his family moved to Alaska when his company folded, so I don't get to see them often. He's always working now but took vacation time to get to visit with me."

She peered toward a dark wall, appearing disinterested in my child.

I would need to find out more about Tetter. But now I wondered about Sue and Jonathan Mill. Had she told us the truth?

"Did you have a full-body massage?" I asked. "Or a facial?"

I imagined Sue, who used to be Stu, covered with a sheet with no underwear and wondered about changes to body parts.

I mentally slapped myself. I did not need to think of such things but often couldn't help wayward thoughts.

"Cealie, I know you and the others don't believe me, but that's what I did. I had a massage. The spa was open." She gulped her drink.

"I believe you. I just wondered how your massage was." I slipped my left hand into my right palm and pinched, reminding myself not to fib.

"It was great. A good-looking woman rubbed me down. I didn't get excited, but I did relax. Until now." On her feet, she headed for the door.

I dashed after her. "I believe you," I repeated, not sure whether that was the truth.

"Let's just forget it. Look, there's Tetter and Jane."

Both women headed toward us. Jane smiled.

I didn't smile back.

"Gil," I said to the man coming behind them.

"Cealie," he said, taking long strides forward.

Hands on hips, I stared at all six foot, three inches of him. Still well-muscled, with thick steel-gray hair and firm cheekbones, he wore an ironed sports shirt and new jeans that would cover soft navy-blue briefs.

He reached for me, attempting to pull me into his arms.

I tugged back. "I can't believe you followed me!"

He grinned. "This is funny."

His grin fueled my anger. "This is *not* funny. You asked me to marry you, and I didn't agree to, so now you're following me, even on a cruise?" I huffed, hearing classmates near me catch their breaths. "I don't even know how you found out I was coming here."

He spread his hands in innocence. "I didn't."

"Right." Staring at his handsome face, recalling hot romance in his arms, I gathered all of my strength. "Gil, I want you to stay away from me."

His lips flattened. His chest swayed back from me. He took a step backward. "I'll abide by your wishes."

"Good."

"I'll see you." He gave me a brief nod. His gaze slid to my classmates, and he strode away.

Sue tugged on my arm. "Who is that?"

"He's a hunk." Jane still eyed him.

Tetter's forehead wrinkled. "Cealie, he wanted to marry you and you turned him down?" She sounded more interested than critical.

A white-haired couple gave me severe looks, like I'd committed the worst sin.

"He followed me," I told them and then led my classmates away from that nosy judgmental couple. We gathered in an open area near the casino. Slot machines pinged and screeched. Dealers' voices carried. This was what I wanted, except for the smoky odor. Noise was better than quiet places where strangers heard every word. Nobody else needed to know about Gil and me.

My classmates' piercing gazes all targeted my eyes. Everyone waited for an explanation for my rude behavior.

"His name is Gil Thurman."

"Sounds good. Where did you meet him?" Jane asked.

"At one of his restaurants."

"*One* of his restaurants?" Sue said.

"The one in Vicksburg, Mississippi. We were attracted to each other."

Sue nodded, apparently satisfied with my answers, but then glanced around as though looking for someone.

"And then you fell in love, and he asked you to marry him." Tetter stated major events from my life as though teaching how to construct a declarative sentence. She waved to get a passing waiter's attention. His tray held stemmed glasses of the day's special: rumrunners. Only Tetter bought a drink, signing to charge her card.

"So then you came on this cruise with us," Jane said.

"Yes, but Gil and I have gotten together in different places where he has restaurants."

Sue shook her head, nose in the air. "You're wrong to do that. You must have led the man on and made him believe you loved him and wanted him, and then you turned him down like that."

"We've had lots of wonderful times together. But I told him from the beginning that after I lost my husband, I realized I had lost myself. I felt paralyzed, like half of a broken easel. The strongest part was gone. I could barely stand on my own any longer. Gil is so sure of himself. I needed to find Cealie again. I'm still trying to rediscover myself, and I can't give in when I'm getting so close."

Tetter, with eyes forlorn, nodded.

"I wish you would have introduced us," Jane said.

"Sorry. It didn't seem like the time."

"I'm going to play the slots," Jane said and headed into the casino.

"I'm going to my cabin." Sue strode away from us.

I took a breath. I'd had enough censure for one day. And I struggled with my feelings. I wanted to be with Gil, but he'd betrayed me. He'd promised he'd let me finish finding myself. And then we might be together for good.

But he lied. Instead of letting me go off with friends, he found out where I was heading and came after me.

I needed to get away from my problems. Now I had Tetter alone. Tetter, who'd been bubbly and open and such fun in school, seemed so troubled I couldn't think about myself. I touched her hand. "How are you?"

"I'm good. How are you?"

"Fine. Tetter, how are you really doing?"

Her eyes widened. "I'm going to find Jane." She scuttled into the casino.

I sank into a cushioned lounge chair. Had Tetter confided in Jane but did not want to discuss her troubling situation with me?

People walked past, people who laughed. Mostly adults, some with children. Everybody else was with someone.

I rose and trudged about, spying people going in and out of shops. Some carried purchases. I stepped to the railing and peered below. The source of many of the voices, people gathered in the vast atrium. Some stood around the grand piano. A long line of people waited to sign up for tours at the excursion desk.

I was alone. Maybe Sue had a good idea. I made my way back to my room.

Inside it, I paced. "He came after me but said he wouldn't," I snapped, confirming my right to be angry. I flounced outside to my balcony. The water looked gray in the night. I dropped to one of the two plastic chairs and crossed my arms and legs. I would see beautiful sights in Alaska, no matter what Gil did. Frigid air slapped my skin and made me shiver.

I returned inside, not caring about sights. The tall one I'd seen was enough. He couldn't chase me. He certainly couldn't try to deceive me.

And what was going on with my classmates? I'd wondered how they might have changed since I'd seen them years ago. It seemed their altered lives could be much more different than I imagined.

Of course, they might feel the same way about me.

I surely never thought they'd invite Sue. When Sue was Stu, none of my friends cared much for him. He was too arrogant. Too different. Maybe because he knew he was, but didn't believe any of us would accept him as a girl?

And did this girl—now my aunt—have anything to do with Jonathan Mill's fall?

I needed to find out.

The boat shifted beneath my feet. Normally I enjoyed that feeling while in bed during a cruise, but I wasn't ready to fall asleep. I needed answers. I had to know what happened to that man and if my relative was involved.

On my wall phone, I located Spa and pressed the number beside it. A pleasant woman's voice answered.

"Hi. Sweetie, can you tell me what time the spa opened today?" I asked.

"I don't have a newsletter right here, but we're open now. Would you like to come in or schedule an appointment for one or more of our services?"

"No, thanks. I know what time the newsletter says you were supposed to open today, but someone told me she'd been in there earlier. I just wanted to check on that."

"Is that person your child?"

"Oh no, my aunt. And she says she had a massage. I just want to know for sure."

A silent moment pulsed. "Ma'am, I'm afraid I can only tell you what's on the newsletter and that we are open now. Thank you for calling." Her voice had lost its gentleness. She hung up.

Okay, I would be more direct. I marched down the hall to Sue's stateroom. I would insist that she tell me the truth and not move away from her room until she did.

I knocked on the door. Nobody answered. I knocked again. "Hey, Sue, it's me, Cealie."

I waited. She might be asleep, but it was much too early for anyone to go to bed. Unless she was ill. If that was the case, I could get her medicine.

"Sue," I called again, pounding harder.

Our stateroom steward stepped out of a room. "She is not in."

"Oh. Thanks." I walked away and turned back. "Did you notice which way she went?"

Indecision crossed his face. Probably he should keep information about guests confidential.

"Please tell me. We're related," I said.

He glanced around, seemingly to make sure nobody heard.

"She might have gone for medical attention. I offered to help, but she wouldn't let me. She left her stateroom with her face bleeding."

THREE

SUE WAS HURT? I rushed to the elevator, found it took too long to arrive and travel down. I eyed the slow-moving numbers, reminding myself that trying to walk down so many decks would have made me also need medical treatment.

The same security guard as before met me as I stepped out of the elevator.

"Ma'am," he said, stretching his arms, ready to stop me again.

"My aunt is in the medical center. She's on the cruise with me, and she's hurt."

He stepped down. "You can go inside."

I dashed to the door and yanked it open. Sue was entering the reception area from the rear hall, holding an ice pack beneath her eye.

"Oh, Sue, you're really hurt," I said.

A man wearing a white uniform with short-cropped gray hair stepped up behind her. "Just keep ice on it for a while. It should be all right."

"I will, Doc."

The doctor spied me. "Can I help you?"

"She's my niece," Sue said. "She just came to check on me. Thanks a lot for everything, Dr. Thurman."

Thurman—like Gil's last name? I wanted to ask him about that and Sue's injury, but she shoved me toward the door. "Go."

We left the office. The guard studied Sue holding the ice

pack to her face. I gave him a told-you-so nod in case he'd doubted what I said.

The elevator door slid open. Sue rushed inside.

"What happened? I wish you would've called me," I said.

She yanked the ice pack off her face. A crimson thread sliced skin under her eye. "He's dead. Jonathan died in that fall."

Staring at the gash on her face, I needed a moment to consider what she told me.

"I'm so sorry. Maybe he tripped and hit his head?" Concern for the man who died and those who loved him made me tremble. "But Sue, you need to take care of yourself, too. Keep that ice on your face. How did that happen?"

She shook her head. "I just stupidly ran into the metal shelf that holds the TV in the corner of my room."

"Ouch. Can I do anything?"

"No." She grimaced each time the elevator stopped on our way up. People stepped in and made comments about her being injured. "I did something brainless, but I'm okay," she answered. She did not look at me again.

On our deck we both stepped out. Neither of us spoke as we strode among people and headed for our hall. No one else was around in our hallway.

"Sue, what happened? I mean, really, what did you do? You only seem concerned about the man you met during our safety drill but not about yourself. You could have lost your eye."

"But I didn't. I'm fine." She headed for her stateroom.

"How did you find out about Jonathan?"

"I asked the nurse."

"And she told you?"

Sue spun and faced me. "She put ice on my face and stopped the bleeding while the doctor was finishing with another patient. I told her I knew the other patient well and knew he was badly hurt. I convinced her to tell me."

"What did she say?"

"That Dr. Thurman would be right with me. He was working with my friend in the morgue."

"Oh, how horrible. Do you know what happened to him?"

She shook her head. "I'm going to rest in my cabin. I'll meet you and the others for breakfast." She pushed her sailing card into the slot of her door.

"Let me know if you need anything," I said, but her door's slam told me she either didn't hear all of my words or didn't care to respond.

I walked down the hall to my room but did not feel like going inside. I didn't know the time since I'd stopped wearing a watch after I decided to take care of me instead of always working. I wasn't sleepy.

Outside my cabin door I found the ship's daily newsletter and scanned it. A welcome from the captain and crew, and a list of many events on the ship available during our sailing day tomorrow. Tonight, of course, the casino opened. Were my classmates still in it? Winning or handing over their cash? The spa supposedly opened a half hour ago, not when Sue told us she went earlier. Other activities taking place tonight were a margarita party, music and dancing on various decks, some in bars. Temporary tattoos would be offered on the Lido Deck, along with a combo playing calypso music. The pools were open, some enclosed and heated.

To perk up some of our group, maybe I could suggest that we get tattoos one day. What a dreadful thought on this sad day. My aunt injured. A man we met dead.

I glanced toward Sue's door. She hadn't come out. I needed to go and find my other classmates to renew friendships more and see what I could discover.

Heading back down and into the smoky casino, I wound my way around flashing slot machines that whirred and called to players, and the card games at tables. No sign of my friends and no idea where I'd find them.

I passed a last small alcove. It held only two slot machines. A lean white-headed man sat in front of one, but reached over and slipped a bill into the machine next to his. His profile seemed familiar. But it couldn't be. I stepped closer.

"Randy?"

"Cealie." He smiled, stood, and hugged me.

"How nice to see you. And what a surprise."

We looked each other over. He was about five-foot-ten, trim, with sparkly brown eyes and a strong chin. Our class had voted him one of the most handsome. He still looked good. I glanced at his left hand. No wedding ring, although a band of skin lighter than his tan crossed his ring finger.

"You haven't changed at all," he said.

"Oh, right." I let out a laugh and shook my head but wanted to believe his words. "You look great. Only your hair color is different. It didn't stay the same, like mine did," I added with a wink, figuring he realized a hairdresser made my hair its current russet color.

"Do you want to sit here?" He indicated the stool beside his.

"No, thanks. I'm not much on gambling. Oh, you'll never guess who else is on this ship." I didn't wait for a guess. "Jane Easterly and Tetter and Sue Ingstrom."

"Sue? I knew *Stu* Ingstrom in our class."

Should I tell him Stu had become Sue?

No. I didn't need to give away anyone's private information.

"I knew about the others. Jane invited me," he said.

"She did?" Jane had told me our old gang was coming. I took it for granted that meant only females. Besides, back then Randy hadn't been a member of our group.

He glanced toward the tables. "She and Tetter were in here

a while ago. We're going to try to meet up for the welcome-aboard show in the amphitheater." He checked his watch. "It's starting about now. Do you want to go?"

"Sure."

He made a couple of more pulls on the machine in front of him, losing the rest of his money. We headed for the theater, finding the crowd had thinned.

"Condense your life since high school," I said with a grin.

"I live in Dallas and have a great wife and two grown kids and two grandkids, and wish I could see them all more often."

"I know what you mean. It's tough to let go of them."

He nodded. "I supervise an oil-field crew, and I'm taking a much-needed vacation." Before I could ask if his wife wouldn't also like this vacation, he added, "I heard that Freddie died. I'm sorry."

"Thank you." I sucked in a breath, not wanting to sink into missing my husband. "He and I started a copyediting agency. I still have it." I didn't say I kept offices throughout the country with great managers running them. A brief concern flashed. I wondered if there *were* any problems with my offices.

No, I wouldn't call any of them to ask if they needed me. The managers all knew how to contact this ship if they required my assistance.

"What do you do for fun?" I asked Randy.

"Work. It's all I ever do."

"That's not good for you."

"I know. How about you?"

"Travel. I've even learned not to mind doing it alone."

We entered the theater with a gaggle of people stepping into the chilled, cavernous, dark room. Most seats were taken. The show had already started. The cruise director, a husky smiling man in a suit and top hat, completed a joke. The audience roared. My knees shook.

"Do you see them?" Randy asked.

What I saw paralyzed my vocal cords. We had entered on the upper level.

I had dreaded balconies ever since I was seven and my twelve-year-old cousin held me over a movie theater's rail, pretending he would toss me down. A recent near-deadly encounter on a balcony accentuated my apprehension.

This upper level held dozens of rows forming a tremendous semicircle. Many rows were visible down on the bottom floor, along with circular cushioned seating areas. I perused faces. There were too many. Staring below, I shivered. This evening I had witnessed a dead man's body down from a fall. Had that fall caused his death? Sue seemed intensely interested in that man, whom she and I met briefly on the Lido Deck.

"I can't find them," Randy said.

I managed to shove words past my teeth. "Did you know a man died on board this afternoon?"

"You're kidding."

"No. He was in the stairwell near where we ate. We saw him."

"That's terrible. Look, there are some places."

We nudged past people to reach empty seats. Working to stave off apprehension, I took in the glamour of our space. Shiny blue-black fabric draped from the center of the huge ceiling also covered the walls. Swirling ceiling lights changed colors, making the fabric glitter in varying hues. The stage was vast. Showgirls dancing across it could have performed on Broadway.

How many people in this room were aware that a man here had died? The people who ate with us this evening knew he fell. So did others who saw him down. I tried for an image of his face but mainly recalled his shirt in the bright shade of pink I'd loved best as a teen.

I glanced around. So many grown-ups and children were up here, many leaning toward the stage.

One face stood out: *Gil's.* He was laughing, head cocked back like it did when he really chuckled. Automatically I checked to see who was with him. Only men. Annoyance overtook my pleasure at seeing him.

I leaned toward Randy. He noticed and eyed me. At least he didn't pull away.

I was not trying to make Gil jealous. Maybe I wanted to let him know that if he lied to me, I would move on. There were probably not many good middle-aged men available, but I didn't want one anyway. I considered my mantra, the slogan I kept trying to believe deep in my heart: *I am woman. I can do anything—alone!*

My peripheral vision let me spy Gil watching me.

I saw a dead man, and something about that is really troubling me. I wanted to telegraph those concerns to my former lover. *I need to talk to someone about it. I need you.*

No, I don't! I nodded as I tried to convince myself.

"They are great, aren't they?" Randy said.

"Terrific." I glanced at the stage. A dance performance was ending.

"Look. There they are." He pointed below at Jane and Tetter seated on a curved sofa.

"I wish we could get their attention," I said.

"We'll do better. Come on. We'll go and sit with them."

I imagined Gil stared at my back as I left my seat and followed this quite handsome man. But I really didn't want jealousy. And I didn't want him. I did want Gil to know my relationship with him was over. Lying to me would never work.

Randy rushed down the stairs. I had a difficult time keeping up and wondered if he always hustled so fast. He reached our friends. "We found y'all."

"Great." Jane pushed over to give us more space. "Sit down. We can squeeze in."

Tetter shifted closer to her.

Randy sat beside Tetter and patted the space left on the seat. "Come on, Cealie. You're little."

"Only in height," I said with a grin.

He and Jane smiled at me. Tetter didn't. Something was truly bothering her. Her restless eyes appeared so tense. Maybe she had more than one situation to solve. I needed to help her.

People applauded for someone on stage. A semi-quiet moment ensued.

I took the opportunity to lean toward Jane. "Are any other guys from our class on board?"

"Not that I know of."

"And you wanted to come," I said to Randy, "without any other friends to hang out with?"

He grimaced and looked offended.

"Other guy friends, I mean. It's just that women like different things. We like to shop and gossip. And did I mention gossip?" I smirked.

He did, too. "That's okay. I'm good with just y'all." Eyes lowered, he appeared to sneak a glance at Tetter.

She faced me. "Where's Sue?"

"In her room. She ran into the shelf holding her TV and cut her cheek. She's okay now but wanted to rest."

"Goodness. I'm glad she's okay," Tetter said.

"But she learned that the man who fell in the stairwell died," I said.

Tetter's jaw dropped. "From what?"

"We don't know. But Sue wanted to rest. We'll see her at breakfast."

Jane faced all of us. "Let's eat in the dining room instead of the buffet. The newsletter says there's going to be a celebrity chef. I want to check out his food."

I kept out of kitchens as much as possible now that I lived alone, and I wasn't especially concerned about chefs. But if

Jane was, we'd go meet one. The orchestra music swelled. Silver and pink and gold lights swirled across a lithe dancer pirouetting onstage.

The show was extravagant, yet I found myself peering up toward where Randy and I previously sat. Streams of light in chartreuse, burgundy, and electric blue flowed over the faces above. Gil was no longer in the area.

Maybe I didn't want to stay around him, but disappointment at not seeing him ruined the rest of the performance for me. As soon as it ended, others in my group agreed that we were ready for bed. None of us wanted to stay around for the late-night performance, a comedy act with adult-only material.

"This adult is too tired for all that," I said, and the others agreed. "I'll slip a note under Sue's door to let her know about our plans."

We parted for our rooms, promising to meet at breakfast.

My stateroom made me smile. The steward had folded back my covers and left two gold-foil-wrapped squares of chocolate on my pillow.

Since no one else would be sleeping with me, I ate the excellent rich candy. I then wrote a note about when and where we'd meet for breakfast, took it to Sue's room, and listened. No sound came from inside. No sliver of light shone under her door. I slid the paper underneath, returned to my room, changed into my gold knit pj's with green dragonflies, and set my alarm clock.

Stretching on the cushiony mattress, I considered Randy. He always seemed a nice-enough person, although I never knew him well. But having him in the mix felt different. Why would Jane invite only one man? And why would one man come along with us?

Of course Stu used to be a guy, but Randy didn't seem to know that he was now Sue. None of us, I figured, had really kept up with each other since our teen years. I'd spoken to some classmates during the first couple of years after we finished school, but then we all went our separate ways for college or jobs and marriage.

Other thoughts from the evening were tumbling through my mind.

A man I met died on this ship.

I wished I could have done something to help him.

What did Sue really know about that man?

Nagging uneasiness told me I was being deceived. People I'd known on board might be hiding too many secrets. Even Gil was not the man I thought he was.

I worried about Tetter. Calamity could greatly alter a person's life. I would make a direct effort to help that wonderful woman with hers.

Gloom set in. I drew the covers to my neck, concerned that more than one person on this ship could meet up with an unhappy situation.

An untimely death?

I needed to find answers and make certain no one I knew was involved in tragedy. I would do that first thing tomorrow.

Shutting my eyes, I twisted and turned and rolled over. Unable to shut worries out of my mind, I switched on the light over my pillow and grabbed the book I'd put on the nightstand. It would get my thoughts on something besides problems and quickly put me to sleep.

Smiling with anticipation, I opened my newest cookbook and began reading recipes. Sleep came within minutes.

FOUR

I AWOKE SURPRISED to discover I'd slept better than I had in a long time. The first three recipes I had perused seemed so exhausting to shop for and prepare, they'd quickly sent me into dreamland. The ship's light rocking had kept me in deep sleep. I showered, dressed in casual attire, shrugged into a light jacket, and opened the door of my stateroom. The scent of coffee and bacon greeted me.

Trays holding leftover breakfast dotted the carpeting outside a few neighboring doors, urging me to grab someone's half-eaten biscuit or rush to the elevator. I tapped on Sue's door first and received no response. Taking an elevator, I rode up, and then spied classmates heading for the dining room. "Jane. Tetter," I called.

They waited for me.

"Good morning," Tetter said, a trace of a smile touching her lips. How nice to see her in a better mood. Now she should share her problems.

Sue bounded out of an elevator. Her heels were high, her skirt short, her makeup thick, especially on the bruised skin under her eye. "I saw we're having a celebrity chef today."

"Oo, that cut. How is your vision?" Jane asked her.

"I was fortunate that I didn't strike my eye. But it's okay."

"Thank goodness," Tetter said as we headed for the dining room.

"Gil," I said, surprised.

He was in the crowd walking with us. He paused but didn't kiss me or even try for a hug. "Hello, Cealie."

"You followed me. You found out where I was going and followed me on this ship! I can't believe you did that."

"And we agreed, didn't we? You would go on your way, trying to rediscover yourself, and I would try to wait until you were done."

"Yes. So why... Never mind. You're hardheaded and determined, and when you want something, you go get it."

"I believe that's one of the things you like about me."

"And I'm trying to imitate. You know yourself and what you want from life."

"Including you." He pointed at my chest.

My friends nestled near, listening to every word of our exchange.

"Yes, including me," I told Gil. "And that's the real killer—you agreed to let me go. And then you rushed after me."

A thought flashed. I did believe there was a killer involved on this ship who brought about the death of Jonathan Mill. I wanted to share this concern with Gil more than any other person. But I was ticked off at him.

He shook his head, eyes steady on mine. "I'm a terrible person. You deserve better."

Why wasn't this getting any easier? How could I argue with him if all he did was agree? I took the break in our discussion—our heated discussion, but only on my part, I realized—to glance at my friends.

Jane grinned at me. Tetter eyed me, no expression to give away how she felt. Sue pushed her lower lip out in a pout. Randy joined us. He smiled extra wide.

I turned to Gil. He was walking away. "Where are you going?" I asked.

"To the dining room. I'll see you later."

"No, you won't."

"Whatever you say."

Darn it, why did he always make me seem like the bad guy? Was I?

My classmates closed in. "He's hot," Jane said.

Randy moved close to me. "Boy, you told him off. Good job."

"I didn't want to tell him off. I—" *Love Gil.* I stopped myself from voicing my whole thought. "I'm just furious with him for telling me one thing and doing the opposite. That's totally wrong."

"It's contemptible," Tetter said.

I nodded and continued toward where we would eat.

"Cealie, you shouldn't have done that." Sue's voice was so loud, the crowd around us stopped and faced me.

"Oh, come on, Sue. He's a great guy. But do you really think it's okay for him to tell me untruths?"

"You're lucky to have someone. And now you're shoving him away."

"I don't have him. I do not have Gil."

"Gil?" a stately well-dressed woman entering the dining room with us said. "What a nice name. What's his surname?"

"Thurman."

"Gil Thurman. Hmm, a strong name. He's probably a strong person." The twinkle in her eye let me know she might be interested in this strong person.

I walked inside with my classmates, a waiter telling us we could sit anywhere this morning. Creatures of habit, we headed for our table to the left. I glanced to the right and spied Gil. He was sitting beside a man, a young family across their table. People streamed inside. Waiters tried to keep up, pouring water and juice in stemmed glasses, filling cups with coffee and hot tea.

I stared at a window to see the promised beauty of nature outside. I spied pale blue water with dark mountainous land beyond. Today we would be heading into a spectacular setting. Nothing yet broke my sour mood. I did not want to take part in more conversation.

Chatter at our table kept up, mainly between Randy and Jane. They spoke of jobs they'd had or still had and marriages and kids and grandkids. Once they reached the ages of their offspring and how terrific the little ones were, I grew extra antsy. I knew *my* children and grandchildren were the best, but wouldn't take away my friends' praises of their own.

Sue made furtive glances in all directions and appeared agitated. I had no idea why, except she mustn't have married, and even with the sex change, she certainly couldn't carry children. Hearing all the talk about others' families might hurt her.

"I hope they take our order soon," I said. "I guess they're a little slow since so many people are coming in at one time. I've been on a few cruises, and most people eat at the buffets in the morning."

"I'm getting kind of hungry myself," Jane said.

"After all you ate last night?" Sue asked, tone annoyed.

"We all ate like it was our last meal," I said, wondering why she was so irritated.

Randy sat quite close to Tetter, their arms pressed together. She didn't seem to notice. She did not shift her arm away but kept an intent look at my face, as though deeply engrossed in what I was saying.

With my mind soothed from my encounter with Gil, I considered how to handle a new concern. I watched passing waiters. Most appeared hesitant, eyes uncertain, like they were learning from those with more experience. I spied one with an assured countenance and waved him over.

"Ma'am, can I do something for you?" he asked, bending toward me.

"You certainly can. I need to know what happened to the man who fell in the stairwell out there last night."

Sue sucked in a loud gulp of air.

The waiter straightened. "I am sorry. I do not know."

"You don't know, or you aren't supposed to tell? We met him. We know he died. I need to know what caused his death," I insisted.

Sue grimaced. Others at our table looked merely inquisitive.

"Please tell me what happened," I said to the waiter.

"I do not have that information."

I thanked him, ignored Sue's angry expression, and considered who else I might try to pry that information from.

Tapping on a microphone in the center of the room created strident noises that claimed our attention. Our tuxedo-clad maître d' stepped to the mike.

"Good morning. I hope all of you enjoyed your first night aboard." A smattering of people clapped. "You will enjoy wonderful foods from throughout the world during your stay with us. I would like to introduce you to the man responsible for all of those meals. Please welcome our executive chef, Mr. Andrew Sandkeep."

A husky man wearing all white, including his tall straight chef's hat, strode forward. Guests applauded. The executive chef took the mike. "I hope you enjoyed your first meal," he said with an accent I couldn't place.

We clapped to show our appreciation for the food his cooks prepared.

"We have a treat for you," he said, although he did not look extra pleased. "This ship has invited a celebrity chef, a man that we are sure you will all appreciate. The person who brought him here will introduce this chef to us. Please welcome Mr. Gil Thurman."

My heart lurched.

Gil stepped up to the microphone.

My tablemates flung gazes at me. I kept my chin up and

tried not to react, although I felt my cheeks flame. Gil had come on this ship for a reason, a reason that didn't include me?

"Thank you," he said. "I'm not a chef. I don't even know how to boil eggs."

Many laughed. Yes, Gil, like me, was not proficient in the kitchen. The main thing I did with stoves was dust them. If we lived together, we would probably starve unless he brought his restaurants' foods home.

"I am fortunate enough to have this chef preparing meals for our customers around New Orleans. He works magic in the kitchen and will do the same thing for you during this trip," Gil said, and a slight man stepped near, the chef's hat enhancing his stature. "This is Adam Hebert, a man who will please your palate."

Gil moved away. He had the decorum not to look at me.

His chef spoke with a Cajun patois. "I'm the lucky man for getting to work in one of Mr. Thurman's Cajun Delights restaurants. During most of your meals on this trip, you will be able to select Cajun dishes. For breakfast, you could have grits and boudin, which is a type of pork sausage, with eggs and biscuits and hash browns made with smothered onions and green onions and potatoes and mushrooms. You might also choose beignets coated in powdered sugar and café au lait. Y'all pass a good time on your trip now and have fun eating."

"I want that," Jane said once the chef quit talking and our waiter approached.

"What?" the waiter asked.

"Everything Chef Hebert mentioned."

The waiter smiled, nodding as each of us ordered the same thing.

"He made me really hungry," Randy told us.

Sue faced me, thick makeup under her eye smudged, the purple area almost black. "So Mr. Thurman came on this ship after you, huh?"

My cheeks burned. "I was so wrong."

"I can't believe you told him off. And all he did was bring a chef on board."

"I need to apologize."

Tetter leaned toward me. "When was the last time you saw him?"

"A few weeks ago."

"And he didn't tell you he was coming on this ship?" Sue asked, tone snippy. "Then you two mustn't be as close as you think you are."

"Lay off, Sue." Jane stretched out her hand as though needing to protect me. "I'm sure Cealie feels bad enough."

I nodded, lips tight, attitude grim. Maybe Sue was right. Gil and I weren't as close as I thought.

"Look at that man's plate. I could snitch a chunk of boudin from it," Randy said.

Tetter grinned. "It does smell good."

"You want me to grab some for you?" Randy asked her, face serious. She lowered her eyes and shook her head. The moment struck me as a flirtatious game between teenagers. But these were adults, and they were married to other people.

A sausage aroma wafted from the next table. Enticing, the scent carried a slight peppery tang. The French toast smelled sugary.

"So are you going to apologize?" Sue asked me.

"To…"

She shook an index finger. "You know who. You know perfectly well what you did to that man. You told him off—right in front of all of us."

"All right, Sue. That's Cealie's business. She can tell him she's sorry or leave things as they are. It's her life," Jane said, face tight with anger.

Sue splayed her fingers on the table and shoved herself to her feet. "All of it is her business, as far as I'm concerned.

And yours. And yours, Randy. You, too, Tetter. I don't even know why I was invited to come on this trip." She whipped toward the entrance and took off, a statuesque figure, tightening her wrap around her shoulders.

"She is so annoying, sometimes I really could kill her." Jane shook her head.

"Don't talk like that." Tetter shuddered, eyes wide. She looked brittle and fragile, not at all like the outgoing chatterbox from our class.

"I mean it. She's just as aggravating now as she was when she was a boy back in school," Jane said.

Skin between Randy's eyes crinkled. "What do you mean, 'was a boy'?"

Tetter shook her head at Jane, probably not wanting her to reveal Sue's secret.

I sipped the orange juice a waiter brought, not taking part in the discussion. I remained too unhappy with myself for having judged Gil's actions. And I had really misjudged them.

Jane faced Randy. "You didn't know that Cealie's Aunt Sue used to be her Uncle Stu from our class?"

Randy roared out a laugh. "I know you're kidding me. The sexy woman who just left here could not be—" He chuckled, glancing at each of us. "No way am I going to believe that."

I was too upset with Sue to try to defend her. I didn't know whether she wanted the truth told about her surgical transformation or if she hid that information. With the way she came on to the man we had met on the Lido Deck, I figured she didn't disclose her past to everyone.

Waiters carried plates to our table. No wonder the toast smelled so appealing. Gil's mother had called it *pain perdu*—lost bread. The bread was drenched in a mixture of egg, milk, sugar, vanilla, and cinnamon, then lightly browned in butter in a skillet.

I scanned the scrambled eggs, hash browns, lost bread,

and boudin. My mouth watered. And then I spied Gil. On the opposite side of the dining room, he headed for the exit.

I rushed after him.

A few stragglers waited near the elevators. So did Gil. People smiled at him, probably recognizing him from his little talk at the mike.

He saw me coming. His smiled faded into a guarded expression.

I strode to him. "I'm sorry."

"It's okay." An elevator door clinked open behind him. He ignored it.

"I had no idea you were coming on this ship or bringing one of your chefs."

"When you and I were in Gatlinburg, Cealie, I asked you to come on a trip with me."

"You wouldn't say where you were going or how long you'd be."

"You didn't give me a chance. You just said no."

"Aw, man," the gray-haired woman behind Gil said. She frowned at me and shook her head, letting me know I had done an awful thing.

"I love him," I told her, "and I believe he loves me. I'm just not quite ready to get tied down yet."

She skimmed my face and figure. "At your age?"

I huffed, and her friend grabbed her arm and pointed toward the restroom. Both women headed there away from me.

Another door opened, revealing an empty elevator. Gil snagged my hand. "Let's get in." He tugged me inside.

"So is it only a happy coincidence that you and I came on the same cruise?" I asked, still not ready to totally give in. "And neither of us knew the other one was coming to Alaska?"

"When did you decide to take this trip?"

"A few weeks ago. Jane Easterly is one of my best friends

from high school. She invited me and said our gang was coming for a kind of small class reunion. We'd all get to visit and especially help our buddy Tetter take care of a severe problem. Of course a major bonus for me is that I'll get to see Tommy in Skagway."

Gil smiled. "I'm sure you're thrilled about getting to see your son and his family."

"I can't wait."

"But did you tell me anything about that invitation from your friend?"

I shook my head. "Since you and I decided we weren't going to stay together, we didn't need to tell each other all of our plans."

"You made that decision." He touched the tip of my nose, making a chill of excitement skitter along my body to my heels. "I want to know everything about you. Where you go. Who you're doing things with. Anything major that happens. Even small daily events."

The elevator door opened. We were gazing at each other. A rush of people stepped inside. We stepped out. Gil and I had entered the Grand Atrium. Scads of people surrounded us, some at the bar, scores of travelers moving across the floor. I glanced above. More of the same, an ant farm of people heading in and out of shops and up and down decks in elevators and on the winding stairway.

Gil pressed close to me.

I placed my hands against his chest to stop him from getting any nearer. "Something major happened on this ship last night. A man died."

"I know." He gripped my hand and led the way toward a wall, one of the few spots away from others.

"I saw him dead at the bottom of the stairwell," I said, voice shaky. "I had met him." The full force of knowing that Jonathan had died made me shiver. Tears heated my eyes.

"He was a man who came on a cruise for a wonderful experience in a breathtaking place. And soon after starting the trip, he died."

"I'm really sorry about that. I didn't see him, but I knew someone died after we embarked. My uncle is the ship's doctor. He invited me to come on a cruise and bring a chef along."

"Oh, that doctor is your dad's brother. No wonder you have the same family name."

"Right. We don't get to see each other often. Getting to spend time with him is the reason I came. And, of course, having one of my chefs prepare Cajun dishes."

I knew it. Gil would not be traveling unless his vacation involved work. I didn't feel so bad now about not agreeing to join him on a trip.

"Cealie, I saw someone rushing away from your table not long before you came out of the dining room. A tall woman. Striking features."

I rolled my eyes. "I'll tell you about her. But what did your uncle say? Why did that man die?"

"He doesn't know yet. It might have been an accident. He could have had a seizure and fallen. He could have died from the fall. They'll need to do tests, some of them onshore. It might take a while for the results."

"I have a bad feeling about his death."

"Maybe the police can use that." He smirked.

"Don't be sarcastic."

"I want to be… Cealie, I get so confused when I'm around you. I want to let you go on with finding yourself, as you say you want to do. But it's so difficult not being with you."

I nodded, my resolve weakening, my body shifting closer. He leaned toward me. "You didn't even kiss me hello."

The next minute I was in Gil's embrace, my body arched knowingly into his. All thoughts of where we were vanished.

I tightened my arms around him, fitting my torso against the right places.

"Oh, wow," I uttered, our lips parting. I meshed my lips again with his, pressing my body even nearer, feeling him wanting me. I wanted him. I definitely wanted him.

"I guess he forgives you," a voice behind me said. Sue's voice.

Gil and I stepped apart.

All of my shipboard classmates circled us.

FIVE

"Gil," I said, and searched for sane words since I remained in the throes of passion, "these are my friends. You saw them."

"Hello, friends." Gil grinned and nodded.

"That's Jane," I said.

"Nice to meet you, Jane." He shook her hand.

"I know their maiden names but forget those married names, so—this is Tetter. That's Sue. And Randy."

Gil shook hands with them. "One man in the group? You're a lucky fellow," he told Randy, sizing him up, giving me a raised eyebrow.

"I am lucky," Randy said. He stood beside Tetter. Lowering his eyes, he shifted his gaze toward her.

"You all got together with Sue?" I asked, surprised that Sue allowed them to join her. She had left in such a tiff.

Tetter shook her head. If she was aware of Randy's nearness, it didn't seem to bother her. "We just saw her standing here behind you."

Great. How long had Sue stood close? The whole time Gil and I shared heated kisses? That thought detracted from our passion.

"Something happened to your eye?" Gil asked.

Sue touched her cheek. "You should have seen the other gal," she said with a wry grin. I'd expected her to end that sentence with *guy* because of the cliché; also because at the angle where I stood, her strong cheekbones and narrow chin made me envision her as I'd known her for years—as Stu, who used to shave that face. This relative of mine could be annoying as either Stu or Sue. "I'm Cealie's aunt," she added.

"And I have an uncle aboard," Gil said and turned his smile at me. "Maybe we could have a family reunion."

Right.

I faced Sue. "Do you want something?"

She shook her head, expression cocky. "I only wanted to see how long you could kiss without coming out for air."

"Did you time us?" Gil asked, apparently amused.

"I will next time," Sue said, and I got ready to give her a sassy retort.

"The next time," Gil said, and wrapped an arm around my shoulder, "we probably won't be out in public."

"Ah," Jane said enthusiastically. "We have an onboard romance brewing."

I noticed Randy's quick smile at Tetter. And her demure glance at him.

A flicker of sadness crossed Sue's face.

Gil tightened his grip around my shoulder. "I'd like to brew romance anyplace this lady wants." He kissed the top of my head. "But right now I have an appointment. I'm sure I'll see all of you later."

"An appointment?" I said.

"Yes." He nudged me a couple of feet from the group, grabbed a cocktail napkin off the bar, used a pen from his pocket and wrote. "Here's my stateroom number. Tell me yours and what time you eat dinner. And do you share your stateroom with anyone?"

I gave him the information, enthusiasm building. "I was supposed to have a roommate, but she didn't show up."

"Next time you talk to her, tell her I said thanks. And give her a kiss from me." He pressed a soft kiss to my lips. "Like that. Or this." He gripped my waist and gave me a deeper kiss.

My legs wobbled. Other parts sprang to life. This wasn't

the time or place if he had to be somewhere else soon. I gave him a tiny wave. "See you later."

"I'll take that as a promise." His voice was husky. Gil flashed me his sexiest smile and sauntered away.

I watched him step inside the nearest glass elevator already filled with people. He stood near the glass and stared out at me while the elevator rose.

Once he was gone from sight, I released a sigh. My class-mates closed in on me.

"Man, there's some really hot stuff going on between you two," Randy said, his smile extra wide.

"Yeah, tell us all about it," Jane urged.

"Come on," Sue said.

Tetter did not say a thing but leaned forward, waiting for my answer.

"I told you we've known each other awhile. But I'd rather not get into any other details. Look, the shops are open. Let's go shopping. Ladies? Randy?" I pointed toward the open doors, attractive giftware and clothing on display in the win-dows.

"Okay, but you need to give us more of the scoop later," Jane said.

Getting the women involved in shopping was easy, except for Tetter. Randy stepped into the shop next to ours, where exquisite men's sports coats were displayed in its showroom window. In the View of the Sea shop, Jane and Sue gathered glittery tops and velvet skirts to try on. Tetter fingered a few items. She didn't look at even one price tag. Her mood was so disinterested, her thoughts seeming so distant, that I wor-ried about her. I needed to discover her problem. But the time and place had to be right. First, I needed her to trust me as she had all of those years when we were close friends. Surely our friendship continued.

"That color would look great on you," I said.

She stood in front of a turquoise cashmere sweater. "Oh, I wasn't looking at that." She shifted away from the rack.

"Don't you like to shop?"

"No. Maybe sometimes." She peered around the store as though discovering it held women's apparel. "I don't see anything I want."

My opening. "What *do* you want, Tetter?"

She pulled back, eyes narrowed.

"I don't want to pry," I said, voice low so I wouldn't antagonize her. "But if you're having difficulties, I would love to help."

Her gaze darted toward the exit. Did she want to run away from me? Or maybe she was looking for someone out there.

"Why do you think I'm having problems?" she asked, not facing me.

Because Jane told me. That enticement first made me consider coming on this ship.

"You were always smiling and laughing. I'd never seen a happier person than you were."

"You were happy, too, Cealie. But things change."

A horrible thought occurred. Terminal illness? "Are you sick?"

"No." Her word was tiny, her voice low.

Was she telling me the truth? She seemed much paler than she did way back then. "Tetter, if you need someone to talk to—about anything—I would love to try to help. Or I could just listen."

Chin quivering, she turned her face away and shook her head.

Had I made her cry? The only thing I knew for certain about her since our school years was that she was married, supposedly happily. Possibly she had money problems? Or the worst challenge—a child with severe difficulties.

Jane and Sue came carrying plastic shopping bags bearing a ship's large anchor.

"We bought some great things." Jane lifted a dress bag.

"We're leaving this store," Tetter said, possibly ready to get away and stop me from bugging her. Her eyes appeared misty.

Randy approached, his wide smile encompassing our group. "Y'all should see what's outside. Let's go to the Lido Deck. The scenery's great."

"We must have reached College Fjord," Jane said.

"Make sure you wear your jacket." Randy helped Tetter slip into the one she carried.

She glanced at his arm wrapping around her and frowned, then rushed ahead of us with many other people waiting for the elevators. "We'll go faster if we take the stairs."

"As long as we don't have to climb too many. I'm getting kind of old, you know," Jane said with a grin, and most of us laughed because we were all the same age.

I willed myself not to glance at the stairwell landing below. Even so, I envisioned Jonathan Mill's crumpled body. What caused his death? It wouldn't do any good for me to ask other people who worked on the ship if the doctor didn't know yet. Still, I would feel much better once I was certain nobody I knew was involved.

We took one flight of stairs and shoved through a doorway into frigid air.

"It's gorgeous." Jane flung her arms wide.

I had taken this trip before and I remembered that nothing compared to the panoramic view of glaciers between snow-draped mountains. Still, the scene stole my breath once again. Our group squeezed into a spot where we could see. Around us, people raved about the magnificent scenery and snapped pictures. The salt-scented wind coated my face with icy droplets.

I peered into water near the ship. When would a casket

holding a body leave? The man who died wouldn't be buried at sea. He'd be kept in a cold holding place. His family was surely mourning and hating to wait to retrieve him from the ship's belly.

"A nature guide will speak to you," a man was announcing over speakers. "He will point out sights of interest."

I strained to hear, since many passengers were talking to each other. Randy garnered my interest. I watched him nudge closer to Tetter.

"Those white dots in the distant water are icebergs that calved off glaciers," the guide said. "While on this trip, you will see Harvard Glacier and Yale Glacier, which have begun to retreat."

Randy gazed at Tetter.

She stared straight down at the water.

"You should note," the guide said, "that the fjord in the northern sector of Prince William Sound contains five tide-water glaciers that terminate in the water, five large valley glaciers, and dozens of smaller ones, most named after East Coast colleges."

"Hmph," Jane said. "Why not name some after other colleges, like those in the South?"

"I agree," Sue said. It was the first time she'd spoken to any of us in a while.

I glanced around. More people came up the stairs. Some passengers left one side of the deck and moved to the other, pointing toward sights.

"Explorers who found the glaciers included a Harvard and an Amherst professor," the guide mentioned. "It's said that they took great delight in ignoring Princeton."

I tuned him out and watched what interested me much more than glaciers. Gil sat at a table near the outdoor pool, drinking coffee with a man whose back was to me.

"I'll be right back," I told my classmates.

Gil spied me coming and smiled. Rising as I neared, he gave me a brief kiss on the lips. "Sit with us." He pulled out a chair. "Cealie, this is my uncle, Dr. Errol Thurman."

The doctor stood. "Gil told me about you, Ms. Gunther. It's so nice to meet you."

"Please call me Cealie." I accepted his handshake.

He grabbed the pager off his belt and studied it. "I'm so sorry I won't be able to stay. I'm needed back at work."

"Doc," I said, not missing an opportunity, "I met the man who died. Do you have any suspicions about what caused his death?"

"I'm sorry I don't yet. His death was distressing. I hope we will learn its cause soon." He placed a hand on Gil's shoulder. Their resemblance was striking. The same strong cheekbones, same broad forehead and gray eyes. "It's great to get to see you, Gil."

"Let me know when you have a few free minutes again," Gil said, and his uncle nodded.

"You look so much like him," I told Gil, watching the doctor stride away.

"Some people think he's my father."

"No wonder you came on board to see him." I squeezed Gil's wide hand.

"Let's go where we can see glaciers," he said with a grin. "And then you might feel so cold, you'll need someone to warm you up."

His attention warmed me inside, much like a steaming mug of cocoa with large melting marshmallows. I led him toward a rail on the side of the ship opposite from where my classmates stood. People snuggled together from the cold. I nudged into a small spot. Gil stood behind me, able to see the view over my head.

"Breathtaking," he said, possibly spying glaciers for the first time.

"This was the epicenter of the Good Friday Earthquake in 1964," the guide announced. "It was the most powerful earthquake in U.S. history."

"Impressive." Gil kissed my ear, creating small earthquakes below my belly.

But a concern gnawed at me. I turned to face him as much as I could with so little space between us. "I'm worried about Sue."

He kissed my lips. "Who?"

"Sue—my aunt—former uncle. My tall attractive classmate. All of my life until two years after our high school graduation, she was my Uncle Stu."

Gil cocked an eyebrow. "Interesting."

"I'd like for you to ask your uncle something."

He smirked. "You aren't thinking of having any changes done, are you? 'Cause I like you exactly the way you are." He nudged closer.

"What a cute couple," a young woman said. Wearing the ship's mauve and sea green colors, she gripped a large camera. "May I take your picture?"

"Sure," Gil said. He wrapped his arms around me and kissed. A long deep kiss.

"Terrific. You'll be able to see your picture displayed on the promenade deck."

Gil waved her off, his tongue still down my throat.

I gasped and broke away. "You want the world to see a picture of us like that?"

"Why not?"

"I don't know." I placed a palm against his chest to keep him from closing in. "But I need your help."

"For what?"

"I told you. Ask your uncle a question or two." I glanced at people crammed on either side of us. "I'd better wait to talk about it."

He noticed what caused my hesitation. "Then let's go down." I peered out at snow-capped mountains and crystalline glaciers with what seemed to be tiny bits of them broken into the sea. The announcer was naming marine life visible in the distance—sea lions and whales, I heard mentioned.

"You don't want to miss this," I told Gil. "We'll only be in this fjord a little while longer."

He glanced out to sea. "It is pretty, but we'll see more glaciers on this trip. And I've already seen these a few times." He urged me ahead toward the elevators. One was already there and empty. We took it down.

"I didn't know you'd ever been here before," I said.

"You never asked."

"Who did you come with?"

"Do you really want to know?"

"Yes." I reconsidered. "No, I don't."

"I can tell you if that's what you really want."

I shook my head, backing toward the corner away from him. We rode without speaking. The elevator dinged, and its door opened. Gil pressed a button for a different deck. The door shut, and we descended.

The first deck he'd gone for had held his stateroom. By the time we'd reached it, he'd certainly realized my mood changed. Any sensual feelings I'd had faded.

The door opened. "After you," he said.

We stepped onto the deck with shops and the library and bars. He pointed toward a seating area in an open-air lounge. The waiter inside it glanced at Gil, who shook his head. "Or did you want something to drink?" he asked me.

"Maybe later, after I find out who you came on all these trips with." I sat back from the small round table and clasped my hands together.

"I can tell you."

I sighed and admitted my thoughts. "Okay, I'm the one

who decided we didn't need to tell each other everything we'd ever done. We weren't kids needing all of that information."

He nodded. "And I believe you said that especially our former love lives didn't matter. We're adults. Mature. Maybe wiser. So you wanted whatever we have together to be at the moment, nothing brought up from before, nothing promised for the future."

I pinched my palm. I did not plan to lie now. It just ached so much inside my chest, I wanted to direct my pain to some other part of my body.

"But," Gil said, "we can change your rules if you'd like."

"No way. Okay, let's forget about who you traveled with before—" I was ready to say *before you met me*. But maybe he had met someone *in between* the times we'd gotten together and gone places with her since. If that were the case, I did not want to know.

"Let's get back to what concerns me the most right now," I said. "Jonathan Mill, the man who died. I'm afraid Sue might be… I don't know what to think."

Gil shook his head. "Sometimes you're rather difficult to read. Tell me about the dead man's connection to Sue."

"She met him while she and I were on the Lido Deck during our safety drill. They were close together and acting flirtatious."

"So you think they got together after that?" Gil's smirk annoyed me.

"Sue wasn't in her room when I tried to get hold of her. She told us she was getting a massage, but the spa wasn't supposed to be open yet."

"And…" His smile was most aggravating, which was fine with me. I did not want to be enticed by him again. "What do you think happened?"

"Do you think they could have—"

"Had sex?" His smile was huge. "How far did they go with Sue's operation?"

"I don't know. I only know what I told you." I hated to admit the rest but needed to tell someone. And no matter who he might have come to Alaska with, I considered him my best friend. "Sue was late meeting the rest of us for dinner last night, and by the time our dessert was served, people were yelling in the hall. That man was dead at the bottom of the stairwell."

Gil gripped his chin and gazed at a distant place, taking in everything I told him. He might have joked before, but he would never take death lightly.

I squirmed, waiting. He was wise. His judgment would be impartial, much better than mine where a member of my family was concerned. Sue was family.

"Sue has a bruise and maybe a cut under her eye. She wouldn't tell me what caused it," he said.

"She said she ran into the stand holding the TV in her room."

"Which is possible." He studied my face. "But you don't believe her."

"I want to. But I had the feeling she did it on purpose so she could see the doctor to find out how Jonathan was."

"Did she see him?"

"Yes. After we saw Jonathan down, we were worried about the extent of his injuries. Sue insisted we go to the medical center."

"That seems like extra concern if she and Jonathan had only met," Gil said, voicing my thoughts.

"A security guard turned us back. They'd only let Jonathan's family members inside or someone with an emergency. Sue and I went up to our rooms. The next time I saw her, she was hurt."

"And she'd been to see the doctor," Gil determined. "She

was hurt near enough to her eye so that her wound constituted an emergency. If she'd hit any closer, she could have lost her eye."

"That's what your uncle told her."

"Are you guessing what I am—that she led Jonathan on? He convinced her to come to his stateroom under the impression that she was all woman—but then discovered she wasn't?"

"I don't know what to believe. That's why I wanted to talk to you. Help me sort out what happened and maybe ask your uncle about that type of surgery."

He rubbed his chin. "After Sue went down there, she learned the injured man was dead, is that correct?" he asked, and I nodded. "Maybe Jonathan had discovered she was still part man and really put her down, crushing her feelings."

I cringed, figuring he would voice the final thing I feared about what happened between Sue and the man who'd died.

"There you are, Cealie," said a voice I knew.

I pushed up to my feet. "Sue," I said with an involuntary shudder.

SIX

I SOUNDED HIGH PITCHED to my own ears, saying Sue's name. I worked to get my tone deeper. "Where are the others? Are we gone from the glaciers?"

"Why? Would I be doing something bad if I stopped watching them?" Sue asked.

Not nearly as bad as what Gil just suggested you might have done.

"Not at all. There will always be glaciers. We hope," Gil said.

"We've moved away from them," Sue said. "Oh, the rest of the gang is way over there, looking around for us. Let me go get them." Taller than most, she marched off, waving her hand above the crowds in the hallway.

"I'm going to leave so you can be with your friends," Gil told me, adding a brief kiss. "I don't imagine you'd want to come over for a nap after lunch?"

My stern eyes gave the reply.

"Got it. Maybe you'll feel better this evening. I'll be in my room before midnight."

Midnight? Where would he be until then? I wouldn't ask him, just like I wasn't going to inquire more about who he'd taken this journey with before.

Sue caught up with the others from my class and pointed toward us, leading the group our way, a huge smile across her face.

Gil leaned closer to me and spoke with a guarded look toward her. "Just be careful. You could be fooling with some-one who's dangerous."

"Why? What do you think happened?"

"She got thoroughly pissed at that man for making de-rogatory comments about her sex change and later saw him coming toward the dining hall. With no one else around, she shoved him down the stairs."

I drew back. Maybe I'd entertained similar thoughts but had nudged them out of my mind. After all, Sue was my blood relative. She wouldn't do anything so sinister. He must be kidding.

"Talk to your uncle," I told Gil.

He gave my classmates a wave and strode in the direction opposite from their approach.

Sue stopped. "He didn't want to be with us?"

"He had an appointment."

"On a ship?"

"Maybe at the spa, just like you did yesterday," Jane said.

Sue appeared puzzled. Seconds later her eyes brightened as a realization seemed to dawn. "Right, for my massage."

"You had a massage? Already?" Randy asked. "Did you come on the ship tense?"

"Doesn't everybody live with tension?" Sue asked in a snippy tone.

"I don't. I have a terrific life." Jane's smile spread toward her ears. "How about you, Tetter?"

"It's okay," she said with a shrug.

"And you seem really happy, Cealie, especially when you and your boyfriend are alone." Randy cocked up his chin, the idea of what he suggested seeming to appeal to him. He slid his gaze toward Tetter.

She took a step away from him.

"I normally keep a positive attitude," I said.

"Good. Okay, gang, so what'll we do now?" Jane asked as

though speaking to teenagers instead of people whose hair was graying beneath the new colors. She yanked the ship's newsletter out of her purse. Unfolding it, she ran a slim finger down the wide sheet. "Let's see, right now there are golf lessons and a lecture on photography and a line dance class and some other stuff. Let's go to line dancing. I love to learn new steps."

"I'm a klutz on my feet," Tetter said.

"Why don't we go to different things that interest us?" Sue suggested, and I had an idea she only wanted to get away from us. Why, I didn't know. But I felt creepy around her now. I probably would until Gil learned some things from his uncle. In the meantime I felt a need to keep her in sight.

Could she harm someone else? Someone with us?

I gave my head a brisk shake. Had I already found her guilty?

I scanned her upswept hairdo and striking face with too much makeup that no longer covered the purplish-yellow bruise and her low-cut neckline. A plastic surgeon had given her double-D cups. I checked out my own breasts. Maybe sufficient, but making a dash toward my waist. Possibly I could speak with her surgeon. Her knit dress was clingy and her heels extra high.

I didn't look forward to dancing now, but I did want to stay close to Tetter. Something was definitely troubling her. She was no longer the vivacious teenager, but even if she was much older, she should still display some of the attributes she'd had. Now her eyes appeared haunted. So far during this trip, she hadn't exuded one ounce of cheer.

If I remained around her, she would know I still considered her a good friend and should confide in me once the time was right.

Tetter, Randy, Sue, and I followed Jane to the Broadcast Lounge. The twang of country music filled the room. The stage area was nearly filled with women. Many spectators sat. Most on the dance floor clumsily missed steps to a line dance.

The song ended. Dancers rested a couple of minutes, most staying where they were.

"Let's go," Jane said and headed for the stage.

Randy smiled, walking behind her.

Sue sat at a small empty table. "I'm not going up there."

"It'll be fun. Come on. We'll all do it," I said.

Tetter took a chair beside Sue. "Not me. I don't dance."

"I'm not much of a dancer, either," I said, torn about what I should do now.

"But you said it would be fun, so don't let us stop you. We'll watch," Tetter said.

I didn't need people I knew watching me make a fool out of myself on a dance floor, but I'd put myself in this position. And this would certainly not be the first or last time I'd made a fool of myself.

"Okay, everyone," said a young man in a ship's uniform, "now we're going to do the Tush Push. We'll show you how first and then we'll all do the steps together."

A lively country song played. Three vibrant crew members pushed their tushes, along with other clever moves.

"Now y'all are going to do it. This is simple." The leader had us mimic a couple of fairly easy steps. "And here you'll put your right foot forward and sway back and forth, pushing your little tushes."

"*His* tush might be little," I told Jane. "But he hasn't checked out mine."

"Yours isn't so big," Randy said. He laid his hand on my butt and squeezed.

"Uh-uh," I said, twisting away. Maybe he wanted to flatter me, but my instinct was to slap his face.

I didn't want to disrupt our reunion, and Jane hadn't noticed him, so I moved away from him, to her opposite side.

I spied Tetter gazing at us. Her expression didn't show that she'd seen him grabbing my behind.

Our instructor showed steps and had us practice without music. I became doubly ill at ease, not catching on to the steps while trying to avoid Randy, even shifting back when it wasn't time to, so I'd keep him out of my peripheral vision.

Everyone tried the Tush Push with music. I didn't push my tush in the correct places and missed some steps, but Jane appeared to get the entire dance right.

"How did you like it?" she asked as we left the stage.

"It was okay." I rushed ahead, not wanting to face Randy. I could only look at him with anger.

Sue stared at me. "One of you should have stayed sitting with us."

I wanted to lash out at her verbally. She was right, but I was already annoyed with Randy. I sucked in a breath and blew out an exhale. "I'm going to do something else." I kept going, out of the room.

In the wide hallway, I breathed easier, less apt to swing at any one of my *friends*.

"It's time for lunch. Let's do buffet." Jane caught up with me, followed by the others. She gave me a friendly wink. "I already knew that dance step."

I responded with all I could give, a smile so tight it made my teeth hurt.

Sue and Randy conversed while Tetter remained silent behind us. We walked the long hall and then went up to the Lido Deck.

My mind carried me back to this area during the safety drill. I pictured where Sue and I had stood until I'd seen that bride in her strapless gown. And I'd spoken to her and the groom, congratulating them. It hadn't seemed long before I'd returned to my previous spot that Sue had also left. I glanced across the nearly empty pool deck now. Yesterday it was crowded with people and their life jackets. And I'd searched for Sue and found her with Jonathan. In that short time, they'd appeared taken with each other. If I hadn't known their encounter was so brief, I would have believed they were a couple.

Soon after we met him, Jonathan died.

"Cealie, are you okay?" Sue bumped into my backside. "Sorry. I was looking away and ran into you. You were just standing there."

"Are you feeling all right, Cealie?" Tetter asked, concern in her eyes.

"I'm great. I was just looking at those young people in their bathing suits," I said, not wanting to mention the thoughts distracting me. We ambled beside an enticing royal blue enclosed heated pool, each corner guarded by ten-foot gilded seahorses.

"Look. Cajun food." Jane reached the buffet, which was decorated with fishing nets and plastic crayfish and crabs.

"My gosh, look at all the choices." Tetter was speaking a little more than she had earlier, maybe starting to feel trustful of us—a good thing.

With some oohing from Jane, we meandered around, picking up items. Most of us chose at least one type of salmon to go along with other dishes.

"Your friend's chef probably fixed those Cajun dishes," Jane said. "Those red beans look tempting. And the corn bread. I'm going to get some."

"I guess they have red beans and sausage because it's Monday," I said.

"You know that because of Gil," Tetter guessed with a brief smile, and I nodded.

Like we had done in school, we all lined up with trays and chose items. I took squash smothered with onions and bell pepper, and red beans over rice.

"Look at this." Randy used tongs to hold up a sizable length of smoked sausage. "Nice, huh?" With a grin, he held it toward Tetter, who turned away, and Sue, staring at him without a smile.

Yanking my tray backward, I shoved my elbow into Randy's ribs.

He yowled and dropped the sausage. It rolled behind the counter.

"Sorry," I said.

He chose a smaller sausage link without comment.

What had he been doing, acting like a young teenage boy with the big sausage thing aimed at Tetter? And when he'd held it up to Sue, he'd certainly been suggesting that as Stu, she'd once had a penis. Maybe she still had one.

My anger flared at Randy. And at myself. He had no business hinting to Sue about her surgery, and I'd had no business speaking about her personal history with anyone.

Sue rushed ahead and set her tray on the table. "Did y'all get lost?" she asked as we neared.

"Randy lost his sausage," I said. "He needed to find another one."

Jane grinned at him. I didn't look, but did not imagine he grinned in return.

My thoughts and discussion about men and their private parts needed to go. There were too many other wonderful things to think about, I considered, using positive self-talk instead of allowing negative vibes to sink in.

All from our group set down their trays. I took drink orders from Sue and Tetter. Jane came with me to get them. "Oh, look who's over there," she said.

It had to be Gil.

He sat alone, sipping water, his plate almost emptied.

Jane nudged me. "Go with him."

"That's okay. I'm with all of you."

"You know you want to."

"I'm not too happy with him," I said, the eye contact with Gil working away at my resolve. "But maybe I'll join him for just a little while." Actually, we hadn't left each other long ago, and I doubted he'd learned anything from his uncle yet. But maybe he had.

I again wondered who he had already seen Alaska with.

I carried drinks to my classmates. "I'm going to talk to Gil. I'll be right back." I lifted my tray.

"Don't hurry," Tetter said. Pink dots colored her cheeks. "I mean, you don't have to. Just do—whatever."

I strode to Gil's table without meeting his gaze and sat across from him. He removed my salad dish from my tray and set it at my place. "Hi. How are you?" he asked, making me look at him.

Direct eye contact gave me a shiver of excitement. His magnetism enticed me. But I was woman. I could avoid him. *I can do anything—alone,* I reminded myself, knowing I needed control to keep from making love with him.

He watched my eyes. His own eyes smoldered with sensuality, making me want him.

Or wait—was that look in his eye confidence? Gil, knowing what he wanted, and he'd get it—whether *it* became a business venture—or me.

I shifted my gaze away from him and ate. "Good red beans," I said, watching my food as though terrified that a slice of squash or a red bean might try to escape.

"I'll tell the chef."

"Please do." I kept my eyes down. He was just a man, I told myself, and he knew exactly what he wanted from life. I, however, did not. *You know what you want. I'm going to continue to rediscover Cealie,* I mentally told him, as I had said aloud before we parted. The wife and mother part of me had lost the knowledge that it was okay to do things just because I wanted to. But now I was regaining that awareness.

I looked him in the eye, meeting as equals and not as man and woman sexually drawn to each other, and lifted a forkful of rice and beans. "Well seasoned."

He watched my lips. I felt squeamish under his gaze, until he reached over and, with a napkin, wiped the corner of my lips. And peered at my eyes.

I thrust my fork down, ready to say I was going for dessert— but Gil's grin let me know what he would suggest if I said that.

"Did you get to speak with your uncle?" I said.

"I did. I asked him about the man who died and Sue. Did he think she hurt herself on purpose so she could get down to the emergency room and find out about Jonathan?" Gil sipped his water. "He said he can't give out personal information. It's confidential."

I sighed. "Did he say anything about Sue?"

"Yes, he's definitely interested."

"Good. What does he think about her? Does he have any idea about motives? No, I don't mean that. I don't really believe she hurt the man or even saw him after we met him on the Lido Deck. But what did your uncle think? And what do you mean—'he's interested'? Does he want to know more about her sex-change surgery?"

"From what I gather, he'd like to make intimate contact and possibly discover that information for himself."

SEVEN

"Gil!" I said, choking on my tea.

"What? You asked. That is what I believe Uncle Errol wants. He seemed genuinely interested in your aunt."

"This is too strange. When did he meet her? Only when she went to his office with her hurt eye?"

"As far as I know. And I only know that because you told me."

"Good grief, what does he see in her?"

"She is a stunning woman. And he's a single man. Divorced." Gil seemed to take delight in this weird conversation.

I leaned toward him. "Doesn't he know she used to be a man?"

"Not until I told him just now. Obviously Sue doesn't announce it to everyone who bandages her cheek."

"And what did your uncle say?"

"That information seemed to make him more intrigued."

I threw my arms up. "Men!"

Gil's grin widened.

His uncle, the ship's doctor, surely knew about transgendered individuals and how troubled their unique situations must make them. Either he didn't care or, more probably, Gil was teasing me, making up this story about his uncle being interested in my aunt.

My classmates were rising, their plates nearly empty. Tetter glanced at me, her expression bland—the usual for this trip. I needed to be around her to try to help her become our

old buddy Tetter again. Surely that fun girl was still somewhere under that troubled demeanor.

"I need to go," I told Gil. "My friends are leaving."

"I hope I'll see you later."

I evaded answering by wiping my mouth with my napkin.
I stood. "I don't guess your uncle believes Sue could have
hurt Jonathan."

"Probably not. I doubt that he's kinky enough to want to
date a killer."

"Oh, I don't know. You men seem to like women, no matter what."

"You do have a point."

I shook my head and headed for my classmates, not believing for a minute that he was serious about his uncle being interested in my aunt. I caught up with the last person, Randy.
He glanced at me, a little fear in his eye, probably thinking
I'd hurt him again. I moved beyond him and fell into step
with Tetter. Moving faster ahead, Jane kept up with Sue's
long strides.

"Where is everybody going in such a hurry?" I asked Tetter.

"There's an art preview at the other end of the ship."

"Who's interested in buying art?"

"I don't know. But you can register to win a piece. And
there's free champagne."

We hustled to the opposite end of the ship, signed in, and
were asked if we wanted a number so we could bid for pieces.
We glanced at each other and shook our heads. We were only
there for entertainment, art and champagne, but didn't say
so. I would sit close to Tetter. Maybe she'd have a drink or
two, and then I could get her to open up about her troubling
situation.

A waitress offered champagne, which we all accepted. We
walked around and scanned intriguing and exotic paintings

on easels grouped in the rear. An attractive woman wearing a suit asked everyone to sit so the bidding could begin.

Jane led the way midway down steps to circular benches and sat. Sue took the next seat and Tetter went next. I tried to scoot behind her, but Randy slipped ahead of me and shoved in. The only seat left was beside him. I didn't get close. Otherwise I might need to really hurt him.

Immediately, Tetter waved for a server and exchanged her already-empty stemmed glass for another one. The rest of us sipped our first drinks.

A man wearing a black suit set a large painting on an easel. The scene was busy, filled with too much activity for me. People in front of us bid. So did a few others to the side. A young woman purchased the art for three hundred and twenty dollars.

As a smaller painting was carried to center stage, Tetter snapped her fingers for the attention of a server with a tray of champagne glasses, some filled but most empty. "Another one, please." Tetter raised her index finger.

Randy grabbed her finger. He placed her hand against his cheek and grinned.

She smiled back at him.

What was this? The champagne was already going to my head, making me slightly tipsy. Maybe that also happened to Tetter. I'd have to watch her so things wouldn't get out of hand with our male classmate.

Our group passed their empty glasses to me, and I handed them to our server.

Beside me, Randy snuggled closer to Tetter. She did not seem to mind and even giggled. She was beginning to resemble the Tetter I'd known from school, always laughing, sometimes a bit of a flirt. But back then, she hadn't been happily married.

"We'll start at three hundred on this piece." The auctioneer aimed a pointer at a tranquil country scene with a bright blue outdoor table that kept drawing my eye to it. The spot of crimson flowers on a trellis near a fence made me also keep looking there. I understood why bidders might want this picture that sold for five hundred dollars to a woman on my right. I glanced behind to see other bidders.

Gil sat three rows back, lowering his card with the number twenty-seven.

I scooted back to sit with him. "You were bidding on that pretty picture," I said.

"I thought you might like it. But that woman seemed to want it so much I decided to let her have it."

The woman he was so kind to rose on spiky red heels and sashayed over to sign for the painting. One section of her platinum hair fell into the plunging neckline of her red dress.

"What a nice person you are," I told Gil.

He nodded with a grin. "If you'd want any painting here, I figured that would be it. But I wasn't sure you would want one. That woman did."

Sue and Jane left their places and with a few others, headed for the exit. Sue rolled her eyes at us. She sauntered on her own strappy heels toward the door.

Gil watched with a man's look of admiration. He faced me, raising his eyebrows. "Hmm, nice," he said, giving his head a nudge toward the exit.

"Oh, come on. She was a he."

"Still, she doesn't look bad."

"Gil, she's my aunt—who used to be my uncle."

He chuckled. "Okay, I'll leave her alone."

"Good," I said, almost certain he'd been kidding about being attracted to her.

The auctioneer snagged my awareness by speaking quite loudly, showing off her new offering, a hideous canvas covered with scattered bits of body parts.

I elbowed Gil. "I'm concerned," I said, keeping my voice low.

"What's wrong?" His forehead wrinkled.

"Look at them." I jabbed my finger toward Tetter and Randy, who'd remained behind after other classmates left. The pair laughed with each other. As bidding began, Tetter gave her empty stemmed glass to a passing waitress, giggled with Randy, and accepted a new glass of champagne.

"What's the problem there?" Gil asked me.

"Look at them. They seem giddy with each other."

He leaned his forehead against mine. Dropping his finger to my neckline, he pulled my top open an inch and peeked inside. "I like giddy."

"But they're married. And not to each other."

He shook his head. "I know you'd like to save the world and keep everyone on the right path. But you can't control everyone, especially in the area of romance."

"But—"

"I know. Your inner urges tell you you're in charge of fixing up couples."

"That's not true. But Tetter is in a good marriage. She told me so," I insisted as bidding increased on the body parts splattered on canvas.

Gil was giving me his annoying smirk.

"What?" I said.

He blew in my ear. "Stay out of other people's love lives."

I drew my head back. "I've fixed up some great couples."

"You did. What about the last ones you tried to fix up?"

"Look at what's happening this time." I yanked up his hand that was holding the card.

"Nine hundred once, twice, sold!" called the exuberant auctioneer. "This beautiful piece goes to bidder number twenty-seven."

Gil peered at his card with the winning numerals. He stared at me.

I lowered his hand. "What a lovely piece you bought. I hope you have the perfect place to put it." I marched out of the room. Away from him, I giggled. I knew the exact place I would put that canvas. Facedown, under my bed, terrifying roaches.

Satisfied with having tricked Gil, I considered the flirtatious looks he gave the curvaceous platinum blond that he allowed to buy the artwork he almost bought for me. He'd given similar admiring glances to Sue.

Disgruntled, I wondered how I might fix myself up to resemble them. I wasn't jealous. Gil recently accused me of wearing a jealous streak. Never!

What could I wear that might help me look better? Plastic surgery was out of the question. It couldn't happen fast enough. I was too chicken, anyway, to have people cut me unless surgery was needed to save my life. I could easily have my hair colored, but I changed it often anyway, so much so I wasn't sure what color it really was.

I'd walked off carpet and now strode across white ceramic, I realized by the *clop-clop* of heels on the harder floor. The louder sound made me also look at people's shoes. Women's shoes.

Gil had been taken with those two attractive women who left the art auction. One thing that added to their bearing was their height. My five feet, two inches would not make any male notice me next to women like that unless he was a little boy. Most females striding past me wore shoes with much height, even on flip-flops.

That's what I needed. Heels. *High* heels. With slender straps crossing my ankles.

Exasperation came, and I slowed. A man just died on this ship—how horrible was that? And I was concerned about my appearance? His death was much more important. But I hadn't really known him. And, as of this moment, I didn't know what I could do about it.

I stepped around a Watch Your Step sign, one of many I noticed today. Possibly other people had perished on this boat. Jonathan Mill may have died from natural causes, but he seemed so young. Jitters skittered around in my chest like Mexican jumping beans because of my true belief: someone killed him.

I needed to make certain that was not someone I knew. Sweat dampened my palms. I swiped them across something black in front of me, then noticed it was a satin gown. The gown hung on a rod next to a tall vat holding a jillion jellybeans.

"Can I help you?" The speaker was one of those spry young women in the ship's uniforms.

I smiled, becoming fully aware that I'd detoured into the glass-fronted shop that sold formal wear. "This is a lovely gown. I don't see a price tag." I wasn't interested in buying a gown but needed to comment.

"This one's been worn before. It's a rental. You can rent formal items here, like for formal nights. We also have many items you can purchase."

This was my kind of store. I could rent clothes and not have to lug them around. The only problem was that the rental shop carried only formals. And lots of candy, especially fine chocolates, and flowers to send to someone special.

I spent a few minutes inside and then left the shop with my purchase under my arm and a smirk draped on my face. Gil might like his women tall—although I did not care what he liked. Tonight the ship would hold its first formal night. I needed to get to my stateroom and practice walking. I might not be as striking as my aunt when our group promenaded this evening, but I refused to wear sparkles and have to scuttle behind them with baby steps to keep up. Maybe I'd run into Gil during the evening, or I could run into a killer. Either way, I would present myself as a lethal figure in my brand-new stilettos.

EIGHT

BACK IN MY STATEROOM, I showered, shampooed with exotic pineapple-scented shampoo, and stepped onto a rug to dry myself. Someone knocked on my door.

I wrapped myself in a thick robe the ship had provided and checked the peephole.

"Jane," I said, letting her in. I glanced out, satisfied not to see Tetter so I could speak with Jane alone.

"What time will you be ready? Maybe we can all have a drink together before dinner." She skimmed my room. "This is so nice and roomy since you don't have a roommate." She rolled her eyes and sat on a cushioned side chair.

"I've wanted to ask about *your* roommate. Have you discovered what Tetter's big problem is?"

"She hasn't told me."

"You must have an idea. You asked me to come and meet with high school buddies on this cruise, and said we'd help Tetter solve a major problem."

Jane grimaced. "At first when I invited her, she said she couldn't come. She was experiencing big trouble."

"Any details?"

"No. She said she was really sorry and would have loved to see us all again. We wrote her off for the trip. A couple of weeks later she called and asked if there was still space for her. I said yes. Barbara and I were supposed to share a room, but her daughter needed her gall bladder removed and she was going to take care of the kids, so I could share my room.

I asked Tetter if her problem had been solved. She said it had only gotten worse, but she'd rather not think about it."

"Good grief. We need to learn what it is."

Jane nodded. She glanced around my room. "You are so lucky you have a stateroom all to yourself."

"It's a lot more spacious, but it can be lonely when there's no one with you."

She grunted. "How about if your roommate sloshes down so much liquor, she snores like a sailor?"

"Is that Tetter's problem? She drinks too much? I saw her downing all that champagne so fast at the art auction."

"I'm not sure. Last night she got to the room and said she was so sleepy, she was going right to bed. She snored like mad. Today she woke up just in time to shower and dress and rush out to breakfast."

I stepped closer to my friend. "When you told me we could help her, I thought that was a given."

"You know Tetter. I figured she'd blab about her entire life the minute we saw her. I had no idea she'd be so different."

I glanced down at my robed figure that had expanded quite a bit since high school. "Not at all like you and me, huh? We've both stayed exactly the same," I said with a smirk.

"Right." She grinned and patted her hips. "And if you don't hurry and do something about your hair, you're going to scare everybody away tonight."

I felt my hair standing up. "Eek. I need to fix this."

"Please do." She smiled. "I'm going to start preparing myself for being beautiful."

"Me, too, and that takes quite a bit of preparation." I clasped her hand. "We need to watch out for our buddy. Something has her deeply troubled. Let's work at repairing that situation."

"We will. See you later."

"Oh, and let's not do drinks before dinner," I suggested, walking her to the door. "That might not be good for Tetter."

"Good idea. See you at dinner."

"One other thing I've wanted to ask in private. Why did you invite one guy from our class to come along?"

"Actually, Randy called me. He'd heard we were having a class reunion and said he wanted to be part of it."

"And you told him only females were coming?"

"Yes, and when I asked who he'd heard about the trip from, he said he had forgotten."

"Do you believe that?" I asked, and she shrugged. I locked the door behind Jane and paused. She'd had me come on this trip believing she knew what troubled Tetter and that like old times, we could help her fix the situation. But they shared a room, and she didn't know our buddy's problem yet?

The old Tetter would have told Jane everything troubling her and possibly made Jane promise not to share the information.

I renewed my resolve to help Tetter become her vivacious self again.

And then I turned and noticed the mirror mounted on the closet door and gawked. I tossed off my robe, jumped back into the shower, and used more shampoo. I towel dried and then crimped my hair with my fingers.

Formal nights on cruises were my favorites. They made me feel like it was prom night, only there was none of the worry about comparing yourself to other females.

Except this time.

This ship carried some of my classmates. I would have thought that because so many years had passed since we were teens, none of us would care about what others wore or looked like, yet my mind's image reminded me of the stilettos Sue and another woman who'd attracted Gil today wore. I grabbed my new purchase.

I coated my body with lightly fragranced lotion and pulled on my black-lace panties and bra. I spent extra time with eye-liner, varying shades of eye shadow, two coats of mascara, blush on the apples of my cheeks and up toward my hairline, and Killer-Red lipstick, then I dressed.

"Not too damned bad, Cealie," I said to the full-length mirror.

My satin deep-blue wrap top shimmered with black shad-ows, the diamond heart on a chain Gil once gave me sparkling at my cleavage. Diamond dangling earrings set off my hair that now behaved. The slit up the front of my long black knit skirt stopped above my knees and exposed my new open-toe black stilettos.

"Let Sue top this," I said, ridiculously reassuring myself that I might look better than my former uncle.

Out in the hall, I glanced both ways, taking in all of the guests in their finery. What made people look best was their smiles. They'd made special effort to look good and appeared satisfied that they'd done their best. Semi-formals overtook formals, although some men wore tuxes, the women accom-panying them wearing evening gowns.

The smiles people gave me, along with scans from my head to my shoes, made me feel good about myself, except for the few times I wobbled on my skinny heels.

Spotted groups wore swimsuits or casual wear, mainly young people who would have late seating for dinner or those who chose not to dress formally tonight.

"You look especially lovely this evening," our maître d' told me at the entrance to our dining room. He probably said that to everyone, yet it made me feel special.

Until I saw Sue.

She stood near our table, bending over while getting into her chair that Randy held out. Sue's breasts would shame basketballs. Possibly that's what the surgeon used to make them stand out like they did. In case anyone missed them, she wore a cherry-red gown with a plunging neckline surrounded by one-inch-square shiny red stones. The gown clung to her slender waist and hips. Her stilettos were higher than mine. And they were crimson.

Randy looked suave in a navy suit and red tie. Jane sat at the table, hair pulled back in twisted 'do with a wide rhinestone clip. She was sleek and sexy in a simple black dress. I took the chair beside hers.

All of us praised the others' appearances. Our table and the whole dining room appeared extra sparkly. Our table steward took the napkin that stood on my plate and opened it across my lap.

I thanked him and asked Jane, "Where's Tetter? Still getting dressed?"

"She never came back to the room."

I faced Randy. "You were with her last. Wasn't she going back to her stateroom to change clothes?"

With wide-eyed innocence, he shrugged. "I have no idea where she went. She left the art gallery not long after you all did. She didn't say where she was going. Maybe she got lost," he said with a grin.

I didn't think his response funny. He knew where she was heading once she left him. Why wasn't he telling us the truth? He'd been flirtatious with her, and when she drank, she acted almost the same way with him.

The sound of someone tapping on a microphone interrupted my concerns. "Good evening, and welcome," our maître d' said from the center of the room. "All of you look elegant tonight. We hope our dinner offering will add to your enjoyment. Executive Chef Andrew Sandkeep is responsible for making this evening's dinner and all of your excellent cuisine."

People applauded as Sandkeep walked up. Surely not everyone had been at the breakfast where he'd been introduced.

Beyond him, I spied Gil. Gil in a tux looked yummier than ever. My heartbeat raced like I was sprinting. He sat at a table with his uncle and a family, apparently a husband and wife and two small children. Gil smiled at something the little girl said. Mmm, what a smile. What a deliciously handsome man.

The executive chef's words washed over me as I focused on something more tempting than his food—until he said the word *Cajun*. He said it with disdain.

Gil's face whipped toward him.

"Since we have invited a Cajun chef during this cruise, tonight you will see the additional choice he prepares that is called 'seafood steak,'" Sandkeep said.

"Yum," Jane and Sue responded.

"It's excellent," I told them.

Many heads nodded, and people appeared pleased about the dish the chef mentioned. Executive Chef Sandkeep gave Gil a swift glance with a grimace. Gil watched him, eyes hard and calculating. "So enjoy your meal and the rest of your evening," Sandkeep said.

Jane gripped my arm. "Tell me about that seafood steak."

I wanted to keep watching Gil. I normally enjoyed eyeing him, especially tonight with him looking fantastic in that tux. But I was most interested in the discontented gazes that had passed between him and Sandkeep.

Our steward handed us open menus with soup, salad, and entrée choices.

"Look, this tells about it," I said to Jane, pointing at the inserted half-page headed *Seafood Steak*.

"Man, that looks good," Sue said, nudging Randy and skimming the description. "It's a fried steak that blends shrimp and crabmeat with many seasonings and topped with a crayfish cream sauce. I want it."

"I don't," Randy said. "I'm having the rib-eye steak."

"You can have beef any day of the week. This is unique." Sue spoke in an argumentative tone. Her lips were tight, her chin lifted. The profile made a bone like an Adam's apple in her neck project, a reminder that parts of her might remain male. I considered Jonathan. Was she with him right before he died? I needed to find out. Gil and I were probably the only people who knew they'd been together some time before Jonathan's death.

"May I take your order?" Our steward's presence calmed the situation at the table.

"Tell me something," I said, and he smiled, glancing at my menu and surely expecting me to ask about a dish on it. "Do you know yet how that man on board died?"

Sue gasped, and our waiter straightened, face solemn. "I know nothing about it."

And you wouldn't say it if you did. I ordered a cup of chicken gumbo and the seafood steak with sweet potato fries, then checked across the room for Gil.

He stood near his table with his uncle, speaking to the executive chef. The chef gave Gil what appeared a drippy handshake, barely touching Gil's hand with his fingers. Aiming a smile at the doctor, the chef exchanged a seemingly firm handshake with him and then strode away.

Gil peered across the room at me. Happy tingles started in my feet and danced higher.

"It's about time," Jane told Tetter, joining us.

"I was checking out things around the boat and didn't notice the time," Tetter said. Our waiter set a napkin on her lap, handed her a menu, and she pointed out dishes.

Her lateness didn't concern me. What surprised me was that on this formal night, she still wore the casual clothes she'd worn all day. Her hair was mussed as though she had just climbed out of bed. Faint mascara smudges stretched beneath her eyes. As her gaze slid to Randy, a demure smile played around her lips.

He beamed at her.

Uh-oh, this didn't look good. I feared they spent lots of time together since we left them, but not at the art auction. They could have spent quality time in Randy's stateroom. And then he spruced up and changed into a suit, leaving her in bed to join us later so they wouldn't walk in at the same time. She could have fallen asleep, awakened, and seen it was so late she decided to come straight here instead of concerning herself with changing clothes.

Or maybe that's just what I would do—if I had been making mad love with Gil.

I glanced back. He was gone.

My disappointment felt like a gloomy day working its way into my chest.

Chitchat at our table no longer interested me. Gumbo, the ultimate comfort food, inched up my mood a pinch. Our entrées came. Randy and Tetter insisted their rib eyes were delicious. The rest of us raved about our seafood. We all completed our meal with the Cajun chef special's bread pudding topped with praline sauce and pecans.

Randy and Tetter kept up shared flirtatious glances, leaving me to wonder if anything really had transpired between them this evening. If so, tomorrow they would probably both be sorry.

We all left the dining room, and Jane needed to make a pit stop. I joined her.

"So what do you think?" I asked once we were inside the small ladies' room. "Do you think something might be going on between Tetter and Randy?"

"Oh, Cealie, just because they're laughing with each other doesn't mean anything." Jane glanced in the mirror and pushed her bangs aside. She ducked into a stall.

"Do you know if she has a good husband?" I called.

Jane came out and washed her hands. "She always talked like they had the perfect marriage."

"So she wouldn't sabotage it with a clandestine relationship, right?"

Jane grinned and shook her head. "Don't make a big deal out of two people doing a little playful flirting. Who knows? I might do some innocent flirting with some of the cute guys on board myself." She reapplied pink lipstick.

"Maybe she's just letting herself go a little so she won't think so much about her troubling situation."

My friend blotted her lipstick and applied another coat. "I think you're right."

I sighed. "Another thing that keeps clawing at my mind is the man who died on the ship."

"That was awful." She combed her hair and adjusted her dress.

"I think Sue spent time with him right before his death."

Jane grabbed my hands. "Cealie, you were always imaginative. Maybe you're thinking too much about all of our classmates having affairs, and your mind is going overboard."

Possibly she was right, I considered as we walked out to join our waiting group.

"Let's go take our picture," Sue said.

"Sounds great," Randy said, glancing at Tetter.

She spoke up. "I'm not dressed. You're all wearing fancy clothes. You take your picture. I'll watch."

"You look great the way you are," I told her.

Tetter shook her head and strolled with us. We took an elevator down and waited in line for a group photo in front of a backdrop of a ship's deck on a star-filled evening. Tetter backed away from our group. Randy remained near the rest of us. He waved to call her, but she kept her eyes down as though not wanting to look at him.

"How many in your group?" the photographer asked.

"Four," Tetter said and stepped farther away.

"Five." I grabbed her hand. "We need you in our picture."

"No. My clothes look horrible next to what you're all wearing."

"Nobody cares," I told her.

"I do."

"Then you can just stand behind Cealie. She's short." Sue stepped to the spot the cameraman indicated. "Come on. Get up here. People are lining up."

"Right, we want the whole group," Randy said with a smile, shifting to make room for her beside him.

"Here we go," I told Tetter. "I'll stand near Randy, and if it makes you feel better, you can get back there between Jane and me."

She did as I suggested.

I leaned my head against Randy's as though we were a couple and smiled.

The photographer snapped our group in various poses. Each time I managed to get between Tetter and Randy.

"Let's go to that next prop," Sue said. She rushed toward a female photographer snapping pictures of people next to a huge vase of roses with petals resembling red velvet atop a Greek-style pedestal.

I tried to catch up with Sue, wobbled on my stilettos, and slowed. Randy gripped Tetter's arm and rushed ahead of me. He took a stance in front of the woman with the camera and kept Tetter close to him. I caught up and squeezed between them.

Our photographer snapped poses, and then Randy stepped aside. We took a picture with only the women, and all of us started away from the set. A man's hand clasped my arm.

"How about one of just us?" Gil said, his rugged enticing face down next to mine.

NINE

"NICE," THE FEMALE photographer said, watching Gil and I gaze into each other's eyes.

She didn't know how nice I felt inside as intimate parts of my body reacted. My urge was to draw Gil closer and keep kissing him.

"Damn, you look sexy," he whispered.

A flash went off in front of us.

He placed a finger under my chin, lifted it, and kissed my lips.

"That's a great one," the woman said, snapping our picture. "Now step behind her and place your arm like this." She moved Gil's arm.

He pressed his body against mine. Ecstasy must have lit up my face.

"Terrific." The woman adjusted her tripod.

Gil blew into my ear. Good grief. The only thing that stopped me from jumping on him was the huge group of people watching, especially Jane and Sue.

I glanced beyond people in our area but didn't see Randy or Tetter.

"Hey," Gil whispered into my ear, "did you like your dinner?"

"Fantastic."

"The seafood tasted fresh, right?"

"How do you know I ordered seafood steak?"

He nipped my ear with his teeth. "There's not much I don't know about you."

I smiled wider. "Yes, the meal was fantastic."

"The executive chef hates Cajun food."

"What?"

"Oops, let's try that one more time," the photographer said. "Ma'am, you stopped smiling. Could you both take that other pose again?"

I was no longer in a mood. I shook my head and thanked her.

"Great poses," Sue told us as we moved away from the camera.

"It looked like y'all already practiced them," Jane said.

"We have," Gil agreed.

"Where are Randy and Tetter?" I asked.

Jane and Sue both glanced around and shrugged.

"Would you all like to join us for a drink?" Gil asked them, his warm hand on the small of my back.

"No, thanks. We'll see you later, Cealie," Jane said with a smile. "Maybe."

Gil led me to a dark cozy bar. He ordered a daiquiri for me, an old-fashioned for himself.

"Now tell me about that executive chef," I said. "What do you mean, he doesn't like Cajun food? He let you and your chef into his kitchen, didn't he?"

"He *hates* Cajun food and only let me and one of my chefs grace his galley because my uncle asked him to."

"Dr. Thurman?"

"Yes. He's wanted me to cruise on a ship that he's working on so we could spend a little time together. Finally he convinced me when his e-mail said the galley staff would be thrilled to have one of my chefs prepare dishes to offer on their menus."

"And you believed that?"

Gil nodded. He swigged from the drink the waiter had brought. "All of the crew members I spoke with said the dishes we've prepared are fantastic. It's only the executive chef who doesn't think so."

"I've eaten a few Southern dishes on cruises before. I wonder why the top chef wouldn't like yours."

"Possibly because many of the galley staff said they're thrilled to be learning authentic recipes from the best."

"Maybe it's jealousy," I suggested, to which Gil nodded. "And does the executive chef always do things your uncle wants him to?"

"I don't think so. I imagine my uncle had already told him about my restaurants, and Sandkeep had a difficult time turning Uncle Errol down for this trip." He placed his hand over mine. "I'm so glad you're here."

"I am, too." I felt mushy inside sharing gazes with him. The jukebox played an old-time favorite by the Platters. I gripped Gil's hand and stood. On the dark dance floor, I wrapped my arms around his neck. He drew me tight against him, his desire matching mine, although mine wasn't as obvious.

"I've missed this," I said, and he nodded against the top of my head. A problem sprang to mind. "Gil, you kidded about your uncle being interested in Aunt Sue. And I hate to even think it, but I really am concerned that she might have been involved with that man's death. Would you seriously try to find out anything your uncle knows about her?"

His phone made three small texting sounds. He read the message. "Problem in the galley. I need to go."

We hurried out the bar. "Let me know what happens," I said with a quick kiss.

"I'll do that. In person." He ran an admiring gaze down my legs. "Great shoes. I've never seen you wear any like those."

"They're just some old things," I said, at which we exchanged grins.

He kissed me again, this time with tongue. I'm sure I

drooled. Gil raced off, and I remained in place, enjoying my intense pleasure. Until a slender bald middle-aged man in flip-flops and a tiny red swimsuit with large pink polka dots stopped in front of me.

"Are you okay? Do you need any help? Can you speak?" he asked, lowering his eyes to the same level with mine.

"Yep."

"Stick out your tongue."

I stared at him.

"I worked on an ambulance awhile. You might have had a stroke."

I had no idea why I might have had a stroke, but if he was trained…I stuck out my tongue.

"Uh-huh, it's straight. Now tell me your name and where you're from."

Okay, I could see where this was going. This man had no affiliation with the medical field. He was trying to hit on me! I couldn't imagine why since there were many gorgeous women on board, surely some without partners. Maybe since he was almost nude, he wanted any woman. Or possibly he'd want my social security number next so he could clean out my bank accounts.

"No, sir, you are not getting my name." I shoved my finger in his chest for emphasis. "And you are not going to learn where I live, either."

"You sure didn't have a stroke. Maybe a seizure. Do you have epilepsy?"

Good grief, you must be desperate.

"I have nothing you're interested in." I stamped away from him. We were near the ship's aft, where few individuals gathered. Knowing more people would be around its center, I rushed forward.

Passengers dressed in finery milled about, many with drinks, singing at open bars. Others waited in lines to have pictures taken. I saw no one I knew but didn't glance back, fearing the maniac could be following.

My foot wobbled. My right foot swerved sideways. I no longer felt a solid floor beneath the heel of that foot. The pencil-thin tall heel of my shoe twisted toward my left foot and my right knee turned out. Flame-like pain shot up my leg.

I flopped to the floor, landing on my right elbow and hip. Tears flooded my eyes.

People yelled. Some knelt to help. "She shouldn't be moved," a woman warned others.

I wished I could be left alone, although without pain. The strap on my shoe had kept my shoe on. Without that strap, my foot might have just slipped out of the shoe instead of twisting.

Crew members rushed forward. "What happened?"— "Don't move."—"We'll get you on a stretcher," various ones said. They shifted me onto a stretcher, the motion making larger tears squeeze from my eyes.

In an elevator, I kept my eyelids shut. If I looked at these helpers, I might have started sobbing. I felt like a baby, wanting someone to coddle me. Jolts from my stretcher's wheels over bumps as we left the elevator and then entered the doctor's office made me grit my teeth to keep from crying out. A young blonde nurse and the doctor waited inside the door.

"Get her to X-ray," the doctor said.

People adjusted my stretcher to squeeze into a smaller room that smelled of vomit and sterilizing solution.

"I'm Dr. Thurman," the man in white told me.

"I met you," I said, and he lifted a thick eyebrow. "You were sitting with Gil and needed to leave right when I got there."

"Oh, so you know my nephew?"

"I've known him awhile."

He tilted his head as though thinking, then glanced at the papers that a man who wheeled me in had given him. "Ah, Cealie Gunther. You must be Gil's Cealie."

I managed a weak smile. "Has Gil spoken about me often?"

"We don't get to talk much with me working on cruise ships. But the way he spoke about you was different from the way I've heard Gil mention any other woman."

"Oh. Has he mentioned many other women?"

"Not at all. Tell me what happened and where you're hurt."

"I twisted this ankle." I touched my right leg. "And fell on my elbow. That hurts, too."

The doctor faced his nurse. "Would you get some pictures of her right foot and her ankle and elbow?"

"Sure," she said, and he left the room. "I'm Erin," she told me and had me fill in a questionnaire. She then X-rayed my painful sections.

"Erin, tell me about the man who died after we left shore." Her eyes opened wider. "Did you know him?"

"We met. One of my friends might have been involved with him."

"Goodness, you need to talk to security."

"Oh, no. It's my aunt. I'm sure she didn't have anything to do with his death." My pounding heartbeat made me want to be certain.

Loud voices came from the front of the office. Dr. Thurman stepped into the room with us and studied my X-rays. "Looks good. I don't see anything broken, although you could have a hairline fracture that we don't see." The noisy office entrance attracted his attention for a moment.

I placed an index finger over my lips and quietly told the nurse, "Shh. Please."

She gave me a firm look, eyes harsh.

The doctor peered at me, his features so much like Gil's. "You need to keep your foot up awhile and put ice packs on your ankle. You probably hit the nerve at the back of your elbow, the spot they call the funny bone, and that really hurts."

"It sure wasn't funny," I said.

"I know. The nurse will give you some muscle relaxers and painkillers for your ankle. They should also help your elbow." He scribbled on paper and handed it to Erin. "As soon as you get what she needs, come help me please. Another passenger needs assistance."

"Will do." She followed him out of the room.

Should I have mentioned anything about Sue to the nurse? I feared she'd blab and get my aunt in trouble. I didn't know anything for certain. I was only asking. And my ankle hurt like mad. My hip was also sore. Excruciating pain flared up my shin to my knee. I shut my eyes, trying to think of anything but aching body parts.

Gil. I could think about him. No, no matter how hard I tried to wrap my thoughts around his great body or his chef's mouth-watering meals, my mind crashed back to anguish. Jonathan dead. My aunt connected?

My bones throbbed.

"This ice pack should help," Erin said, rushing in. She wrapped my ankle with what felt like an iceberg.

"Yow! That hurts more." I jerked my leg, exacerbating the anguish.

"But it'll feel better soon, especially once you start taking this medicine. Here are pain pills. This one's the muscle relaxer."

"Let me take them now," I pleaded.

She retrieved a glass of water, helped me into a wheelchair, and gave me the pills. "Someone will be here soon to get you to your stateroom. You can keep the wheelchair as long as you need it. Oh, here's your other shoe. Where do you want it?"

"Throw it overboard."

"Sorry, we don't pollute the water. I'll put it next to your purse. Let us know if you have any more problems or questions. Your room steward will get more ice whenever you need it." She dashed from the room before I could beg her not to mention my aunt to anyone, especially security.

The nurse's voice carried, along with the doctor's and those of another man from a nearby room. It seemed the man had experienced vertigo and fallen.

Just like me, I thought, concerns drifting. A man fell. Yes, down a stairwell. And possibly I could have prevented it. *How?* I wondered, not so intensely worried as I was moments before. Maybe when I saw the way Jonathan and Sue gazed at each other on the Lido Deck, I could have told him Sue used to be Stu—and might still be, at least partially. Of course, I had no idea what Sue looked like beneath those clothes with her beautiful curves and long legs and high breasts…and we were having a family reunion on this ship with her being my aunt, and Gil's uncle, the doctor. And Randy was trying to hit on Tetter, and she complained because she hadn't worn dressier clothes tonight. Maybe she couldn't afford them…

"Ma'am, I'm wheeling you to your stateroom," a man said, waking me.

Somebody bumped the iceberg freezing my leg and holding my foot down. None of that mattered. All that concerned me was sinking merrily back into my dream world, the land of happy places and cheerful faces. I knew mine was smiling as he let me again sink into reverie, the weight on my leg growing into a breathtaking blue-white glacier.

TEN

"CEALIE. CEALIE, HOW ARE YOU?" Gil's voice, quite low, followed the deafening drumbeat in my head. "Oh, baby."

How sweet of him to call me that. The bed beneath me shifted as he lay near. His warm lips touched my forehead.

"Mmm." I reached for him and grabbed his behind.

"I've been so worried about you."

"We all have," a woman said.

I cracked one eye open. Sue stood near the bed. Jane was with her, shaking her head, forehead creased, eyes concerned.

"Why didn't you call us?" Tetter asked, Randy at her side.

"Where were you?" I mumbled.

"What did she say?" Jane asked Gil.

"I'm not sure." He leaned closer. I kissed his lips. "Thank you, babe, but Jane wants to know what you said."

"Mmm," I uttered, lips tight with my smile. Had I said other words?

"She took that medicine. It's putting her in la-la land," Jane said with a laugh.

La-la-la ran through my mind.

"Do you need any more help?" an unfamiliar man's voice asked.

I managed to get both eyes open. He was a security guard, I saw by his badge and café-au-lait colored uniform. He stood near Aunt Sue. Uh-oh, had I gotten her into trouble? I'd told that nurse something about Sue. Had the nurse told the police?

"No, I think we've got it," Gil told this man. "I'll let you know if she needs anything else. Thanks for letting us in."

The guard spoke to one of them. The door closed and clicked.

"It looks like you took more of these pills during the night." Sue held up two small medicine containers.

I shrugged and glanced at her clothes. Sexy. And below the lovely skirt hugging her hips, did a penis still hang? That would make her feel horrible. No, it must be gone. And that was none of my business—unless somebody died because of it.

"Cealie?" Gil's nose came close to mine. He shook his head. "I think she's out of it. At least those meds are probably keeping her free of pain."

"Where's your…" I asked Gil, but could not get *tux* out. I saw his broad neck, the curly charcoal-gray hair below it that sometimes tickled my cheek. No black tie or vest. I managed to half focus on what I wore. Still my shiny top. Maybe the long skirt.

"She needs rest. I'll stay with her," Gil said.

"Let us know how she's doing," Jane told him, and my classmates left the room.

Gil wrapped his arms around me. I snuggled, content, and gave in to the rocking watery heaven.

"Yow! You're killing me." I shoved Gil's chest. "And I'm freezing."

"Wha— Cealie?" Stretched in bed beside me, Gil blocked my hand and sat up. "I didn't do anything except sleep with you."

His slight morning's growth of whiskers let me know we'd slept a long time. And what hurt was my leg. I reached toward my ankle and discovered my long skirt was gone. Peeking under the covers, I found I wore only a black bra and bikini panties.

"I'm sorry." I shivered and drew the covers up to my neck.

"I'm just remembering what happened. My ankle hurts, and I need to pee. Where are my clothes?"

"They were bothering you. I removed them."

"How did you know they were bothering me?"

"I figured. Oh, and I put more ice in that bag on your leg."

No wonder I was so cold. Numbness fought with ache in my ankle. "Thanks. Now please help me to the bathroom before I wet what few clothes I have on."

He sat me on the side of the bed. "Be careful. Hold on to me."

I placed a hand on his arm and stood. Head spinning, I slid toward the floor.

He grabbed me. "Let's go in the wheelchair. Take your time." He maneuvered me to sit and rolled me toward the bathroom. I snagged a wonderful whiff of coffee. A side table held a coffeepot and a large dish of sliced fruit and overflowing basket of pastries near a vase holding a red rose.

"Yummy," I said. "Oh, my leg aches."

"You need to eat, and I think you can take more medicine soon." Gil wore only briefs. Probably he'd slept with them instead of in the buff as usual, since he might need to call for medical help for me.

"Oh, it hurts. I can't tell you enough how much I appreciate your help."

He helped me into a thick white robe and slipped a matching one from the closet on himself. He refilled my ice pack while I emptied my bladder. "You don't know how worried I was when you didn't answer your door or the phone in your room last night. At first I thought you were just staying out late with your friends, but then you weren't coming back to your room." He helped me sit in front of the food and fixed my coffee. "Take these pills. I can see you're still in a lot of pain."

I felt tension in my face from the throbbing in my leg. The warm coffee and sweet flaky Danish eased my anguish. My head cleared a little. "I saw my classmates in here last night. Why did everyone come?"

He drank coffee and ate a crescent roll. "I found Tetter and Randy in a bar. They hadn't seen you. While I was talking to them, Sue and Jane walked past, so I stopped them. They didn't know where you were, either."

I gobbled the last Danish and grabbed a lush strawberry. "So then I guess you checked with your uncle to find out if I had a medical problem and discovered what happened."

"Yes, and he said the meds would make you really sleepy. He had security let us in here to check on you."

"I'm not sleepy anymore." I nibbled on juicy cantaloupe. "Randy and Tetter were together?"

He nodded, pouring more coffee. "They looked mighty cozy."

"Hmph. But why were you looking for me in the first place?"

"For sex."

"With this pain? How could you even think about sex?"

His face neared mine, a smile tugging the outer edge of his lips. "With the way you were playing with some parts of me last night, how could I not? I'm human."

"Oh," I said and glanced at the bulge in his briefs. His robe had fallen slightly open. Tempting…except for the aches and numbness spreading through my body. I grabbed his thigh.

"Not now, cowboy," he said with a grin, moving my hand away. My head leaned to the side, and he lifted me off the chair and slid me onto the bed. "I'll stay while you sleep."

"I'm not sleepy," I mumbled. Eyes shut, I envisioned him walking away. "Oh, why did you leave me last night? We were in a bar, I think."

"I got paged from the galley. The executive chef was arguing with my chef."

"Why?" I asked, but slept before hearing the reply, which no longer interested me.

"How are you?"

Darkness slipped from my mind, leaving slight fuzziness behind. "I'm okay." My mouth felt like it was filled with thick dry cotton. I still lay in bed.

Gil stood near, fully clothed. "Good. Do you want me to help you shower?"

His offer was tempting with that sensual smile he wore. I knew it would not take him long to toss off his clothes and shower with me. "Not yet," I said, noting the blend of numbness and throbbing in my leg. "I showered yesterday evening before I dressed for formal night."

"You were especially beautiful in your formal."

"And you were terrific in the tux. Oh, would you throw those damn pencil heels I bought in the trash?"

"Maybe you can pass them on to someone—like your aunt—or uncle."

"Sue," I said, again sympathizing with her.

"How about if we go and look for everyone?" He pulled the covers off me and took away the ice pack. My leg felt thirty pounds lighter but hurt more. "Jane called this morning and asked how you were doing. I said to tell your gang you're doing all right. We'd find them sometime today." He opened the closet. "What will you wear?"

"I'd like the white cotton shirt and navy slacks."

"Let's have this red shirt. It's nice and low cut."

Now he was stepping on my nerves. "The white will be fine, thank you."

He brought me the red one. "This might brighten your mood."

I crumpled the shirt and shoved it under the bedspread, then reached out my hand. "My mood is great. The white cotton, please."

He gave me what I wanted, and I rolled around the bed, getting into clothes without having to stand on my throbbing leg. He kept his lips tight and chin set while I dressed. Gil knew what he wanted and normally got it. That was the main source of his not getting his main desire, our getting together for good.

Maybe one day I'd feel secure enough to share my life with a man again. But like right now, Gil went after what he wanted—me wearing the red low-cut shirt. But I needed to get what I wanted, even though the red one might make me feel better. I couldn't give in. *I am woman. I can make my own way—alone!* I considered wrapping myself inside my mantra and my white shirt.

Dressed, I tried to stand. "Yow!"

He shoved the wheelchair behind me before I toppled. "I'll ride you."

"Okay, but I'm going to walk after a while."

"Good. Do you need the prescriptions? My uncle said that by today, over-the-counter meds might be enough and wouldn't make you sleep away your cruise."

"Over-the-counter would be fine. There's some in that drawer. I've been on lots of cruises, but I definitely don't want to miss seeing Tommy and Ramona and the little ones tomorrow. God, I miss them."

Gil helped me into a jacket. "I understand. I know how you love your kids and their families."

"What time is it?"

"Mid-morning. Oh, some plans have changed. You won't see your son and his family tomorrow."

My heart plunged. I opened my mouth to blurt protests.

Gil gave me a gentle smile. "You'll get to see them today."

"Today? Fantastic! But why? Are you sure? Did I sleep through an entire day?"

He laughed. "No, you just dozed a little while. The ship had a slight problem and needs to pick up some equipment, they announced, so they changed plans. This afternoon we're going to Skagway."

"Why? When?" My heart made tom-tom beats. "Oh, I need to change clothes."

"Cealie, you look great. And that outfit is much better for your family than that red sexy thing I wanted." He raised a hand to stop further questions. "It'll be a couple of hours or more before we reach shore. And don't worry. I called Tommy and told him to meet you today instead of tomorrow. He'll be there."

"Oh, wow," I said, trying to take it all in. Within a short time, I would see some of the people I loved most in this world.

"Okay, primp up a little if you want. And then I'm taking you out of this room."

I zipped on a light touch of liquid makeup and peach lipstick. Checking my outfit, I decided it was perfect for meeting the family.

"I love you," I told Gil.

"I know. I love you, too." He wheeled me out of my stateroom, my leg throbbing when the wheels bounced over passageways. "Let's get a little lunch."

"I'm not hungry. I'm too excited to eat."

"I know, but you might get too excited the rest of the day, and you need something in your belly, especially with those meds you've been taking. We'll just get grilled chicken, okay?"

"Fine," I said, and he took me up, exchanging greetings with many jacketed people on the Lido Deck. I felt the smile plastered across my face, not veering away until we were in line for the chicken. Then I noticed the cooks preparing our food. "Gil, earlier you told me there was trouble between… two people. What happened?"

He carried our trays to a table away from others. "The executive chef blamed my chef for trying to take over his galleys. I straightened things out."

"How?"

"Sandkeep and I had a talk." Gil huffed, apparently not wanting to replay the argument he must have had with that man. "I managed to speak to my uncle on the phone a few minutes," he said, changing topics.

"I'm thrilled that we're going to land today instead of to-morrow, but did he tell you what was so important that they needed to get it today?" I nibbled the edge of a dry grilled breast.

"The morgue isn't staying cold enough, and some outside cameras aren't working."

I choked on the chicken. Gil patted my back, and I raised a hand, letting him know I was all right. "I just need some water, and then I'll be okay." I did not want to dwell on what might happen if a morgue wasn't working well. I envisioned Jonathan, blocked out his image. "What else did your uncle tell you?"

"A ship's doctor works on a person presumed dead for sixty to ninety minutes before making the final call."

"Oh." I leaned closer, ready to learn what really happened to the man my aunt met. I needed to make certain she didn't kill him.

"The body is placed in the morgue. The doctor has about six hours of paperwork to complete."

"Goodness. And?"

"He needs to inform the Coast Guard and nearest quar-antine station. If the deceased had fever or any rashes, he'd have to report it." Gil sliced his chicken.

"What about Jonathan Mill?"

"There were needle marks on his arms."

"Wow, so he was a drug user?"

"Right, insulin. He was severely diabetic."

"Your uncle told you that?"

"Actually some people around me last night were talking about him. A man was one of the first to see him down. He'd rushed down the stairs and noticed needle marks on his arms."

"How did he know Jonathan was diabetic?"

"He didn't. That's one of the few things my uncle would tell me about him. He was letting me know that many things could have caused his fall. Maybe he became weak and couldn't grip the stair rail."

"What else?"

"That's all I know. Ready?" He wheeled me from the table, and my mind raced, trying to sort through what he'd said. I wasn't satisfied.

"Wait. Most diabetics give themselves shots in their stomachs or thighs. Are you sure the marks on his arms came from injections for diabetes?"

"No, I'm not."

We returned to the elevator.

"Care to tell me where we're going?" I asked as we descended. We exited on a deck near the photo department and rows of thin stands. Passengers' pictures covered both sides of those stands. A few people ambled around, looking through them.

"I figured you'd like to see some of these." We stopped at a large standing board filled with photos of couples and families looking exceptional in evening wear. Gil wasn't a man to spend time staring at photos of people he didn't know. That wouldn't normally interest me, either, but confined to a wheelchair, I had little else to do while I waited to reach shore.

Gil pointed to what interested him. "How about that one?" It showed him standing behind me.

"You look terrific in a tux. Why don't you wear one every day?" I teased.

"You didn't look bad yourself. Of course, you always look great." He nuzzled my neck. "I believe you were pressing yourself against me for that picture. Does that give you ideas?"

"Yes. I want to get rid of those damned shoes."

He snickered, surely giving up on the idea of sex. "How about you and your friends? One person doesn't look too happy."

I spied photos that my classmates and I took together. In them, Sue and Jane and I appeared fairly glamorous with our fancy dresses and big smiles. Tetter's casual clothes did not stand out since she'd partially hidden behind me. Randy dressed nicely in a suit, but in each picture, he was frowning. He aimed his frown at me.

"Looks like Randy was really unhappy since I stuck myself between him and Tetter," I said. "I told you he seems to want her."

"It seems when she's drinking, she tends to forget she's happily married."

"Well, look at you out of bed," Sue said, striding toward us. In heels and snug black pants with a fluffy red turtleneck and dangling earrings, she looked fantastic.

I couldn't believe a twinge of jealousy ripped up my spine.

"I tried to keep her in bed," Gil said, "but she wouldn't cooperate."

Sue covered her mouth and giggled.

"Where are the others?" I asked.

"I'm going to meet them."

"Then would you mind taking my patient with you?" Gil asked her.

"I'd be glad to."

I whipped my head toward Gil, not believing he wanted to get rid of me, not happy he'd pawn me off on my aunt. "You don't like me anymore?" I said. Surely he couldn't be angry because I didn't want romance at this moment.

"I still like you. I just have a few things to do."

I watched him take long strides away and glanced up at Sue. She rolled my wheelchair toward other pictures.

"Did y'all have a good time last night? I sure wish I could have stayed with you instead of doing what I did," I said, and really grinned.

She glanced to the sides. No one was near. Her face came toward mine, a scowl erasing her beauty. "You did that on purpose."

"What are you talking about?"

"You only twisted your foot so you could get to see the doctor." Her face grew angrier, her tone bitter.

"Why would I do that?"

"So you could find out what happened to Jonathan."

Apprehension skipped across my back. "Are you kidding? Is that why *you* went to see the doctor?"

"I cut my cheek and almost lost my eye. Does that sound like I was being curious?" she snapped, yanking my wheelchair and almost shaking me out.

"Stop. What's wrong with you?" I shot a worried glance around, wishing Gil or another of my other classmates was near.

"I'll tell you what's wrong with me." She wheeled me into a tiny alcove. "People think I'm some type of weird monster."

"You're gorgeous."

"That's just it." Tears squeezed from her eyes. "I look like a beautiful woman—mostly. But I was created as a man."

"Oh, Sue." I reached up to hug her. She bent partway down,

letting her cheek touch mine. My hands barely reached to pat her shoulders.

She straightened. "You have no idea what it's like, all the things I have to put up with."

"Like what? Did something bad happen to you on this ship?"

Her furious glare held on me. She peered toward the left at the stairwell, the long marble stairwell that wound two decks down. She stared at me.

Fear gripped me. Had I stirred up emotions so bitter that she wanted to get rid of me? Had she killed Jonathan and determined I knew? Her fierce look made me believe she wanted to shove my wheelchair off the top of that stairwell.

"Sue," I said, arms straight, as though I could block her if she tried anything. I wondered if I could hop out of my chair. There was no way I could get past her if she wanted to stop me.

Her gaze was skidding to the left.

"So there y'all are. We've been hunting all over for you," Jane said as she and our other classmates arrived. "How are you today, Cealie?"

Confused. Sympathetic. Terrified!

Sue stepped away from me.

"You can tell she's doing much better," Randy said, and smirked. "So you fell off your shoes, huh, Cealie?"

"I did not fall off my shoes."

"Maybe you shouldn't wear heels so high. Young girls wear shoes like that—and Sue." He sent an admiring smile Sue's way and returned his attention to me. "You're not getting any younger, you know." His attitude made any good looks he'd possessed dissipate.

Tetter stepped closer. "Randy, stop it. Cealie has a right to wear anything she wants. Right, Cealie?"

"Right." And what was that little grin she flashed at Randy as she supposedly took my side in this disagreement?

He gave Tetter a wider smile. "Yep, and Cealie fell on her funny bone. I'll bet that didn't make you laugh too much, did it?"

I refused to humor him with a response.

"Look, more pictures are up. Let's go check them out." Jane started toward them.

I opened my mouth to say I'd already seen them, but glanced back. Sue aimed a scowl at me. She might tell them we'd both seen the pictures and then take me away to somewhere sinister.

She started toward me. I wanted to get away from her. Did she believe that when I went to the doctor, I discovered some evidence that let me know she killed that man?

I needed to calm down. Even if she wanted to hurt me, she wouldn't do it in front of everyone.

"Tetter," I said before Sue reached me, "would you mind giving me a hand?"

"Sure." She glanced at Randy as though asking his permission.

Depending on others was too difficult. I wanted to walk, but my ankle still ached so much I knew it was too soon to try.

"Did you hear that we're landing in Skagway after a while?" Jane asked me.

"Yes. My son and his family will meet us there." Excitement fluttered through my chest.

"We'll be glad to see them." Tetter wheeled me in front of the myriad photographs.

"There we are," Jane said. "Don't we all look great, especially Sue, all glamorous?"

We agreed, and Sue lowered her eyes and shook her head. Mock modesty? Or was she sincere? It had been so long since I'd really known her, or possibly I had never known her at all. I'd known the statuesque person standing near me as a teen boy the last time I'd seen her. No wonder she'd been so confused. I certainly was.

"Cealie and I already saw these pictures." Sue stepped around my chair and bumped into my extended foot.

Knifelike pain shot up my leg. I yelped.

"I'm sorry." Sue patted my knee.

I held my breath, dreading that she might accidentally bump me again. I reminded myself of the positive aspect of this day. Our ship would dock, and I would see Tommy, his sweet wife, Ramona, and my grandkids, little Tom and Kim. Excitement snagged me.

Passengers swaggered past us, heading for elevators. Glancing over the handrail, I spied groups of people waiting to disembark once we reached shore.

"We won't be in town as long as was planned, though," Jane told me, "and our time in Glacier Bay tomorrow will be shorter, too. This afternoon passengers won't have enough time for most of the tours, so if you scheduled any, you'll get a refund."

"The only thing I had scheduled in Skagway was spending time with my family. I'm getting giddy, I'm so anxious to see them."

"Ah." Randy moved to another wall of pictures. "Check this out. Cealie and her dude look mighty cozy."

Our group shifted over to see. I held Sue's gaze, making sure she knew I watched her so she wouldn't hurt me again. She moved behind us. I would've needed to turn all the way around to keep her in view.

"Hot stuff here." Jane touched her fingertip on Gil's midsection pressed behind mine.

"Cealie." Tetter spoke in a quiet voice. "How long has the relationship between you two been going on?" She stared at our photo, expression pensive, nothing suggestive about her tone.

Randy watched her, admiration in his eyes.

I felt the ship slowing to a stop and wanted to concentrate on my loved ones. But Tetter waited for a response. "We've been together and apart for quite a while. We fell in love. But I've been trying to leave Gil alone until I know exactly what I want from the rest of my life."

"And how can you know that?"

I considered and then shook my head. "I'm not sure. I can only try."

With a thoughtful expression, she nodded.

Oh, darn. I didn't want to suggest that what Gil and I had been going through might mimic a relationship Randy wanted to start with her. Probably I should listen to Gil and stay the heck away from their situation and let her work things out for herself. Except she was asking me questions now. Maybe I was progressing in getting her to trust me again.

Randy ran his gaze down her backside.

"Good grief." Jane stepped farther along the wall of photographs. "Why are y'all being so serious? I came on this cruise to play. Don't you all want to have fun?"

"I'm ready to have fun," Sue said. "Let's go ashore and play."

"I can't wait to introduce you all to this part of my family," I told everyone.

"Great. And then I want to shop." Jane hefted her purse. "Let's get in line."

We took an elevator down and waited in the long line for the ship to dock, the heavy ropes to be tied, and the finalization of all of the ship's other tasks.

Enthusiasm built inside me so much I couldn't stop smiling.

Jane noticed and gripped my arm, smiling with me. She, at least, seemed to understand my elation.

Finally we moved along with other departing passengers, going through security into salt-scented air.

"Stop a minute and get your picture taken," a photographer near the gangway said.

Wanting to find family members, I said, "No, thanks."

"This'll just take a minute." Randy drew my wheelchair to our group.

"Smile," Jane urged.

I glanced onshore, searching the scads of people for a young girl and her smaller brother, both with their mother's shiny black curls. Their mother would be with them and my handsome son, Tommy.

Excitement swelled when I spied Tommy.

He waved at me, a meek smile on his lips. No kids tugged at his sides. And I didn't see his wife.

"Hey, Mom." He rushed to me as I rolled ashore. "What happened to you?"

"I just twisted my ankle. Where's your family? They came, didn't they?" I kissed him and shared a tight hug, pleased with the feel of my son. Lifting my chin, I searched farther into the distance, my classmates stopping around me.

"Yes." Tommy spoke almost apologetically, making apprehension spike up my spine. "My family is here."

A blond Viking-type man strolled forward.

"The others quit talking to me," Tommy said. "Mom, meet my life partner, Patterson Vanderhorn."

ELEVEN

"Patterson what?" I asked and then said, "No, Tommy, do not tell me this man is your life partner. Ramona is your partner."

Sue, who had transformed from my uncle into my aunt, stood beside me and snickered.

"This is not funny, Sue!" I whipped my head toward her from my wheelchair.

"It's okay, Mom." Tommy touched my shoulder. "Don't blow a fuse."

"I'll blow a fuse if I want to—and if it's needed—and right now, it's needed." Unusual for me with one of my children, I nudged my arm away from his touch. "Stop trying to be clever and tell me where she is. And you can quit playing around and get the kids to come out. That was funny. Ha-ha. Now get them out here." I pushed up as high as I could while seated and twisted my head in an attempt to find them.

Unsuccessful, I leaned back in the wheelchair and studied Tommy's face. He was gifted with his paternal grandfather's red hair and a smattering of freckles. His tight-lipped expression held. But he had to be kidding.

I kicked aside the footrests on my chair and shoved up to my feet. "Ow," I cried, falling sideways.

Tommy caught me. "I don't think you can stand, Mom. Be careful." My son slid his arm around my waist and supported me with a tight grip. Reminding me of times I'd helped him stand when he was a toddler who sometimes fell, he sat me back on the chair.

I slid a teary-eyed glance toward my school friends. Jane,

Tetter, and Randy stared with eyes wide, looking shell-shocked. That was how I felt. Their confusion could only be a fraction of mine.

Patterson stepped closer, his hand sliding forward to meet mine in greeting.

Unable to shake hands with him, I kept my hand down and eyes diverted.

"Tommy, where are they? Where are the wife you promised to love and honor for the rest of your life and the beautiful children you two created?"

He hung his head. I never wanted to see my child sad. This time was different. This time he meant leaving the rest of the family he'd given me and that I now cherished. My Tommy could not have replaced that adored wife and children with a man.

He looked away. "Ramona's gone to stay with her parents."

"She and the precious grandchildren I've been dying to see are out near the Grand Canyon?"

He nodded, a sad withering nod.

"I hurt," I said, grabbing my leg. "My ankle hurts. I need to go back to my room." Hating to exchange gazes with my friends, I said, "Jane, would you mind taking me?"

"Sure." She came to my wheelchair. "Are you ready? Or..." She glanced at Tommy, but I could not look him in the eye any longer.

"I'm ready," I said.

She pushed me toward the gangway.

"We'll wait for you here, Jane," Randy called.

"I won't be long," she yelled back to the group.

"I love you, Mom," Tommy called out.

His words drifted into and out of my consciousness. I sucked my child's sentiments into my soul and vacuumed them out of my mind. I could not envision my son and his family apart.

Jane and I sent our purses and cameras through X-ray and gave our sailing cards to security members. She maneuvered me into an elevator, going up. "Cealie, I'm so sorry," she said, stooping beside me.

"Oh, no problem." I shrugged. "Whatever he wants."

We ascended more decks in silence. My thoughts cried out to my son. *I adore your wife. I cherish those kids—and you. You can't do this to them and to me and yourself.*

"Are you sure you'll be okay?" Jane rolled me into my room. "I could stay with you." Her words sounded sincere, but her tone did not. I couldn't blame her.

"No, thanks. But if you could grab those pain pills and muscle relaxers and help me slide into bed, that'd be great. I need some sleep."

She handed me one of each pill and a glass of water. I took the meds, stood on one leg, wobbled, and sat on the edge of my bed. "I sure hope you feel better," she said.

I could only respond with a weary smile. Both of us knew the real source of my pain.

"Get some rest. I'll lock the door."

"Jane, I…" All I could do was shake my head.

She hugged me. "We'll talk later. Rest now."

Respect for my friend hiked up five notches. I nodded, stretched in bed, and drew the covers to my neck.

"No!" A WOMAN YELLED.

I opened my eyes. I lay in bed. The voice probably came from a dream.

Eyeing the sheer curtain at the window, I realized the sun still shone, although it seemed lower than before, and daylight might take place well into the night in Alaska.

"No, I won't!" The woman's words definitely came from outside my stateroom. The voice sounded like Tetter's.

"Tetter," I called, sitting up. "Do you need help?"

I quieted my breaths and focused on listening.

All grew silent.

I swung my legs around to the floor. Pain in my right ankle made me yelp. Yanking that leg back, I tested it, found it held me up, and placed it gingerly on the carpet. Using the wheelchair as a walker, I shoved it before me to the door.

Looking out the peephole, I found no one in view. I opened the door.

Nobody was visible down the long hall. Most passengers had gone into town.

I checked the pockets of my slacks, found my room card still there, and slipped out the door. "Tetter," I called, leaning close to each shut door around mine. "Tetter, are you in there?"

A family of four and then a young couple came down the hall, some carrying packages with bags displaying the names of Skagway shops.

I inched along, pushing my wheelchair to the elevator, trying not to put much weight on my right foot, and peered around for Tetter. Unsure of where to go, I decided on the promenade deck, so I could check passengers leaving the ship and returning. At the central circle, I glanced down to the base of the Atrium. More people than I'd surmised were milling around, some having drinks, others talking in clumps, most moving through to various fun places on board.

Worried about my friend, I watched the stream of passengers returning from town. Many wore sweatshirts and jackets with *Alaska* and an outdoor scene with a bear or a whale. Had Tetter come back on the ship? Tetter, Sue, Randy, and Jane got off here. Of course, so did I. But I'd quickly returned—as quickly as I knew my son was telling me the truth. Instead of living with his terrific wife and children, Tommy was now paired under a roof with a man.

Unbelievable.

I hated that man and my son. No! I could never hate any child of mine. I cherished my children. But I could get angry with them. And I was. Despair sank deeper into my heart. Fat tears wet my cheeks. I attempted to dry my face. Streams kept it wet.

"Oh, ma'am, here, let me help you." A young man wearing the ship's colors clasped my arm.

"I'm okay. I'm fine," I said as he helped me sit in the wheelchair.

"Maybe you are, but you seem in such pain. I believe it might be best if the doctor checks you out. Is that okay? I'll bring you to him."

I opened my mouth to protest, but reconsidered. Maybe by now Dr. Thurman had information about Jonathan Mill that he would share. Of course physicians needed to keep some information about patients confidential, but much of what they learned often became public. I would urge him to tell me what he discovered.

"I appreciate your help," I said to the young man.

He rolled me into an elevator and down to the medical center. A nurse I hadn't met sat at the reception desk. Six people sat in chairs in the waiting area.

"This lady is really hurting," my helper told the nurse. He glanced at other patients and softly added, "I'd appreciate it if you could rush her in."

The nurse beamed at him. Was something going on between them? She was attractive. So was he.

"I'll try," she told him and handed me a form. "Would you fill in this information?"

"I'll just leave you right here," my helper said, backing my chair to the wall. "They'll help you. Good luck."

I filled in the form, noting I'd already been seen by this doctor after I twisted my ankle. I did not mention that I'd fallen off those stupid stiletto heels I'd stuck my feet into in an attempt to impress Gil, and I did that ridiculous deed to compete with my aunt who used to be my uncle.

Not feeling too good about myself, I finished the forms and handed them in. Trying to refocus my thoughts, I flipped through papers available for patients. I read what passengers should do if they became seasick. Room stewards and the medical center could provide pills. Patches for nausea were not the favored solution, I read, surprised.

"Mrs. Gunther." The nurse made me notice I'd drifted off, my head lolling to the side. "The doctor will see you now."

Much time must have passed for me to have fallen asleep. I glanced at the people waiting. They were the same faces I'd seen when I came in. The patient with the doctor must have a big problem. I wondered what it might be—broken bone, heart problem, stroke?

Gil emerged from a rear room with the doctor.

"Cealie," Gil said, smile automatic. But then his forehead creased. "What's wrong? Your leg got worse?"

I touched my cheeks and was glad not to find dampness remaining. At least he wasn't seeing my tears. "No, I'm... Why are you in here? You have a problem?"

"Yes. But not physical."

"Mrs. Gunther, maybe I can check you in an examining room," Dr. Thurman said. His eyes flitted toward all of the other people waiting. He wheeled me down the narrow hall and glanced at Gil, following us.

"You won't see any part of her that I haven't already seen," Gil told him. "And I'd be happy to view it all again now." He gave me a suggestive grin.

I didn't smile back. "Doc, I'm okay. My ankle is just still a little sore from—" Nope, I would not mention my fall off the shoes.

"I remember," the doctor said. He inspected my ankle and touched various places. "Does this hurt? How about here?"

"It really isn't bad. I don't need this wheelchair. I think I can walk okay."

"Or I can help." Gil's smile spread.

"Get serious," I said, thinking of the problem I'd met on-shore. Tommy was no longer with his family. This wasn't the place to discuss it with him.

Gil's smile vanished. One eye crinkled in an expression of confusion.

"How about this?" the doctor said, surely wanting to get on to all of those other patients. "Why don't you try walking with a boot? It's something people with broken bones often use."

"A boot?" I considered asking him if I could get matching ones, and if they came in cute colors with heels, but I knew Gil would jump on that with some cutesy response. Normally I would enjoy a cutesy response from him—we often enjoyed trading quips and laughing—but today I wasn't in the mood. Today my child told me he'd split from his wife and my grandkids.

Dr. Thurman held a boot in front of me. "Like this."

"That's fine. I'll try it."

He hooked it on while giving instructions on how to get it off and on. "Would you like to try crutches with this?"

"No way. No crutches." Visions came of all the dancing I'd planned to do during this trip. Crutches did not fit into that picture. And my mood excluded wanting to dance.

"I'll help her get started," Gil said.

"Doc," I said, clasping his hand, "my friend Jonathan Mill died on this ship." My peripheral vision let me see Gil giving me a double take, certainly wondering if the man truly had been my friend. "I need to know what caused his death."

"I need to know that, too." Gil's uncle supported my arm and walked me to the door. "I hope to have an autopsy report soon."

"Then you really aren't sure?"

Lips tight, he shook his head, looking so much like Gil. "No answers yet. Let me know if you need anything else. And be careful. Gil, you're going to help support her?"

"I sure will. Thanks for everything." They shook hands, and Gil gripped my arm as I hobbled through the outer office. The boot felt like a weight strapped onto my ankle. It kept me from lifting my foot too high.

A prune-faced woman in a wheelchair wrinkled her nose at me. She had been sitting there with others since I entered and was probably angry because I managed to see the doctor before any of them. Also, Gil had been back there before, taking up a lot of time. Now he walked briskly out the door.

I would wait until we were alone to speak with him. I'd tell him all about Tommy and his family, and ask Gil what I could do. I surely needed to intervene, to help Tommy and his family get back together.

First, though, I should help Gil get his own difficulty off his mind.

We stepped into an empty elevator. "What's troubling you?" I asked.

He kept a grip on my hand. "The executive chef is really hassling my chef. I butted heads with the man, and I'm ready to pull all of our dishes off the menu and let him have what he wants in the kitchen."

"The galley," I reminded, though the look he gave me said he didn't like being corrected at the moment. It was habit and not my fault. I owned a copyediting agency, and although managers ran my offices, I sometimes needed to correct their grammar. I didn't always think or use correct grammar, because some of it sounded too snobbish. But everyone needed to know what was right for our customers.

"I went and asked my uncle for his advice about dealing with Mr. Sandkeep," Gil said. "He told me I should do whatever made me feel best. And that would be punching Chef Sandkeep."

"You won't do that. I'll bet you don't give up, either. That's not your style."

He let go of my hand. The elevator stopped, people stepped inside, and we ascended. I was not going to talk about my son in front of strangers. It would be hard enough talking about it to Gil. Or anyone. Mainly because Tommy's changed relationship would mean he and I would probably lose all of those others in his family that for so many years we'd adored.

An ache burned in my chest like a smoldering volcano.

How long had my son been away from Ramona and little Tom and Kim?

I wanted my child so badly. Why had I walked away from him? I treasured Tommy and yearned to stay around him as long as I could.

Gil bent close to my ear. "What about that fellow Randy?"

The elevator stopped, and the door opened. No one got in or out. The door shut. We moved on.

It took that time for my mind to grasp who Randy was, at first considering he might be the blond giant with my son. "He was in our class in high school," I said.

"Why would you women have only one guy with you?" His lips pressed into a tight line.

Gil was afraid Randy might be involved with me? At some other time, I might appreciate his jealousy. Occasionally men still did give me appreciative looks, but those were mainly antiquated ones needing thicker trifocals.

"I had no idea Randy was coming," I said. "I just learned he invited himself."

Passengers with us got off the elevator once it stopped. More people stepped on.

I didn't know where we were going, but we moved again. My mind took in a troubling situation. "I'm afraid he might have come along because he learned Tetter was coming," I said, voice low.

Gil's forehead smoothed. The line of his mouth relaxed. He was pleased that Randy might be after some woman besides me.

"But that's not a good thing," I assured him. "Remember, they're both married."

"Right. But what can you do about it?"

"I can try to keep him away from her." I didn't notice my angry voice lifted until I spied the girl backed into the corner staring at me. I gave her a tight-mouthed smile. Her mother tugged her hand, making the child focus away from me.

"You can't get involved in everyone's relationships," Gil said.

"Excuse me. This is not matchmaking. This is keeping families intact."

"Which would work great in a perfect world filled with perfect people. But that isn't what we have."

"We certainly do not," I snapped, my son's family coming to mind. I fought the sting behind my eyes.

"Cealie…"

The elevator door dinged open. I stepped out. He tried to follow, but I raised my hand. "Don't try to come with me. Go and break up every marriage on the ship. Who cares about happy families anymore?"

He remained on the elevator. Everyone else stepped out before the door closed. Adults glanced at me over their shoulders.

I stood in place and let my tears flow. Was I so concerned about my classmates? Or did the wet searing my cheeks stem from what my son had told me?

Buffing off tears, I realized I hadn't even gotten to share that major concern with Gil, who normally supported me.

My ankle ached like a tooth yanked without anesthesia. My

foot felt too high, shoving my hip up out of place. I wanted to help all of the other people with problems, but wasn't sure what I could do.

"Can I help you?" a young woman asked. She was dressed in ship colors with a name tag that said *Lily*.

"I wish you could." I shook my head.

"Come on. We'll do what we can. Do you want to go to your room?"

"Yes," I said and gave her the number.

She gripped my hand and led me in turtle-slow steps. The pleasant scent of almond vanilla permeated the air.

A few feet to our left, a small waterfall was mounted on bamboo wallpaper. "What is that?" I asked.

"The spa. Maybe you'll want to use some of its services once you're feeling better."

"Take me there now, please." Pulse speeding, I figured I should be able to solve at least one mystery. I could discover whether my aunt had truly been in there during the time Jonathan Mill died. I hoped she was.

TWELVE

"Oh, wait," I said to Lily, guiding me toward rows of workout equipment in the gym. "I can't do that."

"We can start easy at first," she said. "I see your leg is hurt. We can get you working to strengthen your upper body."

"Why would I want to do that?"

A sleek college-age girl, pressing her bent arms forward in one of those machines, stopped working. She gave me a curious look, like why *wouldn't* I want to do that?

"We used to do exercises like those when I was much younger, but most of us didn't have machines," I said. "We did that to try to increase our bust size. Silly, huh?"

"Did it work?"

"I don't know. I think what increased my size after time was eating too much."

She exchanged a smile with me, and the girl went back to work, maybe pushing herself a little harder than before.

I hobbled farther into the gym. Women and men on treadmills gazed out of massive windows. I saw the pretty town where my son had just crushed my heart. Near me, two men stretched on their backs on low benches and lifted free weights.

"I don't guess you're interested in that," my escort Lily said, and we moved on.

A door marked Spa made my heart race. I stopped. "Lily, what time did the spa open after we sailed?"

"That would be written on your newsletter."

"I know what the newsletter said, but someone told me she had a massage here earlier than the time on that page."

"In here?"

"Yes," I said and reconsidered. Sue had told us she'd had a massage. Did she say who'd given it to her?

Lily gave me a weak smile. "And?"

And if Sue did not come during that earlier time, she might have been killing a man instead. I don't want that to be true.

"And," I said, trying to come up with some believable excuse, "she's my good friend, and I'd like to know if she was really so stressed that she needed a massage right after she came on the ship."

Lily tugged my arm to move me forward. She glanced over her shoulder, probably seeing whether anyone in the gym needed her. "Most people come on cruises to get away from everyday cares and relax. Some get a drink the minute they step on board. Some take naps by the pool. Some get a massage the second we open."

"Could you check for me? I'd love to know when she came."

Lily stood still. Her expression turned serious. "I don't have access to the names of people who came in the gym before today. That's a matter of privacy for our passengers."

"But—"

She raised a hand to stop my words. "Those pages are locked up. You wouldn't want everyone on board to have access to everything you do all the while you're here, would you?"

I considered my fall from my stilt heels caused by jealousy of my aunt. I also lusted after Gil and argued with him. I considered my trip ashore to visit my son and my quick boarding again because of what I discovered.

"No, I wouldn't want the world to know what I do."

I didn't see anyone else working that I might try to press

for information. Spying the exit, I hobbled toward it. "So what takes place on a cruise ship…"

"Stays on that ship. If we can be of service to you any time, let us know," Lily said in her previous pleasant light tone.

Sure. Thanks a lot.

I took an elevator away from the area filled with buff bodies and stepped off on a deck with a name I recognized, although I wasn't familiar with all of the deck names yet. After a few steps, I noticed scores of people shopping.

I wasn't in a mood to shop for clothes or souvenirs, but I dipped in near the checkout of a small place and bought chocolate. Ordinarily I didn't eat much candy, but today I didn't feel like fighting temptation. I needed comfort. Neither Gil nor my son gave that to me. I ripped the bag open and let the colorful sweet, nutty candy satisfy my immediate need.

Limping along while popping more candy into my mouth, I checked show windows of dress shops, hoping to spy friends inside.

Instead, I spotted Randy through the window of a men's shop. He lifted a sports coat from a rack.

"Hey," I said, walking in, "how was today for you?"

A pink tinge flashed to his cheeks. "Really nice." Seeming to recover from whatever caused him to blush, he said, "How's your leg?"

"Getting better. Where is everyone?"

"I'm not sure."

"Randy, I was concerned about something today." I leaned against the wall to get pressure off my achy leg. "I was in my room and heard a woman yelling."

"You know how some women are," he said with a smirk. "They can't help but yell when they're in the throes of passion."

"She sounded like Tetter."

"Tetter?" His lips pressed tighter. His eyes pulled closer together. "Did you see if it was her? What happened?"

"I don't know. I went out in the hall but didn't see anyone, so I called her name at doors of surrounding staterooms. Nobody answered."

His chest lowered as he blew out a breath. "Her room isn't around yours, is it?"

"No. We're on different decks."

His eyes went out of focus as though he was trying to figure out what to do. Randy appeared to notice he held a jacket on a coat hanger. He spun aside and randomly grabbed an armload of other jackets from a rack. "If you'll excuse me, I have to try these on. I'll see you later." He rushed off to a fitting room. It would not take him much time to try on those last jackets. Without paying attention, he'd yanked them from a section marked Big and Tall. He was neither.

But he wanted to get away from me.

I waited, wondering what caused his reaction. Why would he want to avoid me? Did he want to reach Tetter and not have me around?

My next thought made chills spike along my spine. Could he have been with her and made her yell? And then he was surprised to learn my room was close by?

Staring at the fitting room entrance, I anticipated speaking with him more. What had he and Tetter done in town? Had they stayed with the others? Or had they done like me and returned on board soon after they disembarked?

"Hello. Are you waiting for your husband?" a man in a suit and wearing a name tag asked. "Or were you looking for something special?"

I mumbled and shook my head, shoving away from the wall I'd leaned against. I looked over a shelf that held wallets and glanced at the dressing room entrance in time to see the top of a man's head pulling back, Randy's head.

He didn't want to talk to me again, which made me want to talk with him even more. What was he hiding? I doubted he'd tell me the truth even if I thought of appropriate questions, and my leg throbbed from the sole of my foot to my knee.

I wobbled out of the shop. Supporting myself on the rail surrounding the Grand Atrium, I wondered what I could do to find out what Randy might want to keep secret. I especially needed to so I might keep from considering what had happened to my family.

"Cealie! Hey, Cealie." Jane's voice barely filtered up through the din of people talking and laughing below. She and Sue stood beside the open bar. Jane lifted a stemmed glass with a pink drink toward me.

I signaled that I was coming down.

I took a glass-enclosed elevator, apprehension snaring my shoulder muscles. I was glad I'd have Jane to talk to but didn't relish speaking about anything significant in front of Sue.

How sad was that? Sue was family. I adored my family. But the trepidation building as I approached reminded me that I wasn't sure of my feelings about her.

"Hey, girl," Jane said when I reached her and Sue. "How are you doing now?"

"Better."

"And how's your leg?" Sue asked.

I shrugged and nodded, feeling my chin jut out. Sue made me realize that Jane may have been inquiring about my son's news instead of my injured body part. My inner pain was much worse, but I wasn't ready to share that information with this relative. "I traded in my wheelchair for this boot."

"Here, sit." Jane shoved a bar stool behind me. "One of these will take the edge off." She indicated to the waitress that I wanted a drink similar to hers.

I sat, satisfied to get off my leg. The Killer Daiquiri drink of the day came. Jane gave the waitress her sailing card and signed the bill. I thanked her and sipped the sweet drink. Icy cold rushed down my throat. Rum relaxed me a little.

"Did you eat much today?" Sue asked me and let the waitress know she wanted another drink.

"I did," I said, recalling those candies. I spied peanuts in a crystal dish on the bar and nibbled a handful.

Jane signed the bill for Sue's drink. "We didn't do any tours, but shopped and bought the cutest things. That town is adorable."

"I've been here," I said, and then was sorry. I didn't want to discuss Tommy now. "Freddy and I often took this cruise."

Ignoring the mention of my deceased husband, Jane said, "I bought the neatest lap blanket and a sweatshirt and fleece vest."

"Nice. And what did you get?" I asked Sue, satisfied to have something to discuss with her.

"Bear claws for everyone. They're flat and wooden, and you can use them to toss salads or pasta."

"What a great idea." I took a couple more sips of my drink. My unease lightened but remained. Crowds grew around us and on the visible section of the deck above. I noticed Jane looking at and away from me. Was she concerned that I might start an uncomfortable discussion about Tommy's changed lifestyle? Or had she and Sue been talking about that when they spied me?

Another concern took precedence over what they thought about me or my family. "Okay, this is bothering me," I said. "Has Tetter told either of you what her problem is?"

Jane shook her head. "We still don't know."

"I'm starting to not care." Sue took a large swallow from her glass.

Annoyed with her response, I asked, "What did she and Randy do onshore? Did they shop with you two?"

"Uh-uh." Sue set down her glass. "They had other things to do."

"By the time I rolled you to your room and went back to shore, they had gone off. Sue sat waiting for me at an outdoor table under a thatched roof."

"Randy told me they would see us later," Sue said. "He said they might take in a tour."

"Did he say which one? Or did he ask whether y'all wanted to go with them?" I asked.

Sue shook her head, wearing a wry grin. "I don't think Tetter knew anything about that tour. Randy probably didn't, either. I believe he didn't want us with them."

"Did you see them again?" I asked.

Both women shook their heads.

"They might still be together. Doing *fun* stuff," Sue suggested, eyeing a good-looking hulk of a man edging to the bar and ordering a drink. He glanced at her, apparently knowing she watched him. Their gazes lingered on each other. A smile traced his lips, a wider smile growing on hers.

Uh-oh. Was Sue going to pick up this man? The last one I saw her flirt with had a tragic ending.

A more immediate concern was another classmate. "I just saw Randy shopping up there." I pointed to the upper deck. "But I didn't see Tetter."

"Maybe she was exhausted and needed to rest. I'll drink to that." Sue lifted her glass in a salute and finished her drink. "One more, please," she said to the waitress, and pointed to my glass and Jane's, asking whether we wanted more.

I shook my head.

The ship's horn blasted three times, making Sue jump.

"Three bells. That's just how a ship calls people to come back to the ship," I said. "Maybe Tetter is at a gift shop in town and will be one of the last stragglers returning."

"Maybe so." Jane offered a weak smile.

Sue met the rugged man's gaze with a sultry gaze of her own, making me more apprehensive. "I need to move. I'll see you all at dinner," she told us and sashayed away, slender hips rolling. She strolled like a model. I wished I could move so suavely on heels—until she stumbled. Actually her foot swayed like she was going to fall off her shoe. She righted her foot and lowered her face in a seeming attempt to discreetly see if we noticed.

I considered glancing away but *bad* me stared at her face and grin. I added a slight shrug with an oh-well-we-all-sometimes-do-that expression.

I was not always the virtuous person I would like to be, and often worked on improving myself toward that end. Today was not one of those days.

Sue glared at me, spun, and took off. Her hips did not roll as she marched ahead, stomping on those heels as if they had become army boots.

The handsome man at the bar watched her go.

"She was your Uncle Stu, right?" Jane asked.

I nodded. "Isn't that strange?"

Jane shook her head. "Unbelievable. I wish I looked like her."

"Yes, but I'm worried." I immediately wished I hadn't said that. What had come to mind was my concern about the possibility of Sue shoving Jonathan down the stairwell. *No!* I told myself. She couldn't purposely hurt the man. Maybe she accidentally did it. Or, as she told me, she might have been nowhere around.

Either way, I desperately needed to find out. At this bar Sue had just flirted with the man who kept grinning as she moved away. I stared at him—smoldering blue eyes and chiseled face with a patch of ebony hair dropping over his forehead. Jitters up my spine assured me that I considered he could become another victim.

Or with his substantial size, if Sue tried anything, he would surely wind up the victor and maybe hurt her.

I gazed ahead, noticing nothing. Was I really considering the possibility of part of my family and murder?

"And you're worried about—" Jane peered at my face that I felt wore a grimace.

But she couldn't know the answer. I did not want to blemish Sue's name if she was innocent. "Tetter," I said, concern about our high school friend resurfacing. I preferred not to talk about my son and his new partner and the beloved people I'd lose because of that relationship.

"I'll check our stateroom and find out if she's in there now." Jane rooted around in her large metal-studded gold handbag and dug out a cell phone.

"I never bring my phone on ships," I said as she waited for Tetter to answer her call.

"These are expensive to use here, but I don't care. Maybe 'cause I've been drinking," Jane added with a grin. She listened a minute longer and closed her phone. "She's not answering."

"Let's go look for her.... Oops." I stepped away from the bar and felt the ship shift under my foot.

"Do you need a wheelchair? I'm sure we can get one."

"I can walk. It's the liquor mixing with my brain and equilibrium. Or we're moving. I'm fine."

"Where do you think we should go? I swear I'm rooming with the woman, but so far I haven't found out a thing about her, at least nothing important."

"Like what major problem does she have that we are here to solve," I said.

Jane nodded. "Tetter isn't the chatterbox she used to be in school. For me to get her to talk, I have to ask questions and pull every word out of her. I haven't gotten her to tell me anything personal."

"Maybe we need to confront her. It's time. And I'm afraid our friend Randy might be the cause of her stress."

"Are you serious?"

"Surely, you've noticed."

"I think he's doing a little innocent flirting, but they're just friends. I came on this cruise to relax and have fun. Tetter's trouble concerned me, too, but I thought with her as my roommate, I'd get her to open up fast and then we could fix things. That isn't happening yet. She only clutters the place."

"There's another possibility of what might be her troubling situation." I spoke more quietly, and Jane leaned close. "She didn't change into dressy clothes for formal night but kept on what she'd worn. Do you think maybe she doesn't have dressier things and can't afford them?"

"I hadn't considered that possibility." Jane's vision appeared to go inward. "Maybe that's why at first she said she couldn't come. But then she wanted to join us so badly and learned she could share a room and the costs with me."

"Exactly my thoughts."

"Her husband might have lost his job or any number of possibilities."

I nodded. "She didn't seem interested in shopping and didn't even check out any prices on clothes."

"You might have something there, Cealie. If so, you and I might at least treat her to some things on board."

"Discreetly. And then if we learn she or her husband needs employment, maybe they'd fit well at one of my offices." I glanced at growing numbers of people ambling around our area, but didn't spot Tetter. Peering at open areas of the decks above, I didn't see her near the rail. "Let's go up," I said. "Randy was shopping. Maybe she's in one of those stores."

On the next deck above, we checked shops, searching for Tetter. Jane bought a pair of garnet earrings. No Tetter. We checked the library. Three young women and an elderly couple perused books. A foursome of teens sprawled on sofas, playing Monopoly.

"Let's try the next deck up," I said.

We stepped off the elevator and glanced at an open bar with passengers sitting on bar stools and singing along with a guitarist who was playing a medley of '60s and '70s songs. Hearing tunes we grew up with, Jane and I gripped each other, sang, and swayed to the beat. I hated to leave the music but knew we wouldn't find Tetter if we remained.

Grudgingly, I led the way on. We passed a game room for kids and heard their cheerful voices, then neared the casino.

"Randy was in there when I first saw him," I said.

"Let's see if he's there now." She stepped inside and checked people at machines.

I peered at the players around card tables and shooting craps. The din of machines assailed my ears. Quarters and nickels clattered in trays of machines in one of the few places that still allowed coins. I swallowed secondhand smoke and coughed.

"Tetter!" Jane said from inside a cranny.

I rushed to her.

Tetter glanced at us from her stool in front of a red, white, and blue 7 machine. The machine accepted quarters. She played the Max button. "Are you all playing?" she asked, and the sevens on her machine quit spinning. One white and two blues.

"No, actually—" Jane said.

"We're just looking around," I said, butting in, "and glad we found you." I didn't want to let her know how frantic I was to do that, mainly to make sure she was all right.

Where did that thought come from? Had I really feared for her? We hadn't been in a rush to find her, but probably that scream I'd thought was hers lingered in the back of my mind.

"Did you think I was lost?" Tetter asked.

Jane glanced at me before answering, saw me shaking my head no, and did the same with hers before speaking. "We just hadn't seen you in a while."

"The casino just opened after we left shore, and I'm playing a little. Are y'all trying your luck, too?" Tetter pressed the Play Max button, and her sevens spun. I hoped she'd have luck, but knew the odds were against it. One white and two reds stopped. She'd already lost almost a dollar to watch those numbers spin.

"I don't play," I said, "except once in a while I might decide to throw a few dollars away. Today's not my day."

Jane gave the same type of response, and I took the opportunity to glance around, seeing if I'd spot Randy. I didn't, but he could be in another part of the casino.

"We were passing through and checking out things to do now," I told Tetter, which was almost the truth. "Do you want to join us?"

"No, I'll keep trying my luck." She punched the button again to let the machine swallow seventy-five cents. "I'll see you all at dinner."

"Good luck," Jane said, and I tilted my head toward the rear of the casino, letting her know I wanted to go that way.

Out of Tetter's hearing, I said, "Let's find out if Randy's here."

Jane eyed me strangely, like what's-the-deal, but we trailed through rows of machines. We found smoke and clanging machines, many with funny creatures and oil wells and jewels and such, but no Randy.

"I only noticed a few people winning. I like to hear the coins fall," she said, "but I don't like the mess or smell of coins on my hands."

"And we didn't find Randy."

"Maybe you're way off about something going on between him and Tetter."

"You could be right," I said, but still believed my first instinct about the pair.

We reached the rear of the ship. The only thing open behind the casino was that sports bar. I snuck a peek inside. Almost everyone watched baseball on the wall-mounted TV. No familiar faces.

We ambled back the way we'd come. Tetter still punched the large button on the right, Play Max.

"Maybe her problem is gambling," I suggested. "She seems to get really into the game. That machine is swallowing lots of her money. It's time for us to find out what's wrong with her."

I glanced back. Three white sevens rolled to a stop across her screen. Tetter threw both arms up and pumped her fists, the most excited I'd seen her on this ship. "I doubt that we can get her attention enough right now to leave her machine and confide in us. Let's get her later."

"I'll get her to talk first," Jane said with a grin.

"No, I will."

She stopped walking and crooked out her pinkie finger, waiting to hook it on mine.

I hadn't made a pinky bet since childhood. Doing it brought out my smile and also, I found, my youthful attitude. Ordinarily I felt younger than my actual age, but the leg I'd injured from my trying to act like a really young woman, and my concerns about people on this boat, but especially off the boat—Tommy—all drained my spirit.

I didn't want to think about my son and what I could or could not do about his troubling situation. I missed staying around him and seeing the rest of his family.

"Let's sing," I said as we neared the crooning guitar player in his corner near the open-air bar. Singing would help rid us of tension. Then probably clearer thoughts would come. The young man belted out "Hey, Jude" by the Beatles. Women our age, older, and younger gripped tall glasses with tiny umbrellas and swayed and sang with him, as did many people at the bar.

Jane held me around the waist. "This will be just like in high school."

I knew the next words of the song and spotted Randy and Sue on bar stools next to each other. Each one held a glass of foam-topped beer. Strange to see those two together.

"Hey, come sing with us," I called to them.

"It'll be like old times," Jane said, tugging Sue's hand.

Sue drew her hand away. "I'll watch you all and try to remember," she said rather nastily.

Randy shook his head. He swigged his drink and motioned that we should go ahead with our song and dance.

Jane drew me closer toward the singer in the corner. She swayed, leaning in toward my shoulder. "So what do you think now? Do you believe Randy and Sue also have something going on together?" she asked with a giant grin.

I drew my eyebrows together with a don't-be-silly grimace and shook my head. I faced the musician and belted out the last words of the song with him, pretending I was totally vested in the music.

People applauded as the song ended. Those on the dance area remained in place, sipping drinks, watching the musician prepare for the next number.

I began imagining what *old times in school* probably meant to Sue. Back then she had been Stu, short for Stuart. He'd been cute in a simple sort of way, like the boy next door, tall with an average build and average looks, nothing to stand out or repel a person. But his personality annoyed most guys and girls, and eventually we discovered why. He'd always felt like a girl trapped inside a boy's body. How tough that must have been. How alone he must have felt. And who accepted him right after doctor's scalpels altered his body into the lovely, curvaceous Sue?

My school friends and I had been shocked. We were so young, more concerned with our own bodies and lives than with anyone else's.

Recalling those days filled me with shame. Probably no one in the rowdy crowd with us noticed, but I felt my cheeks flush. With renewed empathy, I glanced at Sue, leaning her head toward Randy, still beside her at the bar. I gave her a big smile and wave.

Meeting my gaze, Randy nodded.

Sue's face remained solemn. She did not reward me with any type of acknowledgment.

I turned away, shame clinging like a leech. I was not in a mood to dance or remain around cheerful music. "I'm going to my room," I told Jane, whose eyes brightened and shoulders swung as the singer belted out "Yellow Submarine."

She placed her face close to mine. Eyebrows lifted, she sang the song's refrain, certainly trying to tempt me to stay.

I did love the music. These were songs we danced to while we fell in love over and over when we were young. Now concerns about my horrible attitude toward Sue drained me. "I need to go and rest my leg before dinner," I said in Jane's ear.

She snapped her fingers and danced in place, answering me with a nod.

I hobbled off, wobbling more than I needed to. I was hurting inside and maybe that made my body match my mood. I did wrong by not taking up for Stu when we were kids, and not being his friend now that he'd come out to be himself, a gorgeous woman calling herself Sue.

I had even been jealous of her looks and, maybe because of that, judged her to be capable of killing a man who fell down the stairwell, which was probably accidental.

"Sad. Sad, Cealie," I muttered, not meeting the gazes of adolescents in swimsuits riding down with me. Surely they thought I was mentally unstable. They could be right.

Shoulders drooping, I wobbled to my stateroom. I grabbed the ship's newsletter in the plastic mailbox near the door, slid my key card into the slot, and pushed inside.

Tossing papers across the bed, I was ready to lie in bed and rest my leg. I needed to rid my mind of concerns. I would love a nap, even though it was late evening. I could sleep through dinner, which might be a good thing. Then I wouldn't need to face Sue with all the others.

I had to apologize for all of the years I didn't show my support for what she was going through as Stu. I wouldn't do that in front of everyone.

I threw my hips back onto the bed.

And then noticed something different in my room.

It was not that it was cleaner than before, which it certainly was. A jacket I'd carelessly let drop this morning now hung on the back of a chair. The ship's robe that I'd worn and left on the bed wasn't there. Someone surely hung it in my closet. Items I'd left on the built-in vanity remained, but much more orderly than before. The ice bucket was still up there. But instead of it being closed, the top had been removed. Leaning inside it was a tall green bottle with a ribbon tied near its cork.

"Champagne!" I said, hopping off the bed.

I had missed Gil after he left me today. Obviously he'd also missed me.

Fresh ice filled the bucket, chilling the champagne. The long stems of two fluted glasses crossed each other near the bottle.

Giddiness replaced my doldrums. I grabbed the phone on my wall, charged the call to my room, and punched in numbers for Gil's cell.

"Hey, Cealie," he answered after the second ring. "Can I call you back later? I'm caught up in a meeting right now."

"Call as soon as you can. Or come up to my room. We can

share what you sent me." I laughed and lowered my voice in a sexy tone. "You naughty boy."

"Naughty?" Quiet seconds ensued. "What did I send you?"

"Don't play around with me, although you might do that after we share a glass or two. Champagne bubbles do tend to make me sizzle. I might take some clothes off."

"What are you talking about?" Irritation filled his tone.

I didn't understand why he was getting riled. I slid on my bifocals and read the card attached to the bow on the bottle. The card said A GIFT FOR YOU.

"Who sent you champagne?" Gil sounded incensed.

"You," I said, but then read the signature aloud. "Executive Chef Andrew Sandkeep."

"What? Why would he send you champagne?" Gil huffed.

Why, indeed?

THIRTEEN

"Cealie, you and Sandkeep met each other?" Gil asked on the phone in an accusing tone.

I gripped the stem of the cold champagne bottle and spun it between my fingers. How exciting to receive champagne, even if I had no idea why.

"We sort of met," I said. Like everyone else, I'd seen that chef and heard him speak briefly in the dining room. I had no idea how the ship's top chef knew me. But I did not like Gil's tone. Did he think I had done something wrong?

"How did you sort of meet him? And where was I?"

I stomped my foot, the bad one. My ankle throbbed. "Do I have to tell you everywhere I go and everyone I meet? I never agreed to report every incident about my life," I snapped, more so because I'd hurt myself.

"Calm down. I'm not trying to check on you. You know I want you to live your life as you see fit, whatever that means."

"Don't you have a meeting to see about right now? Didn't I interrupt something?"

"I'll get back to it in a minute. I'll talk to you later," he said, tone as soothing as if he were trying to settle a colicky baby.

"I'm not a child, you know. I am a grown woman."

"I know. And you can do your own thing."

"Right."

"Have a glass for me," he said and clicked off.

"Wait," I said to the dead phone in my hand. I wanted to make sure he knew he couldn't rule me.

Actually, I would have wanted Gil near so that I could

share my inner pain. Ever since we met, he'd been the person I could turn to whenever trouble heaped itself upon me. Normally I caused it, but he never made me feel that way.

"I am woman, able to make my own way—alone," I absently said, trying to make myself believe the words.

Had I been mean to him? I didn't think so. I believed I justly stood up for my rights. But being right did not make me feel good.

I grabbed the champagne and flipped the card open. A printer had created *Bon Voyage* in large letters on top. Smaller print underneath said, *Name of Guest, Stateroom,* and *Sailing Date.* The person who had printed the chef's name on the front of the card wrote the date we sailed, my stateroom number, and *Cealie Gunther &* _____.

What was that about? He could have written Gil's name. He certainly knew who Gil was. It seemed he always complained about Gil's Cajun food being on this ship.

Or maybe he figured I would share champagne with one of my friends.

Wait. He didn't know my friends. He didn't know me, either, as far as I knew.

Could he have noticed me and found out who I was and decided to send me some bubbly—maybe figuring I might share a glass with him?

"Oh, right, Cealie," I said with a chuckle. I was wise enough to know that if there was ever a time when a stranger might notice me enough to send champagne, that day had long ago zipped by.

Then why had the chef sent me this bottle and two glasses?

With no idea and my leg tired from standing, I sat on the bed. Velcro screeched as I removed the boot from my foot. Relieved with my ankle free, I stretched on the comfy mattress. Maybe I could figure out what that chef was doing. Was he trying to get at Gil by sending me the nice gift?

But how would he know I had any connection to Gil? Gil would not go around announcing my name and our past relationship to every person he met, especially the man who'd quickly become his nemesis on this ship.

I AWOKE, NOT SURPRISED to find I'd slept. The wall clock showed that I had just about missed my table's evening seating.

Sloughing sleep from my brain, I considered alternatives to going to the dining room. I could order a juicy steak in the exquisite Gold Dining Room, although a seating in that restaurant extraordinaire required reservations. I could order room service and have terrific dishes brought up to my room. Or I could go for sandwiches or pizza.

But my main reason for this cruise was to help Tetter through a dire situation. I needed to get around her every chance I could to convince her to open up. Jane and I had done that pinkie bet about who'd convince her to spill her problem first, I considered with a grin. But Tetter's difficulty was certainly serious. I needed to discover what it was and do all I could to help.

Tommy flashed into my inner vision. With every fiber of my being, I yearned to wrap my arms around my son, hold him close and then at arm's length so I could gaze at him. But in that picture also came his wonderful wife and children. I didn't care about anyone being gay. I just wanted my child with his family, whom I missed and who would miss him.

I had seen Tommy so briefly. I mentally flailed myself and shoved up off the bed. I needed to get out around people so I could lose some awareness of the hole in my heart. Maybe it wasn't too late to catch up with classmates.

Classmates—Sue. Oh, my gosh. I hoped she hadn't gone off to meet that attractive man from the bar in his room. Or could Randy be trying to make out with her?

Possibly Jane was right. I was only imaging that any of my classmates were really fooling around. I would try to cling to her belief.

I caged my foot into its boot, pulled my fingers through my waves, and eyed the champagne in the melting ice. Would Executive Chef Sandkeep be in our dining room?

If so, how should I react to him? What would I say? *Thank you for the champagne. Why did you send it? Do you have the hots for me?*

The thirtyish couple ahead of me in the hall turned and glanced at me strangely, surely wondering what my problem was, since I was laughing so much while walking by myself.

I reached our dining room and saw through the massive glass doors that many people had already vacated their seats, or maybe fewer than normal had shown up to eat.

I drew my carriage upright, imagining the executive chef might be standing right beyond the solid wall panel near the entrance. Trying to recall how he looked, I could pick out only a couple of tidbits: mid-fifties, rounded cheeks, slightly hefty and tall, wearing all white.

Was I trying to impress him?

Possibly, I decided, remembering Gil's anger about the man sending me champagne. And maybe the chef was better looking than I recalled.

I stepped into the dining room, skimming the area as far as I could see. The white chef's hat should be easy to spot.

I found myself peering across to the opposite side of the huge dining room where Gil had sat. My lips tugged down at the corners when I didn't see him or a chef.

Our waitress stepped near. "You wanted to dine with your friends?"

"Yes. It isn't too late, is it?"

"Of course not, although they are almost finished with their meal. I will get you a menu."

I approached my table, disgruntled to find only Sue and Jane. Sue picked at her fruit cup. At least she wasn't off with a man. Jane appeared content, devouring a spongy chocolate cake coated with what seemed to be a raspberry sauce.

"The second seating is almost ready to come in," Sue said as I sat, the smile I'd tried to form wiping from my lips.

"Hi to you, too. I'll eat fast." I wasn't too hungry and would not want to keep the staff hustling between the first and second seating. Everyone was so polite and striving to please us that I surely didn't want them to run late because of me. Our table assistant grabbed the cloth napkin standing on my plate and set it across my lap. I thanked him.

"Get this dessert," Jane told me. "It's exquisite."

"I'll skip dessert. But maybe I'll hit the ice cream bar later."

"Maybe I'll join you," she said.

"Good grief. How can you eat so much?" Sue set down her fork, a purple grape stuck on its tines.

I was saved from giving her a blunt response by our waitress handing me an open entrée menu.

"I'll just take whatever's quickest," I said. "No soup or salad or breads or dessert. No wine, either."

"Are you certain? Everything would take about the same amount of time."

"Yes, please. Surprise me." I returned the menu.

"Why are you so late?" Jane asked.

"I fell asleep. Where are the others?"

"This isn't our day to keep track of them." Sue dabbed her napkin to her lips. She placed it across her dessert dish, which still held strawberries, grapes, and cheese. "And I'm sorry, but I need to move around. I can't sit and wait until you eat."

"No problem. Maybe we'll see you later."

She gave us a brief nod and tottered away on spiky heels.

Jane gazed at me. "Was she always so bitchy? I don't remember her being so annoying when she was Stu."

"She was, but aggravating to us in other ways. Now she's moody. Maybe she needs different hormones."

"I wouldn't have invited her along if I'd remembered that. But you know how it is—you don't remember everything about the people you went to school with."

"Right, and even so, maturity and adult experiences made us all change."

"But none of us as much as Sue, right? Going from Stu to Sue." She ginned with a wink, and a poignant moment made me sympathize with Sue. What misery she must have gone through, believing she was female in a male's body.

"Jane, where are the others? Did they come to eat?"

"Randy and Tetter? Neither one showed up. Sue said she didn't know where Randy went."

"Do you think Tetter could still be in the casino?"

"Possibly. And do I believe she could have a gambling problem."

"She also drank lots of champagne awfully quickly at the art auction. She could have a gambling and drinking problem, which causes some people to lose even their homes. Or maybe she uses those as crutches to distract herself from other painful situations."

Jane slid her dessert fork along her dish, scraping up the last bits of drizzled chocolate. "You and I have our bet. After you eat, we'll check out the casino. If our girl is in there, we can yank her out and give her a good talking to."

"We might have to do an intervention."

Our table steward stepped up with a covered dish, her smile uncertain. "Here is your meal, Ms. Gunther. I hope you enjoy it."

"I'm sure I will. That was quick. Thank you so much."

She removed the cover from my plate. The exquisite scent of bacon-wrapped steak thrilled my nostrils.

"Dang." Jane ogled my plate. "Filet mignon and fancy potatoes and garlic asparagus. That wasn't offered on tonight's menu."

"Are you sure?" I leaned over my thick steak and inhaled. "This smells fantastic. Let me share some of it with you."

"If I could fit another bite in my stomach, I would. Go ahead. I'll ask for that tomorrow night."

"I'll hurry," I said, noting that most tables had cleared. The staff quickly took up used plates and utensils and glasses. I easily sliced into my three-quarter inch steak. The meat was pink in the middle and tasted especially flavorful. "Yum." I raised my eyebrows at Jane, pointing to ask if she wanted some, but she shook her head. The cheesy garlic potatoes and crunchy asparagus went down before I noticed.

"Do you want to search for our friend?" Jane asked the minute I set down my napkin. "Or would you like ice cream first?"

"No way could I eat anything else. The only food that might make my belly happier now would be boiled crayfish," I said on our way out.

"Huh?" she said, cringing.

The idea of crayfish made me think of Gil. Its direct opposite, filet mignon, made me consider the executive chef.

"Wait, I have to do something," I told Jane and headed back to the dining room. I'd ask a staff member if Chef Sandkeep was around and say I wanted to talk to him.

The doors had been locked.

"What are you doing?" Jane asked.

Without answering, I peered through the glass doors. Staff members rushed, replacing ironed linen tablecloths, straightening the chairs, and vacuuming carpet. Beyond this rush of people, I spied a tall white hat.

Taking steps to the left, I rose on tiptoe and could see his face. I waved so hard I could have been trying to get Mardi Gras float riders to throw me beads.

Executive Chef Sandkeep peered at me from across the room.

Ready to pound on the glass door to ask a staff member to let me back in, I gave the chef a huge smile and a thumbs-up.

His expression didn't change.

"It's me, Cealie," I called through the glass and pointed at myself, though he was too far away to hear.

He turned and walked out of sight.

"Cealie." Jane grabbed my hand. "Are you all right? What's wrong with you?"

I tromped toward the deck of elevators. "That man," I said, glancing back to see if he might come out of those doors since he'd seen me. "He sent champagne to my room. And also that steak, I'll bet."

"What man? You had *champagne?* And didn't share it with your friend?"

"*That* man." I pointed at the large frame beside the elevators that held photographs with names of the ship's main staff: Captain. Purser. Hotel manager. Executive chef.

"He has pretty teeth," Jane said. "Okay, I know you like to play pranks, or I guess you still do. Because now you're telling me the man in charge of all the food on this ship likes you enough to send you great food and drink?"

"But he's not in charge of all the food on this trip. Gil also has a chef on board."

"Terrific." Jane flung up her hands. "I don't have anyone who knows how to cook, and you have two great cooks fighting over you?"

"Don't be silly. That can't be happening," I said, realizing that what Jane inferred could be right. Of course Gil couldn't cook, but his chefs could. "I'll tell you about the champagne later. Let's find our friend."

"We're searching for Tetter, right?" Jane's finger poised over the wall slate of elevator buttons.

"Yes. If she's been in the same place all that time, we may have guessed some of our buddy's problem, whether she wants to admit it or not. And then we'll determine how to solve it."

Jane spoke up. "And I'll beg for a scrumptious dinner tomorrow if we come across one of your chef boyfriends along the way."

Hmm, what if we came across both of them?

FOURTEEN

"I DON'T KNOW ABOUT THIS," Jane said as we approached the smoky casino. "Lots of people gamble for hours on end, and they aren't addicted. My Aunt Lucille did it once a month with the same group of ladies who rode on a bus."

"But they probably never claimed to have a major problem. Tetter did," I said.

"True."

"We'll just take a quick run through here. There are lots of places with other entertainment she might be enjoying on this ship."

We plunged ahead between tables, whipping our heads one way and the other to try to spot our friend. I aimed into a section in the far right corner, and Jane turned toward the left. Coins jangled as they tumbled from a machine I neared, a voice in the machine yelling, "You've scored!" I wished those machines would also tell players how much they lost each time they pushed a button.

The coins' recipient snagged my interest much more than the quarters he was collecting in his plastic bucket.

"Randy," I said. "You did great."

"It's about time. I put a lot more than this in the machine."

"Really?" I took a second to calculate that he must have spent lots of time and cash in this spot. "Have you seen—"

"Have you seen Tetter?" he asked, the question I'd started to ask him.

"No, she didn't come to dinner. Neither did you," I said.

Frown lines creased his forehead. "I didn't feel like a big

meal, so I went through the fast line on the Lido Deck and grabbed a grilled chicken breast."

Exactly what I should have done instead of pigging out on that bacon-wrapped filet mignon and accessories the executive chef must have specially prepared for me. The thought of that possibility made me wonder, as I watched Randy scoop the last piles of coins from the machine's tray into his bucket. *Had* the chef made that meal just for me? I'd shown up in the dining room late and without checking the menu, asked our waitress to bring whatever was quickest so I wouldn't hold the staff back from preparing for the second seating of their guests.

If Sandkeep did prepare a meal for me and send me champagne, what did that mean?

"This ought to tide me over for a while." Randy smiled, struggling to balance his filled bucket on his lap.

"Nice. You might buy some jewelry at the Floating Jewels sale tonight with all of that cash. You could get something nice for your wife," I suggested.

"That's an idea." He spoke disinterestedly and wrapped both arms around his bucket. "I'm going to cash this in."

"Great. So what did you and Tetter do in town today?"

He glanced at me, eyes more serious. "We walked on that boardwalk and went in a couple of neat shops with false fronts. Then she wanted to check out some store where I didn't care to go. We said we'd see each other later. I haven't seen her again, but I'm sure she came back before we left shore."

He carried his coins toward a cashier's cage.

I rushed toward Jane, who was dropping coins into a penny machine.

"I didn't see Tetter," she said, "but I saw this machine. Look at how these frogs jump."

"I found Randy over there." I filled her in on the details. "I'm not sure I believe him."

"Well, he's a big boy, and she's a big girl."

That wasn't good enough for me, not if Tetter had told Jane she had a major difficulty and it had gotten worse right before our cruise.

"Why don't you play awhile? There are lots of fun machines."

"Machines always win when I play. I'm going to look around the boat. I'll see you later, maybe for the performance in an hour or so in the theater. Good luck," I said.

Gil was in a meeting and unhappy about my champagne when I last spoke to him.

What I really needed to do was check on two people—my friend and my aunt.

Did Tetter want help with a problem? If so, she certainly wasn't sharing that information.

Worry clung like a spider attaching itself to my shoulders and scalp when I considered my aunt and the man who died on board. I wanted to believe she had nothing to do with his death. But a nagging fear reminded me they had flirted with each other.

And today she'd flirted with that large man at the bar.

Tommy's face came into mind, and I yearned to be with him. But I couldn't achieve that desire right now. Feeling the boat seeming to pick up speed, I scuttled in search of Tetter or Sue.

I'd start with some of the public places on this deck. People walked and sat and talked everywhere. I ducked into the Regal Lounge and smiled at the bartender, the only person inside. Scouting faces again in the wide hallway, I peeked into the library. A dozen or so people searched for reading material. I ambled farther, and the boat dipped, making my booted foot slide a pinch sideways. It struck the leg of a stool at the open bar where we had sung.

Gil sat on the next stool.

"Great. You're falling for me." He clasped my wrist before I fell over and helped me straighten on my feet.

I widened my stance to keep my balance and surveyed people sitting with him. All three were men, making me relax. They wore dressy casual with light jackets or sweaters. No-nonsense drinks without umbrellas stood in front of each of them.

"I need to fall for someone," I told Gil, "and you happen to be in the right place." I gave him a smile in which I attempted to give away nothing. These men didn't need to know he knew me, if that's what he chose, and I could move on, continuing my purpose. He could continue whatever he was doing with these people.

"It looks like you hurt yourself." With a serious face, Gil pointed to my boot. "Do you need some help, ma'am? I could help you get somewhere—maybe to your room."

I stared at his eyes. No smile lines near them. I checked his lips. Not a hint of a grin.

He wasn't trying to get me back to my stateroom for sex. What was Gil up to?

I wasn't in a romantic mood, although that could easily change when he came around. He wore that look of something-serious-is-filling-my-brain-now-so-let-me-work-it-out.

I wanted to know what that serious thing was.

"I appreciate your offer," I said, pretending he was a stranger. "I'm not ready to go to my room yet, but I was hoping to get to that place." I pointed aft, trying to recall what might be back there on this deck.

"Oh, the Wake Lounge," he said.

"That's the one. My friends are waiting." I saw his gaze follow my left hand slipping into my right palm, and spied his smirk as he watched me pinch, knowing I'd brewed a lie.

"I'll help her get there and be right back," he told the men on the bar stools.

"Take your time," one wearing thick bifocals said.

"Give us all another round, would you?" Gil asked the bartender, surely to keep these people in their places till he returned.

He gripped my arm. I bent toward him as I walked, doing my best imitation of a woman in pain needing a man to lean on.

"This is so nice of you, sir," I said, gazing at my feet.

"Does your foot really hurt?"

"No, I slid. I was just lucky I stopped against Sir Galahad."

"Damn, I miss you." His gaze met mine. "I would much rather be with you than any of them."

"So why are you with them? Why not stay with me?"

We passed through the smaller hallway beside one of the dining rooms. Out of view from the men he'd left, Gil wrapped his arms around me and kissed. Long. Deep kisses. My torso sprang to life.

"Yummy," I said as he drew back. A couple with small children was passing. Gil, the gentleman, would not let them see us getting too passionate. My mind all but dissipated. Body parts sent him invisible magnets.

He pushed a lock of hair away from my forehead and placed a soft kiss there.

I reached out for him.

He kept at arm's length. "Those men are telling me about something that could become a real problem. I need to get back to them."

"Can I help?"

He kissed my nose. "Maybe if you could whip up lots of fantastic Cajun dishes."

I grinned and made my shoulders droop. "Mom's fault. She didn't create a cook."

"I know. Not even a good microwaver." He smirked, but

then wore a serious expression. "It seems your friend Chef Sandkeep has a special intolerance for Cajun food."

"So? Lots of passengers love it."

"Yes, but some people have been getting sick. He seems to be blaming their illnesses on the food my chef prepares."

I considered his statements. "What does your uncle say?"

"That's one problem. Uncle Errol keeps so busy with all of the sick passengers we haven't had time to talk. His reply to my email said he hasn't seen any proof that any Cajun dishes are causing the problem."

"Well, there."

"That doesn't rule it out. They just don't know yet."

"I'm sure your food is fine. The executive chef is wrong. He's just jealous of your chef's cooking."

Gil lifted my chin. "And maybe of my girl, too."

"Excuse me?"

"What's this deal about him sending you champagne?"

"And two stemmed glasses."

He didn't look happier. "Why did he send them?"

I shrugged. "Who knows?"

"A man doesn't send champagne to a woman he isn't trying to impress."

Huffiness expanded in my chest. "What are you suggesting?"

"There must have been a card with his gift. What did it say?"

"The date we sailed and my stateroom." His eyes glazed over as I told this info I knew he didn't care about. "And then it said, 'To Cealie Gunther and blank.'"

"Blank?"

"Yes, like whoever I was going to drink with."

His gray eyes hardened. "And that person is..."

"What? Do you think he wants me?"

"I don't know why he wouldn't."

"This is me, Cealie, with the flabby boobs and droopy skin and crow's feet gathering near her eyes. And my middle keeps spreading but not my height."

He grabbed my hands. "To me, you look fantastic. I love you. I don't want any other man to do that. I could never stand to lose you."

Flattered, I didn't know what to say. Should I tell him I never wanted another man to admire me?

Absolutely not. Would I want to lose Gil? No way. I just didn't want to remain with him all the time until I fully knew myself again, and I was so close.

I kept my lips tight.

He kissed my cheek. "I need to get back there. Maybe I'll get to see you later."

"Thanks for the help, mister," I called and entered the lounge.

Everyone sat in large black leather chairs forming a semi-circle that faced a huge flat-screen wall TV. People drank, smoked, and watched baseball.

Tetter sat in the room. And she had a problem that I was about to help solve.

FIFTEEN

TETTER WATCHED MY APPROACH from her leather club chair. She sat in the last row of the semicircle of people gathered in the loud smoky bar, eyes appearing harder as I neared. No one sat beside her.

A few bar patrons glanced at me but returned their attention to the baseball game on television.

I located a chair similar to Tetter's, drew it beside hers, and sat. "Hello," I said.

"Hello." She gave me the briefest nod and faced the game.

"Can I buy you a drink?" I pointed to the margarita glass she held. Her frozen drink was almost gone, its thick salt rim disturbed in only one spot.

"Sure."

I met the male bartender's gaze, pointed to Tetter's glass, and held up two fingers. Surprising me, he twisted his lips in a sort of frown. Then he nodded. Why wouldn't he want to get us both drinks? Or maybe I was reading something into his expression that meant nothing.

Voices lifted in the game. Some people in the bar cheered. Others complained.

Tetter stared at the set, not changing her expression. She sipped her drink.

I watched her long moments. Still facing forward, she checked me through the corner of her eye.

The waiter brought our drinks. I gave him my sailing card and signed the bill.

Tetter nodded her thanks to me. She took big swallows to finish her other drink and handed her glass to the bartender.

He swung his gaze to me and then to her full glass and the empty one she set on his tray. I felt he was telling me she'd had a few, and he was concerned.

"We missed you at dinner," I told Tetter.

She stared at the game.

"Which of them do you like?" I asked.

She squinted at me, eyebrows cocked like she was confused.

"Do you like both of them?"

Her eyes widened. She turned away and stared at the TV. I could have sworn that was the first time she noticed two teams played baseball. What did she think I was talking about?

"They're both good." She removed the tiny umbrella from her glass and swilled her drink.

I sipped my frozen drink, the coarse salt on the rim making me need to lick some grit off my teeth. *Thwack* came from the TV. People with us cheered and griped. Some urged players on. Others quieted and waited.

I touched Tetter's forearm. "I'd like to help."

She drew her arm away and gulped down more liquor. "With what?"

"The situation troubling you."

Her gaze met mine. Worry lines crinkled skin between her eyes, which now revealed fear. She breathed, not saying a word but she appeared more like the Tetter I knew as a teen, the buddy who was ready to tell all and help all or ask for help if she required it.

A smoke tendril drifted between us as a woman in front fired up her cigarette.

I fanned the smoke aside, momentarily considering my cousin I'd visited not long ago in Gatlinburg, who recently quit smoking. I would have to call or email and find out how she was doing with that and her new love life.

Tetter's expression stayed tense. "Cealie…."

"Yes." I leaned close so she could speak without fear of being overheard.

She shook her head, her gaze seeming to go inward, where a decision was made.

"I have to leave." She pushed up to her feet. Standing, she swayed.

I grabbed her arm. "Maybe you need to sit awhile longer."

"No." She set her drink down and picked up her purse. "I'm okay."

I kept my margarita and followed her out of the bar. My booted foot made keeping up with her quick steps especially difficult. She glanced from side to side at people as though searching for someone, and did not slow for me.

"Can we go somewhere to talk?" I touched her elbow.

"I'd rather not." Her voice slurred, probably from tequila. Maybe she had been drinking awhile. Her eyes looked red.

We sped past the open bar where Gil sat. His back was toward us. He leaned, listening to one of the men with him, and did not notice us passing.

Tetter reached an area with few people.

"Stop," I ordered.

She paused so quickly I almost rammed into her. "What?"

I grabbed her hand. "Tell me what's wrong with you."

"I had a few drinks. Is that all right?"

"Were you watching baseball?"

"Where?" Her eyes focused on a near spot as though she were locating the sport I mentioned. "Oh, in the bar. No, I don't give a diddly-squat about baseball."

This sounded more like the Tetter I knew. "So what were you doing in there?"

"I was thinking, okay?"

"It's not okay." I didn't realize I'd raised my voice until people passing turned to stare.

Clutching my friend's hand, I guided her into an empty alcove that held stands with pictures. "I'm your friend. I have been your friend ever since we were twelve, and I felt I could tell you anything. I thought you were the same way with me."

"I was."

"And now you're different?"

"Are you kidding me?" She turned her face sideways, gazed up, and shook her head. She stared at me. "You don't actually think any of us are the same people we were in junior or senior high school?"

"Well, no, but… Yes, we are the same people inside. We couldn't have changed that much here, right?" I balled up my hand and pressed it to my chest.

Her eyes tightened into smaller orbs. They saddened. She grew quiet, her vacant gaze taking in the air surrounding me. Her mind, I hoped, was helping her decide what her heart probably told her, that she should confide in me. This troubled woman needed to share the weight in her soul with someone. Why not a trusted friend?

She seemed to decide. Yanking her purse open, she dug inside.

I swallowed a sip of margarita, wetting my throat for the counseling session I was about to share with her.

Her gaze into her purse made me wonder what she so intently searched for. Possibly a letter from someone that made her fearful. A doctor's diagnosis of an incurable disease? That would be especially horrible. Maybe instead she had kept track of how many times she'd done something she regretted, like too much gambling.

The moment after I sipped my margarita, I regretted it.

What if the problem she was ready to tell me about was alcoholism? I lowered my glass and held it toward my rear.

She dug a small rectangular plastic item out of her purse and handed it to me.

A mirror.

"Is that the person you once were?" she asked.

Overhead lights meant to brighten the photographs that were set on the boards struck the mirror, making it glitter and highlight my wrinkles. That was the main thing I saw. And there was the under-eye puffiness. The skin that no longer appeared fresh.

"Ugh." I yanked the mirror down as though it were on fire and handed it back to her. "I hope I looked better than this at one time."

"I hope the same thing for me." She slipped the vicious mirror back into her bag.

"Okay, we don't look anywhere as young as we did back then."

"We sure don't." She leaned forward. "That was decades ago, Cealie."

"Right, but we still have the same basic values, the same things we consider right or wrong."

"Sometimes those change, too." She zipped her purse. "I really need to go."

"Please don't."

Three women approached. They smiled at us and studied the pictures, probably searching for themselves.

I touched Tetter's forearm. "Let's talk somewhere." I almost suggested one of the quieter bars but thought better of it in case her difficulty included liquor. "We could sit by the pool or go to my room."

She moved her arm away from my hand. "I don't know what Jane told you about me, but I'm fine. I don't have anything serious that I want to talk to anyone about. I'm only on this cruise to see a few classmates and relax. And you sure aren't contributing to my relaxation."

I raised both hands as though in surrender, although one still held my drink. "I'm sorry. I thought you might want to confide in an old friend."

"*Old* is the operative word."

"Damn, Tetter, you've changed."

"Yes, and so have you. When I'm in a better mood, I'll pry into your life and try to dig out every little situation you've been through during the last decades, and we'll see if they're all pretty."

"No, I've done things—"

"So have I." She stomped off.

The women standing near stared at me with my mouth hanging open. My good friend had told me off.

I forced my jaw closed and hobbled away. My feelings were hurt. I wanted sympathy.

I wasn't sure Gil could sympathize, since he normally told me I should keep my nose away from other people's troubles unless they asked for help. A female friend would understand. Females, even from an early age, instinctively knew that you stuck your nose into others' business whether they wanted it or not.

Deciding I'd like Gil's shoulder to lean on even if he didn't grasp my inner ache, I aimed for the bar where I'd seen him. He'd talked to those guys long enough. If I couldn't pry him away, I would join them until they were done with their discussion. And then I could snuggle in one of the nearby comfy lounge chairs with Gil, having him hold me.

Darn. His bar stool was empty. The men he'd spoken with were also gone.

"A man sat here talking to some other guys," I said to the young bartender and pointed to Gil's bar stool. "He's a nice-looking man about my age. Did you happen to see which way he went?"

"Sorry, ma'am, I didn't notice."

I would find Jane instead and tell her about my encounter with Tetter. Maybe together we could decide if we should just leave her alone.

Jane was no longer in the casino. The boat dipped under my feet. I gripped the edge of a video-poker machine. An elderly man playing it eyed me, and I smiled. Then glanced at his watch.

The show in the theater began minutes ago. That was probably where most of my friends were.

I headed there, skimming faces, most of them cheerful, but none I recognized.

I inadvertently entered the theater's top deck. House lights were down, and everything was dark except for the spotlighted stage. The orchestra played. Dancers in pink and red swirled around the floor.

A swell of fear shot trembles to my shoulders and snaked past my elbows to my fingers. The sway in my torso and legs made me fear I'd slip down. I gulped and gulped, working to stave off my terror of balconies. *Your big cousin will not hold you over the edge, pretending he'll toss you down. You're a big girl now, Cealie.*

And, I reminded myself with my head taller, I'd stood on a balcony not that long ago. Of course then I'd faced a killer. But I had won.

I'd purposely climbed to that balcony to protect my grandchild and then made it back down again just fine, I considered. Until I recalled I hadn't been able to get down alone.

Oops.

And I had come up here before, but not by myself.

A glittering ball made slow spins above, shooting rays of brilliance off sequins in velvety folds of dark fabric. Music swelled in a popular Broadway tune, which my numbing mind refused to name. My arms felt stuck out like a penguin's. Knowing I blocked the center of the entrance, I could not force my legs to move me.

I swung my gaze sideways. Smiling passengers filled rows that trailed upward, ever higher into what appeared a black abyss capable of swallowing them whole. People came in and nudged past, apologizing for squeezing by. I nodded and swept my head toward the opposite side of the balcony, where hundreds more people sat.

The music livened as I stood in place.

I chanced a glance below. People on the right filled circular cushioned seats stretching from the center of the huge area. Sectional seating took up the sides, the dark shadowed sides. If I could make out a person I knew, one of my classmates or Gil, I could probably get down there and stay around. But here…

"Can I help you find a seat?" A blond male steward gave me a smile. "There are a few empty ones down those rows."

Without turning to see where he meant, I shook my head. More latecomers brushed in beside me.

"If you'd prefer to stand back here, you might want to get to the side," the steward said. "Then people won't bump you."

I stared at him. My mind grasped what he told me. It was something I knew without hearing the words. Yet even as I realized I needed to move, I could not.

"Ma'am, are you all right?" He peered into my panicky eyes. Was he going to offer a straightjacket? Or strap me into one without asking?

"That's okay. I've got her." Sue stepped near and snagged my arm. Turning me around, she led me like an old woman out of the theater.

Bright lights in the wide corridor made me relax. I released a deep sigh.

She kept a grip on my arm. "Isn't it time you got over it?"

"Thanks for the help. You can let go of my arm now," I said, grateful for her aid but not ready for chastisement.

She let go and followed as I walked farther from the balcony. "It's a good show. You'd like it. I could take you back inside downstairs."

"I know that show's terrific. I saw it the last time I came on this trip."

Sue bent her head toward me, her look doubtful. I also doubted whether it was the same performance I'd seen, but did not pinch my palm in case I was telling the truth. I figured it was at least similar to one I'd viewed. Most performances on cruises were so great I couldn't believe all of that entertainment was included in the price of the trip.

"Then we can do something else." Sue spoke begrudgingly.

"You go back in. I don't need a sitter."

"Sometimes you do." She strode beside me.

I frowned, stepping my booted foot ahead as quickly as I could.

Her legs moved faster. "I remember when my mom kept you," she said, making me slow and glance at her. "You could be quite a brat."

"I could not."

A slow smile spread across her lips. "We had fun playing together, didn't we?"

"Usually." I considered Sue's mother and those great crab cakes she made and all of those spongy angel food cakes. We seesawed on their gym set many times. Of course the person beside me had been Stu, wearing baseball caps and T-shirts. Now she wore great heels and slimming dresses over a slender woman's curves.

"I can go to the later performance," she said. "Let's get a drink."

Maybe Tetter hadn't drunk in excess, I considered, realizing most cruise ships contained many bars, probably because lots of us imbibed in them more than we did at home.

We entered the well-lit Party Tyme, holding many younger people. Rock music resounded. We sat on bar stools and ordered margaritas.

"I don't do well with many of these," I said once I received my frozen drink and clinked large-bowled glasses with my aunt. "And this isn't my first tonight."

"Good. Then maybe you'll be friendly."

"Me? You're the one who keeps withdrawing."

"You've been apprehensive about me since the minute you walked on board."

"You told me off. You said I was old and fat." I glanced at my stomach. Maybe she wasn't far off. And although I wasn't young, she was the same age.

"I was kidding. Jeez, can't you take a joke anymore? People used to be able to kid with you."

And this relative of mine had been annoying and always told jokes that weren't funny. In school, we'd normally faked smiles.

"I didn't kill that man." Her tone was loud. The words flew out of her mouth as a song ended. Certainly she hadn't meant to have everyone hear her, but the bar grew quiet. Every person stared at her.

"I'm sure you didn't," I said. "Would you like to go somewhere else?"

She nodded. Carrying our drinks, we strolled out.

"Oh, that was great." She swallowed big gulps of her margarita.

"Sue, were you with him when he died?"

"Absolutely not!"

"Did you know him? I mean, you know...."

"Intimately?" She grimaced.

I started to shake my head no, but decided to forge ahead. "Yes."

"Cealie—"

"Cealie, Sue. There y'all are." Randy strolled to us.

Sue flung an angry glance at me, her chin tight, maybe warning me to shut up about our discussion.

"You weren't going to the performance in the theater?" I asked Randy, ready to send him away. I had begun asking Sue things I really wanted to know and wasn't ready to let her go yet. I wasn't mildly curious. I was concerned about a dead man and praying my blood relative hadn't killed him.

Since I knew of their relationship, I might be the only person who could lead authorities to her. If my fears were correct.

I checked her through the corner of my eye. Her lips shoved out in a pout.

"I'm going to the late performance. Y'all want to come?" Randy asked.

I envisioned my older cousin holding seven-year-old me over the balcony ledge. A massive shiver shook my body. "I'm not going."

"Are you sick? Or is it your ankle?" He peered at my booted foot.

"I need the restroom," Sue said and spurted away from us. I figured she wouldn't come back. In fact, she might try to avoid me for the rest of the trip.

"I went shopping," Randy said, his face breaking into a large smile reminiscent of the handsome teen he was in school. "Look what I found for the grandkids." He opened a bag and drew out a tiny pink dress with a cruise ship embroidered across its bodice. Pride sparkled in his eyes.

"That's adorable."

"And look at this one." He pulled out a boy's knit shirt,

about size ten, navy with a cruise ship plastered on the left side of the chest.

"Nice," I said, wondering if the kid wasn't too old to want a boat on his shirt.

"And I got them some other things. Some headband thingies for her and a huge ship puzzle for him."

I smiled, for the first time on this cruise seeing him in a new light. He was a grandparent. Just like me, sometime after he left school he became blessed with the wonderful gift of becoming a parent. After that, he was chosen for the joyful task of becoming a grandparent.

"You did a great job of shopping," I said.

He beamed, closing his bag almost reverently. "They're my joy."

"I understand. We can love them and send them home without all of the responsibility we had when their parents were little."

He nodded and glanced around. "Have you seen Tetter? Or Jane?"

"I guess they're watching the performance unless they decided to see it later."

His brow creased. He took on a pensive look, as if he was trying to decide where to go. And search for Tetter, I imagined.

"I was heading for the Lido Deck," I said, slipping my left fingernails into my right palm and pinching. Lies like this came too easily. I had no idea where I'd been heading. "How about joining me?"

His creases deepened, definitely not a sign that he wanted to come with me.

But I wanted to question him. What the hell was he doing with Tetter during this trip? Had he created her major problem?

"I could use some help getting around up there." My lie

slipped out as effortlessly as hair spray from an aerosol can. The only positive thing about these fibs was that I was sorry I told them. Darn, I wished I could be flawless.

Randy appeared deeper in thought. He needed a nudge to keep him with me.

"I wouldn't be surprised if Tetter was up there." I pinched the hell out of my palm for that downright lie. The Lido Deck was the last place she might be. "Jane, too," I added so he wouldn't surmise I suspected him of having the hots for Tetter.

"I guess I could go with you." He glanced at the boot on my foot and clasped my elbow.

Gritting my teeth, I allowed his assistance as we walked.

"Oh, but we forgot Sue." He peered backward. "You think she's all right?"

I was not going to spit out another lie. "She wanted to go somewhere else. I'm not sure where, but she was anxious to go." She definitely was anxious to get away from my grilling.

But here was someone else I wanted to question. Tetter needed help with a problem. The man leading me like a guard dog could be its cause.

We waited for the elevator, exchanging pleasantries with people gathering to wait. Randy avoided looking at me. He gave friendly smiles, like I did, to people riding up with us.

We stepped out into brisk frigid air, much colder than earlier in the day. The late evening wasn't dark but carried in a hazy dusk. Snow-dappled mountains in the distance made me breathless from their beauty.

"It's cold out here. Would you mind going inside near the pool? We can look at sights through the glass," I said.

"Sure. I guess it's colder since we're heading toward Glacier Bay." He turned his head in a circular motion as though wanting to check out every person on this open deck. Many lined the sides of the ship, staring into the sea and at the gorgeous terrain. Most people wore fleece or heavy jackets. Many men snuggled against their women.

I wanted to snuggle with Gil.

"I'm going to catch a drink," Randy said, glancing at the pool bar. "You're having frozen margaritas, right?"

"Right." I took the opportunity to stare at passengers in this area, hoping I'd find one I really wanted to see.

Gil.

But maybe I didn't only want to see him. Maybe I *wanted* him.

Yep, that's what it was, I decided, finishing off my second drink. Or was it my third? Or... Well, those frozen things added to my chill and need for warmth.

Randy returned with a frosty glass for me and a beer for himself. "Wine probably would have warmed you up more," he said, glancing at my shaking arms.

"So would sex."

His eyes brightened. His mouth formed the slightest grin.

"I don't mean with you."

He chuckled. "It might not be so bad. At least that's what they tell me." He pulled the door open, and we stepped inside a humid room with the fantastic swimming pool. The odor of bleach permeated the air. Children's laughter rang out from the water.

"Tell me about those people," I said, brushing a section of thick salt aside on my glass's rim. I swallowed a sip.

Randy laughed self-consciously. "What do you want me to say—I'm good in bed? That would be kind of bragging." He sipped his beer.

"Okay." I located a spot to stand near the window. "Who would tell me how good you are in bed?"

He choked on his beer. "What's the deal, Cealie? Are you going to write a column for the school paper? Why do you want to know about that?"

"You and sex?" I swallowed a sip of margarita. Thoughts swam around my head. Exactly how would I ask whether he and Tetter were having an affair? Maybe I did not need this last drink.

"Are you okay?" Randy asked.

Did he think I was going bonkers? Getting early-onset dementia?

"Nope, I am *jussst* fine." I slurred a pinch and pressed my finger into his chest to accentuate my statement. "How many people are you having sex with?"

"Huh?" he said, nose wrinkled.

"I didn't exactly mean people. I don't think you're messing around with any guys, but how about our friend?"

He chugged half of his beer. I drank from my glass, getting a mouthful of bitter coarse salt along with sweet tequila. He stared out of the glass wall. I did, too, noticing we passed more white-tipped mountains. Lovely.

"Are you asking about anyone in particular? Or do you think I'm taking advantage of all the women with us? Or maybe you're thinking of some back home? There were a lot of girls in our class."

"Nope. I mean besides your wife. How about one of the women with us for our little reunion?"

He turned away. Randy placed his empty hand and the one holding his beer glass against the window. He stared outside. I didn't think he noticed the water or mountains.

I watched and waited, angry with him, sympathy shoving that emotion aside. This was a husband, a father, a grandpa. He appeared lost. Empty. Wanting.

Wanting who? Or *whom?* I thought, unwillingly correcting my own grammar.

I couldn't hold my tongue any longer. "I know what I see. You want Tetter."

He drew his head back, arms stiff toward the window where his eyes continued to aim, although they gazed lower than before.

"You want her. Or maybe you've already had her." Words bubbling across my tongue as fast as tequila could slide into my mouth. "I saw you trying to get her attention ever since we came on board," I blurted, adding a chuckle. "All of the pictures of our group together are so funny, or horrible actually, with you frowning at me because I stuck myself between you and her."

"You have no idea." He spoke in a quiet tone.

"Sure, I do. You had a crush on her in junior high and then she started going out with Ted Rader, and he was five years older and you thought you didn't stand a chance, so you never asked her to go out."

Clattering silverware drew our attention. A steward dumped used silverware onto a cart.

"Let's go back outside," Randy suggested. He indicated we should go to the opposite side of the ship, where there was only a slim outer walkway. He opened the door, and we stepped into icy air.

Empty tables and chairs stood along the shiny teak floor. Beyond lifeboats farther along, a young man polished windows. A naturalist spoke over the loudspeaker, telling about the sights. He mentioned whales breeching on starboard, where we stood. I peered out and spied a small waterspout. A tail flipped atop the water. Without binoculars, I could have sworn I watched a porpoise instead of a whale. But I had seen many of both. And my friend Tetter was much more important.

Standing near the outer rail, I nudged Randy's arm, shivered, and took a small sip of my drink. "At first on this ship, Tetter seemed unhappy about your advances," I said, picking up on what I was determined to pry out of him. "But lately she seems to enjoy the attention. I believe it's just now that she's gotten older, she likes the interest of a man. But that's it. She's flattered because a guy still finds her attractive."

Randy's face tensed. He stared beyond me.

The naturalist announced puffins and sea lions in view on icebergs close by.

Ooohs and aaahs carried from people on higher decks.

I peered at white chunks in the water far below, able to see only small brownish figures. With a strange feeling of apprehension, I set down my glass, reached into my purse, and slid on my bifocals. I stared at nearby water and grinned at three sea lions lying on their backs on ice with their chins up, as though they slept on soft pillows. I also spied colorful seabirds with thick beaks and felt my eyeglasses slipping. They reached the tip of my nose. I grabbed them before they fell into the water.

"You almost had a tragedy there," Randy said. "It seems like you really need those glasses."

"You don't wear any?"

"I have contacts."

Was he still so concerned about his looks? A moment after I considered that question, I envisioned my sexy outfits and spiked heels. Touché.

Without bending over the side this time, I glanced at receding icebergs, which looked tiny as this massive ship slipped past them. I spied a puffin sliding off one and wished I could see the bird up close. But the main thing I needed to do was keep Randy involved in conversation. I had to find out if he created Tetter's problem, and if he did, I'd do everything in my power to keep him away from her.

"It seems like we're rushing to Glacier Bay, I guess because of the change of schedule," I said. "We must have picked up whatever parts were needed from Sitka." I considered what they needed to fix—mainly the morgue—and hoped they did it immediately. Jonathan was probably still in there.

Randy peered into the distance ahead, apparently not concerned about ship repairs or puffins or whales. "I love my kids and grandkids."

"I love mine, too." Tommy's face sprang to mind, along with others in my family. I wanted to say how much I'd screwed up by not spending time with my son when I had the chance. Instead, I'd judged him and the man he was with. I could have tried to accept what my son told me—he was with someone else now—and then I could have spent time with them and also scheduled time later to visit my daughter-in-law and their children.

Ready to pour out those woes, I glanced at Randy.

Eyes harsh, he gave me an angry stare. "You just don't know."

"Then tell me. You are in love with Tetter. Or in lust with her. She has this major problem I'd hoped to help her with, but she won't tell any of us about her trouble, so we can't help until she does. I imagine it could be gambling or maybe drinking. Or you."

"Me?" he asked with a snicker.

"Yes. You're a happily married man, and she's a happily married woman, and now you're pressing her to have an affair."

He snorted. "Where do you get your information?"

"From you. Or her. I don't know." I realized my mind was fuzzy, maybe from eyeing ice-crested waves. With help from salt-crusted margaritas.

Randy jabbed a finger toward me

I drew my head back, thinking he might strike me.

A man's voice grew in volume but did not sound like anyone on the sound system. Cigarette smoke carried from one of two tall men walking toward us. The person speaking and smoking wore all white.

Executive Chef Sandkeep.

He was speaking with Gil.

SIXTEEN

"HELLO." GIL LIFTED HIS HAND in a small wave at me. His gaze shifted toward the man I stood alone with on this area of the deck. His smile gave way to a somber expression, eyes unhappy, chin jutting like a man preparing for a fight.

When Gil became jealous, it told me he thought I might be attractive enough in some way to get another man's attention. Funny.

I did not like it a bit when he brought out my jealousy of him around a woman.

Chef Sandkeep smoked beside Gil. Should I thank him now for the champagne?

I'd want to ask who he thought I should drink it with, and what did he mean on that card, *For Cealie Gunther and....* Could he have been thinking of himself?

Glancing at the harshness in Gil's eyes, I decided now wasn't the time to ask those questions. Gil appeared to take sharper breaths in fast succession, as though getting pumped up for something not nice.

The chef ran his gaze over Randy and me with no change in expression. He didn't appear to recognize either of us and seemed more interested in his cigarette.

"Hello," Randy told them. "I need to go," he said to me.

"Wait," I said, but he rushed away.

What an awkward situation. If I ran after him, he probably wouldn't talk anymore now. And I'd also be thinking about Gil, knowing how I'd feel if the situation were reversed. I decided since I'd gotten Randy to start talking about him and Tetter, I should easily get him to continue once I had him alone again.

Chef Sandkeep sucked in a long drag from his cigarette, blew out smoke, and tapped the butt in an ashtray on a plastic table. He tossed the butt over the rail.

"No! You're not supposed to throw a cigarette out there," I said, hands flailing in his face.

"I put the thing out."

"You just stubbed it in the ashtray. It wasn't all the way out. Suppose your cigarette starts a fire on this ship? What'll we do?"

"It won't start a fire."

Gil stepped between me and the chef. He lifted his hands as though trying to intercept my hands that balled into fists. "It's okay, Cealie. Let it go."

"It's not okay. The literature tells people not to throw anything from the ship, especially cigarettes. They can start fires. And then what?"

"And then people would put them out." Gil gripped my fists.

I smiled at him. "That would be nice."

"Yes, and so are you, now be nice to this gentleman. He makes sure all of your food tastes good."

"And *your* food? Your wonderful Cajun dishes?"

I eyed the executive chef who could stop Gil's chef from preparing meals in his galley. I was ready to turn on that white-hatted dude. Maybe he was big, but I could kick. And pinch. And stomp on his feet.

Gil nodded, slowly backing me up. "All of the food's good. And I believe someone enjoyed a few drinks today." He gave me a wider smile.

"Yep, margaritas."

"Ah, and more than one of those makes your thoughts fuzzy."

"And my tongue thick. Wanna see?" I wagged it at him.

"Yes, but in private," his deep voice rumbled in my ear. "Yummy."

Gil turned to the chef. "I'll see you later. Not tonight," he added with a wink. Taking my hand, he guided me through the glass door into the buffet.

"It's nice and warm in here," I said.

"I know a place where it'll be even warmer." He nuzzled my ear.

I reached back, grabbing for a vital part of him, my hand brushing his thigh.

He pushed my hand toward my side. "Too many people in here. But I can get you to your room in a flash."

"I can't wait for a flash." I leaned my head back as I walked. "Let's do it when we get on the elevator."

"There's an idea. Nobody else is waiting for one." He pressed the down button.

I backed against the wall; people's voices and reggae music in the distance. Grabbing Gil's shirt, I fingered his buttons. "As soon as we get in there, I'll go for your slacks."

"I can get that faster than you can." He kissed my forehead, leaving me to wonder if he really meant we would try to have a sexual encounter in the moving elevator. We'd had quickies before, but how many seconds would an elevator take between decks?

I felt I could sizzle as soon as his hot body met mine. The idea of getting it done on this trip downstairs grew more appealing. I slid my fingers inside his shirt and smiled up at him.

His sultry eyes sucked me deeper into his space.

"It's here," he said, making me notice the *ding* as the elevator door opened.

My anticipation shot into higher gear.

"Y'all come on in. We'll make room." A woman wearing a black-and-gold Saints T-shirt and cap waved us inside. Other people shifted over, giving Gil and me space.

He thanked them, but I didn't feel like saying a thing to those people. Selfish me wanted a romantic experience. Now.

The trip down took forever as we made stops on every deck for someone to get on or off. On one deck, a woman waiting on the floor spoke when the door opened. "Oh, you're going down. I wanted to go up. I'll get the next one."

I'm not getting what I wanted, either, I wanted to shout. *Now let us get to my room!*

My body felt droopy by the time we reached my deck.

Gil guided me down the hall. "We're almost there. You're still in the mood, right?"

"Why shouldn't I be in the mood?"

"You seem a little tipsy. I thought you might fall over while we were walking out here."

I had felt that sway right before he gripped my hand tighter. "That was from the waves. And my boot."

"How is your ankle? And can I have your key?"

"My ankle's fine. The whole leg's fine. You'll see in a minute. I'm ready to stop wearing this thing." I pointed to the boot, dug out my key, and gave it to him.

"I look forward to seeing it all," he said, tone deeper.

"I need to tell you about some things, too."

He held the door open to let me enter first. "What kinds of things?" He finished unbuttoning his shirt, stepping toward me. Deftly, he unbuttoned mine.

"There's a killer on this boat."

His fingers stopped. He stared at my eyes. "Who did he kill?"

"That man, Jonathan. I think." I considered Randy and Tetter. "But I do know there's an adulterer."

"Probably lots more than one."

"Don't stop." I put his fingers back on my buttons. "I really want you."

"And I want you, Cealie. I always want you." He slid my

top off. Gil's satisfied smile at my bared breasts made me certain that my droop and waist flab had disappeared.

"You are so nice." I sat on the side of the bed, loosed my foot from its boot cage, and patted the sheet beside me.

Gil sat. He looked me over. "Are you sure you're okay?"

"Yep." A frown tugged at my lips. "No. I almost got to visit with Tommy, but I turned my back on him and sent him away." Sniffles worked to the tip of my nose.

Gil handed me his handkerchief. "It's not too late."

"Yes, it is. I turned him away—or turned myself away from him. I miss my boy." Tears swelled in my eyes, burning them. I hiccuped, making my chest hurt.

Gil drew back his head. "Tequila breath," he explained and reached toward my pillow. "How about a chocolate?" He lifted a square silver-wrapped one that the room steward left.

I opened it and sank my teeth into the rich chocolate. He handed me another one. I ate it.

"Chocolate is good for your soul," he said, patting my pillow.

I leaned toward it. He lifted my legs and set them on the bed. My head sank deep into the soft bedding.

"Let's get your slacks off, too." He worked magic, sliding them and my panties off without disturbing my upper body.

"You're great," I murmured.

"We can solve all of those other problems later."

He stretched in the bed beside me.

Sex or not? I wasn't sure yet.

FLAMES ROARED, SWEEPING across the bottom deck, licking up each higher one, until red-yellow heat engulfed the whole ship. Then we sank. Like passengers and crew from the *Titanic,* we scrambled in the icy sea, clawing to grab hold of icebergs. I shook from cold and fear, struggling against panic.

And heard myself snort. A louder snore followed. I sank deeper into sleep, satisfied that the cold and the fire faded.

I popped my eyes open. Gil had been in my bed. Where was he?

I touch the sheet where he'd lain. Cool. He'd left that space some time ago. I sat up, hoping to find him in my room, but didn't. My mind scuttled for thoughts. I'd wanted him. He'd wanted me. Did we make out? He certainly wasn't a man to wham, bam, thank you, ma'am, and leave.

"Gil," I called.

Maybe he was in the bathroom, ready for a shower. I hoped he was nude in the shower. I would hop in there with him.

Okay, we hadn't had sex yet. And he didn't answer. I glanced around the room.

A small page with the ship's logo lay on the pillow next to mine.

Sorry, I had to go. Gil's strong handwriting made me smile. *Baby, you snored so loud, I think you kept people awake on the deck above us. Hope you got lots of rest. I'll find you later, and we'll catch up where we left off. I love you, Gil.*

I slid out of bed and glanced down. Naked. The man could look at this body with its wrinkles and dimples where dimples weren't appealing—and still say he loved me.

But I did not want to love him so much, because I had started to depend on him. I'd depended on Gil last night, I recalled. I'd wanted him to help me solve all of my troubling situations. One concerned Tetter and probably Randy. A member of my family might have caused a death. I didn't want to even think about that one but needed to.

Some of my friends had started to depend on relatives as they'd gotten older. I refused to do that, thus often trying to avoid family members, most of whom I adored. Sue, however, was giving me a special challenge.

And there was Tommy. I hadn't seen my son in much too

long. I imagined the feel of his muscular body inside my arms and against my chest. Why hadn't I even squeezed him in a real hug?

I was a mess.

But I would work things out. And I would not depend on family members or Gil. I called up my mantra: *I am woman. I can do anything—alone.*

The words didn't have a strong enough impact.

Today I would take positive steps to take care of some problems. I'd get hold of Randy again and learn all of the truth. And I would confront Sue and discover for sure whether she killed Jonathan.

I recalled that last night Gil and the executive chef were talking together. What was that about? Previously, Sandkeep seemed almost hostile toward Gil.

Needing to uncover many truths, I heard my stomach grouse. Food would help straighten my thoughts. I lifted the phone to call room service, then figured we could be in Glacier Bay. I didn't want to miss any of that site's beauty. Dressing quickly, I snagged an elevator and found Jane riding inside.

"Good morning!" she said, voice much too chirpy. "How surprising to see you up at this time."

"I couldn't sleep anymore. Maybe because I fell asleep early, courtesy of margaritas."

Jane grinned. She wore a navy jogging suit with lime green stripes down the sides and running shoes. I had shrugged on a heavy sweater and covered it with a thick quilted jacket.

"Do you want to come and work out?" she asked.

"You must be kidding. You are not climbing out of bed and dashing up there to run around the ship?" Of course, I'd recently visited a cousin who did that at her gym. I'd tried with her once. Maybe I could work out a little, but not so early or with so much enthusiasm.

"I love to run and to play tennis. Do you play?" Jane asked.

"Good grief, didn't you get any older since we finished school? I have grandkids who play tennis, but I gave up the sport after my knees suggested I stop."

"Oh." She peered toward my knees as though she could see any difficulty through my slacks. "Do you have arthritis?" she asked, nose scrunched.

"I don't think so, but I imagine some of the people we graduated with must be suffering with that affliction by now."

She straightened, appearing to accentuate that she had no physical afflictions. "Darn, Cealie, the way you talk, you'd think we were ancient."

"And you play tennis. You can still do all of the things you did when we were in high school?"

"Probably. You can't?"

Our elevator stopped. I regretted that we weren't on the Lido Deck yet, so I could get away from this conversation.

Two women with deeply wrinkled faces and white hair smiled and stepped inside. "Are y'all going up to eat?" one of them asked.

"We sure are," I said.

"Not me. I'm going to run." Jane jogged in place.

"Tell me," I said to our passengers, "do you think she and I should still be running?"

They checked out both of us. "You're the same age?" the one with frizzy hair asked, bespectacled eyes narrowed.

Jane sucked in her stomach and threw back her shoulders. She lifted her chin as though a rope pulled her straight and tall.

I could do straight, but not tall.

"Who did you think was older?" Jane asked the woman whose trifocals I could have smashed when her gaze slid toward me.

A blessed *ding* rang out.

"Oops, we're here. Nice talking to you," I said to the women and hustled out before they could give Jane a reply. She came out, too. I liked Jane, always had, and walked away from the elevator telling myself I would get with the program, some kind of physical program. Running didn't tempt me, but I watched her pumping her arms, going up a set of outdoor stairs, ready to run around wherever people ran on these ships. I would start working out. One of these days.

"See you later," Jane called, and I waved, heading for the buffet that gave off enticing aromas of biscuits and bacon when someone opened the door. The buffet would also offer strawberries and cantaloupe and sweet rolls and salmon prepared various ways. And buttered grits, among other tempting dishes.

More people than I would have imagined headed out of the enclosed area, having already eaten.

Dawn sprinkled out a few early sunrays. They glittered through a dusky frigid mist that settled on my hair and across my eyelashes. Mountains topped by snow that we drifted past could have been scoops of ice cream dipped in chocolate and coated with whipped cream. Soon we should see majestic blue-white glaciers.

A sound system crackled to life. The surrounding voice of an onboard naturalist welcoming people on outdoor areas of the ship startled me. I realized I must miss a lot by normally sleeping late. An astonishing number of passengers already stood along the boat's railings.

I found it difficult to hear much of the speaker's words. He mentioned glaciers that we were approaching and the icebergs our captain was slowly steering us through, most of them looking so tiny way below that they could have been shaved ice.

A collective gasp roared.

Passengers standing at the port rail screamed. They stared down near the boat, pointing and yelling.

I dashed to that side of the deck and worked my way through people to see.

The ship's whistle gave one long bone-chilling blast that could not mean anything good.

The deck shifted under my feet and it felt like we were stopping.

A man near me bellowed, "It's a person!"

"Oh, my God!" people screamed. Footsteps stomped on outdoor stairs and along the deck as more passengers and staff members dashed out. All around, people snapped pictures with cameras and phones.

I viewed the larger iceberg we'd passed that looked so small. A tiny dark object that could have been a sea lion stretched along its side. My teeth chattered, striking each other. My head shook. Waves of shivers ran to my fingertips. My back swayed, legs ready to give way. I could not steady myself and was sure I would fall—I hoped not all the way down there, where I feared one of my high school classmates lay.

Jane.

She ran up those stairs moments ago, planning to jog around the upper deck. Had she slid off? Been running and not been able to slow or stop?

I hadn't seen the face or even been able to determine if the person on the iceberg was male or female. I didn't know if that person still lived.

"We're going to stop, and they'll go get him," a man near me said.

"Him? Did you see the person?" I asked. "Is it a man?"

He shook his head, long black hair swaying. "It always is. Don't you know that?"

"What's always a man?" I asked, legs a little more steady.

"People who jump or are stabbed by their spouses and then pushed off a ship."

A cluster of passengers around us nodded their agreement.

I gained little respite from his words. I glanced at faces and the clothes passengers in my view wore. No face or jogging suit was Jane's.

That doesn't mean she's down there. The person on that ice could just as easily be a man.

I imagined the face of the man I knew best on this ship. My legs trembled.

The person lying across that iceberg could be Gil.

SEVENTEEN

ALL OF US along the ship's port side watched action in the water.

I stood among the thickening crowd in the crispy cold, trying to hold on to a surreal feeling of interest but not attachment. A sharp wind whistled and slapped us. Our ship had stopped between assorted jagged dots of ice. A platform flapped open at the ship's bottom.

Passengers around me all quieted.

I wished I'd brought my phone, yet even as I heard people speaking on theirs and saw them snapping pictures, I could not ask to use one. My interest and concern focused on the person in the water. If Gil or one of my school friends was not in his or her room, I did not want to know.

Many people on this ship would be aware of this tragic event by now. They'd be standing on their balconies and various decks with outside walkways to watch what transpired. I'd prefer to watch unfolding events from a lower deck but could not tear myself away from the rail. The elevators must be filled, taking too much time. I wished I were in shape to run down flights of stairs.

The sound of a small motor came to life. A boat emerged from where a platform opened near the bottom of our ship.

People roared. "They're going to get the body," a man said.

The body. Was Jane lying on the ice?

It couldn't be Gil.

I squeezed my lips together to keep from crying out.

The small boat held a few crew members. From what I could see, they all wore white.

Was one of them Gil's uncle? How upsetting it would be if he found the person out there was his nephew.

"What's wrong? You need to get inside," a man called. The ends of his long red hair flew into his face as he leaned toward me, grabbing my arms before I hit the floor.

"Why do I need to get inside?" I wanted to ask, but all that came from my mouth was a jumble of sounds made by the knocking of my teeth against each other. I trembled so hard from fear that I couldn't get my balance to stand straight.

"Give her room," the red-headed man said. He and a smaller man helped me sit and not fall on my face. People around backed away. Many glanced at me but then scooted to the side to watch the much-more-interesting action in the water.

"I need to see," I uttered, pointing toward where the little boat headed.

"You need to get where it's warmer," the second man helping me said.

"We'll get you inside." The redhead scooped his arms under my shoulders and, with his assistant, got me to my feet. "You might be sick, but the doctor's probably too busy with the body out there to see about someone with fever. We'll ask the nurse."

They gripped my arms, walking me toward the elevators.

"No!" I got in the redhead's face. "I need to see him!"

Both men backed down, possibly thinking I was a maniac. At the moment, I was. If Gil was on that ice, I needed to see him, to be close for him.

I dashed toward the rail. People let me through.

Some men from the rescue boat knelt on the ice, checking the person lying on it. Was that person alive? I wanted to be down there to know for myself. Was it Jane? Gil?

A giant trembling swept through me. I swayed, then gripped the rail, struggling to steady myself. Glancing at the men who'd helped me, I speared them with my glare, threatening lethal harm if they tried to take me away.

They backed down, apprehensive eyes letting me know they would let me fall rather than try to help me again.

In the water the rescue boat headed back toward our ship. I couldn't see clearly but made out some of the men in white in that boat bending to work on a person lying beneath them.

I, and hundreds of others, leaned over the rail as far as possible to watch the rescue boat enter the hatch at the bottom of our ship. Its platform lifted and shut.

Passengers remained quiet for long moments. We waited, hoping to hear exactly what had happened. Who did they pick up?

No announcement came.

The boat shifted. We were moving again. Everyone started talking.

"Do you have any idea of who that was?" an elderly woman asked, skimming faces. No one volunteered an answer.

"Was that a male or female?" another woman asked, and people shrugged.

"Did someone jump?" a teen asked.

"You hear of women stabbing their new husbands and throwing them over," a thirtyish woman said, making me hope our newlyweds were all right.

Crew members who took the person inside must have headed for the intensive care unit, where the doctor and other medical staff would perform emergency services.

"No use trying to get an elevator now," someone ahead of me told others. "Everybody up here will be trying to get down somewhere. We'd just as soon watch the sights and go downstairs later."

I wasn't interested in sights or sounds, unless I saw all of the people I cared about or heard they were all right. I meshed into the group waiting for elevators. The air became sparse in my tiny area, surrounded by a crush of people. Many remained silent. Some kept guessing about the *body*.

"They picked up a *person*," I said so all around could hear. "We don't know whether that person was alive or dead."

The speaker system crackled, followed by the blare of a man's solemn voice. "We are certain most of you know that someone was found on an iceberg near the ship." A moment of silence ensued, as though showing reverence. "Our security team will begin working to determine what happened. And our full medical staff is working hard to help the person."

I felt slight relief to hear this man say *person*. I hoped he would soon mention whether that person was male or female.

"I guess that's supposed to make us feel better," a woman near me said.

"Hush," I hissed. "Listen." I pointed back, as though I knew exactly where the voice of the man on the speaker system was coming from.

He continued. "We can assure you that all care will be taken to secure the safety of all of our passengers. Please let a crew member know if you need any assistance," he said, causing people around me to nod at each other. They appeared pleased to know they would remain safe. "We hope all of you will keep the person who was in the water in your thoughts. And if you believe in prayers, please pray for our injured guest."

Injured! I'd never heard such a powerful adjective.

I squeezed my eyes shut, focusing all of my attention on prayer. I prayed like mad, apologizing to God I'd too often taken for granted. I used such intensity I missed hearing an elevator door open. I only noticed when a person on it said they were full.

I snapped my eyes open. The elevator door shut. I cursed.

Sorry, I whispered to the God I'd just said all of those nice things to. But I believed He was kind and understanding. He would certainly understand how badly I wanted to get in that elevator to ride down to the medical center to check on Gil.

My heart felt empty, my body stiff as I thought of his name, almost certain he was the victim the medical team retrieved from that ice.

"I need to get through. I need to get on the next elevator," I said. Pushing forward, I found people letting me move forward. Finally I stood in a tiny space.

"Cealie. Hey, Cealie," a voice near me cried.

Jane's voice.

She waved from the crowd five feet away from me.

"Oh, wow, it's you, Jane. I am so glad to see you. I was afraid you'd fallen off the boat from where you were running."

"Couldn't you see who it was?"

People around watched her, faces anxious, all waiting.

I dreaded hearing his name. But needed to know. "Was it Gil?" I quit breathing, waiting for her answer.

"No."

I could have shouted *Halleluja!* Instead I cried, "Yes!"

Jane's eyes squeezed tighter. "They picked up Tetter."

EIGHTEEN

I COULDN'T BELIEVE my good friend had been the person lying on the edge of that iceberg.

"Oh, my God, Jane," I cried. We stood feet apart, both squeezed into the crowd waiting for an elevator. The air was cold, but I was smashed inside the group, warm from not getting much air, hotter still from hearing this news about our buddy. "Are you sure it was Tetter?"

Passengers turned their faces from me to Jane. All of them wanted to learn everything they could about the person who had gone overboard.

A young woman pulled out a pad and pen. She eyed us and appeared to take notes of whatever we said.

I did not want to say much with this crowd listening. Some of them might be reporters. Surely many would call, email, and text others, sensationalizing the event.

A light flashed in my face. And then another. Folks around us appeared to take ideas from the first ones snapping pictures of Jane and me. We knew the woman who went overboard.

I turned my face forward, almost against the shut elevator door.

"Hey, look this way," a male teenager called.

"Over here," another one said.

I cringed. Nausea swept through me.

"How do you know the victim?" a man near me asked.

I ignored him so I wouldn't slam my fist up his nose.

"How about you?" he asked, and I knew he'd directed his

question to Jane and that most of the faces around us swerved from me toward her.

"None of your business," she said.

I inwardly cried *Yes*. I didn't want to be ugly to anyone since I figured most of them just cared. And like most of us, they were curious. But I did not want them so curious about my friend. The elevator door opened.

I stepped inside, more at ease when Jane grabbed my arm. "Hey, friend," she said, giving it a squeeze.

I wrapped my arms around her, snuggled my head against hers, and whimpered. "I can't believe it."

"I know. Me neither."

"She has to be okay," I said, and Jane nodded.

"Ooh, look," someone with us said in a quiet tone before snapping a picture of us. Others followed suit.

"Okay, stop it!" I snarled.

All picture taking stopped. People stepped off at different decks, asking if we wanted the deck where they stopped. I felt certain most of them wished we'd get off with them so they might have us alone to question about our buddy who'd gone overboard.

We kept descending. Those with us quieted. I felt safe enough to peek at the few who remained. Only an adolescent freckled girl with a small boy whose hair was orange.

"Hi," I told them, trying for a friendly smile, only able to create a tiny one.

The girl held up a red phone and snapped my picture. She snapped one of Jane.

"Turncoat," I said.

We stopped, and the girl grabbed her brother's hand and darted out. Maybe she was scared we'd dash after her and yank her camera away, a consideration that crossed my mind. The door shut. Jane and I watched each other. Neither spoke.

I figured she felt like I did, drained from seeing a person we deeply cared about lying on the ice. And then trying to stop strangers from questioning us or snapping our pictures.

My friend and I weren't popular. We just knew the deceased. *Deceased?* Was she? Our friend, everybody's buddy Tetter Hargroove, could not be dead.

I urged the elevator to rush. It carried us to deck 3. We ran to the medical center.

Security guards with stern faces stretched their arms and raised their hands. "You can't come in here," the tallest of them said.

"What about medical emergencies?" I asked, wondering what emergency I might create. Chest pains? No one could dispute that. In fact, anxiety made my chest tight.

"If you have an emergency, please phone this center. Someone will direct you on how to handle your situation." He yanked a page out of a rack holding papers on the wall. "This gives the number to call and tells what to do for common complaints."

I grabbed his paper, keeping eye contact. "And does it tell you what to do if your best friend falls off the ship and lands on an iceberg?"

"She was your friend?"

"Was?" The word caught in my throat. Its meaning slammed against my brain.

"It's only a term," he said. "I mean, is she your friend?"

"She is, so let us go in there to see her."

"You can't. The doctor is working on her. You can't help him."

"We can try," Jane said.

"We can touch her and call her name, telling Tetter it's us, so she'll remember. We all finished high school together, and we're having a class reunion," I said.

"Then you need to go up to the library. A security team is questioning people who knew her or saw her last."

Last. What exactly did that mean? Muscles across my back knotted.

The guard who hadn't spoken to us before told us what deck the library was on. I'd been in there before but couldn't have gotten thoughts straight if I tried.

Jane and I and rode up to the library's deck, quietly holding hands. The door opened, and we looked at each other, not moving. I feared once I left this space and entered the room with many security guards, I would be asked questions too painful to answer. And I might learn things I did not want to know.

Tightening my grip on Jane's hand, I moved with her into the wide corridor.

Too many onlookers crowded outside the library, probably waiting for any information they could get about the person who'd fallen.

Or jumped? Or been shoved? How had she gotten out there?

Some in the crowd pointed at us. Many snapped our pictures. A guard stood outside the shut library door, shoulders wide and arms akimbo.

"We are her friends," I told him. "We're with Tetter, the woman who fell."

He moved aside, tapped twice on the library door, and opened it. "Please go in," he told us.

I gulped, attempting to moisten my mouth so I would be able to speak. Letting go of Jane's hand, I stepped into the room where I wanted to hear but dreaded knowing the fate of my beloved friend.

"Gil!" I said, seeing him and trying to rush across the room.

A solemn guard stopped me. "I need to see some ID."

He produced a pad on which he'd written other names and information.

"I'm Cealie Gunther. I went to school with the woman you all picked up from the iceberg." I handed him my driver's license and sailing card.

He took forever to write the information, while I peered helplessly at Gil. He stood beside a large rack of mystery novels. His gray eyes met my gaze, his face giving away nothing about Tetter's fate. Possibly he didn't know it.

I did a quick scan of the room.

A number of passengers sat on sofas and chairs, their apprehension like static charges filling up the space. They checked us out, maybe wanting to learn about our connection to Tetter, exactly as I was wondering about them.

And why was Gil here?

"You're with her?" the guard asked Jane, returning my license and card. He put a hand up in front of me, which seemed to mean I should wait with her.

"Yes, we both went to school with Tetter." Jane handed him the card with her information, glanced at Gil, and gave him a little wave.

Tight-lipped, he nodded in return.

The officer gave back Jane's things, and I stepped aside, ready to rush to Gil. I needed his arms around me and his sturdy chest on which to rest my head.

"Come this way, please," the officer told me, extending his hand toward the door we had entered.

I peered back at Gil and shrugged. He gave me a small reassuring smile before I followed the officer out the door. The crowd parted for us, making comments. I kept my eyes forward. I did not want to see faces of people I would try to avoid later. My leader spoke into a small device I couldn't see well and said words I couldn't make out.

Three rooms down the hall, a door opened to conference

room C. A bulldog of an officer with unyielding eyes let me in. My guide departed.

"I'm Mitchell Hayden, in charge of investigating what happened to your friend. These are members of our security team." He swept his arm out to indicate men and women in uniform around the room. I'd seen many of them getting information from passengers when we'd entered and left the ship. One was a bartender at the Ginger Bar. "Please sit," Hayden said, pulling a wooden chair back from a table.

I sat. He took the chair next to me, a tape recorder, pen, and pad at his place. "Do I have your permission to tape our conversation?" he asked, and I nodded. He pressed a button on the recorder. Saying his name and mine and the date, he again asked for permission to tape what we said, and I agreed.

"Why am I in here alone?" I asked, then glanced at all of the other guards and back at him. "You know what I mean."

"We're questioning people who had some connection to our guest who was found on the iceberg—people who knew her and those who might have seen her last."

"Tetter Hargroove. She's my good friend. How is she?"

"I'm not at liberty to say at this time."

"Then at what time can you say?" I shouted, shoving my hands into the air. "At nine o'clock? Ten? When? She's one of my dearest friends," I said, and considered that statement. I'd hardly seen Tetter since our graduation. "At least she was in high school. I need to know if she'll be all right."

His Adam's apple slid up and down as he bided time. His gaze remained speared with mine. "I can tell you the doctor is still examining your friend."

Tears bit my eyes. Sudden relief flooded through me when he called her my friend, not *the body.*

"We are questioning people one at a time," he continued, "and want to know everything you can tell us that might help in our investigation of what happened to her."

Words bubbled from my mouth. I told about when I'd first met Tetter in seventh grade. Jane had called me over to come in this circle of kids in the schoolyard at recess. Tetter was there, having everyone's attention, a sparkle in her eye as she told a joke, and all of us laughed. She gave me a huge smile. Later that week, I saw her in the hall and introduced myself. She hugged me and made me, at twelve, glad I attended that school. She'd been the life of the crowd, cheering up everyone, a friend to every person she met.

He jotted notes on his pad, maybe not wanting to listen later to everything people said on the recorder. He might be noting comments he thought could be important.

"And she continued to be cheerful and friendly with everyone all through her life?" he asked.

I nodded, then stopped. "I'm sure she was. I hadn't really had a lot of contact with her these last years. But people don't change much, do they?"

"You tell me." His gaze nailed my fingers, which I quit moving once I noticed his stare at them. I wanted to squirm but figured he would consider me guilty of something.

"She's been having a major problem," I said, and then told about why I decided to come on the trip. He questioned me more, and I gave details about trying to pry into her difficulties so I could help, to no avail. "But our good friend Jane Easterly, who's Tetter's roommate on the trip, tried and didn't get anything out of her, either."

He pushed, asking about my experiences with Tetter during this cruise, and when I'd last seen her. Exhaustion in my brain extended into every tissue of my body by the time he dismissed me from the room.

"We might call on you again with other questions," he warned.

Out in the corridor, I peered toward the library, where Gil and Jane and those others still waited. I couldn't get in there if I wanted to, I figured, seeing the crowd still gathered around that door an officer guarded. Voices mumbled from the group. A woman noticed me leaving the conference room and pointed. People raised excited voices.

I stamped away in the opposite direction. I'd prefer to shove through that crowd and reach Gil. I'd rest my head against his shoulder and feel his reassuring hand massage my back. He'd know what I needed.

What I did not need were more questions from all of the people waiting for answers and snapping pictures of me, and I didn't need reprimanding from the guard at the door. I limped away from all of them, my ankle aching. I needed to know what happened to Tetter. My gosh, I'd come aboard this ship to help her.

Needing to leave this deck, I stepped into an elevator's open door.

"Good morning. You're going down. What deck?" a buff man inside asked.

The question made my shoulders tense, my brain numb. Where was I heading? I needed to go somewhere. My stateroom? No, too depressing to stay alone now.

"Uh, that one," I said, pointing one button down from the lit one.

"You've seen enough beautiful mountains and ice this morning?" he asked, and I nodded, wishing I could stop envisioning the woman draped over an iceberg.

"I'm picking up someone and then going up higher. You have a good one," he said, holding the door open so I could get out first.

I nodded and aimlessly walked, hoping useful ideas would take hold. On the wall beyond the restrooms, signs pointed to room numbers fore and aft. I walked the opposite way, where art lined the walls. The pieces lost their appeal. All were now gaudy baubles.

Reaching the base of the Grand Atrium, I was satisfied to find few people. The atrium's wide open expanse felt less confining than my room would. I went for a heavily cushioned sofa, needing all of the comfort I could find.

Looking sharp in dressy casuals, Sue strutted out from a hall of staterooms.

"Sue," I called.

"Hey, where are you going?"

"Do you know what happened?" I dreaded telling her.

"To Tetter?"

"Yes. You heard?" I felt my eyes squeeze together and my forehead tighten. An ache started in my right temple and wrapped itself around my scalp, squeezing as quickly as a python might snag victims. We were talking about our precious lifelong friend.

"I saw her down there." Sue's mouth pinched into a frown. "What a pity."

"It's awful." I grabbed her in a hug.

She patted my back and stepped away.

"Did you go upstairs and tell the security team what you know?" I asked.

"What do you mean, what I know? I don't know anything." Her stance stiffened.

"I don't mean you'd know anything about her fall. I mean what you know about her as a person. If you haven't yet, you should go to the library and tell them you know her. They'll ask questions, and you can tell them about our friendship and meeting her on the ship. Or anything else you might know about her, like when you last saw her."

Sue jerked her head back. "What are you insinuating?"

It took a moment for what she meant to sink in.

"Darn, Sue, you're my aunt. I'm not suggesting a thing. I just think you ought to talk to the security team if you haven't already done so. I did."

Tension in her face relaxed. "You spoke to them? Then I don't need to. I don't know anything more than you do. She died. That's it."

"*Died?*" My pulse stopped. Breaths trapped in my throat.

"You don't think she died from that fall?"

"Oh, nobody told you she was dead?" I breathed again after Sue shook her head. "Until I hear anything official, I can hold on to hope that she made it."

"Whatever makes you happy." She glanced at the few people in our area. "I'm going outside to see the sights. Want to come?"

"Not now." I watched her flounce off toward the door to the outer deck. Drawn to the paisley-printed sofa, I plopped, instantly satisfied, onto its soft cushioning. What did not make me satisfied was Sue's belief that Tetter was dead. I chose to believe otherwise. I closed my eyes, trying to shut out the glittery lights and marble staircase and moving people and classical music, and I called up prayers for my friend.

"Are you Buddha?" a man asked.

I snapped my eyelids apart. "Randy."

"You looked mighty funny with your eyes closed and hands together in your lap like you were praying."

"I was."

"Good. I guess I should still do that. Hey, you want to do lunch?"

"Lunch?" I asked, surprised that it might be time to eat.

"Or dinner, whatever you call it." He glanced around the atrium. "I haven't seen anybody else in our group yet."

Surely he meant Tetter. And he hadn't heard.

I patted the section of sofa beside me. "Sit down a minute."

He sat, and I took a breath. "This morning—"

Loud voices and commotion from cameramen and women lugging huge cameras and other bulky equipment in from outside snagged our attention. Members of the ship's crew escorted them. One man wearing a GNZ News jacket trained his camera on the opulent atrium. He moved his focus along the glass elevator carrying passengers and aimed up at the massive chandelier. Their story of the passenger who fell from this ship might start by showing much of its beauty. And then they would move to the awful part about Tetter down on the ice.

"I wonder what that's all about," Randy said.

I snapped my head toward him, unable to believe he didn't know, and gripped his cool hand. "You didn't hear that someone from our ship fell overboard?"

"You're kidding." His eyes narrowed in a look of disbelief. "When?"

"This morning. Or— I don't know. Yes, it must have happened early this morning since our ship was still near her."

"Her? A female?" He leaned back, drawing his hand away from mine.

How could I tell him, especially since he seemed to care so much about Tetter? Maybe he was in love with her.

She's okay. She'll be all right, I repeated to myself. I swallowed. Sucked in a deep breath. Considered how to tell him it was Tetter.

The cameraman swooped his lens down from the ceiling and trained it on us.

I swung my face away. For long minutes, I kept my head turned, a strong pulse beating alongside my scalp.

By the time I determined the camera moved away from us, I had formulated questions. I peeked and saw the film crew moving on.

"Randy, you really never heard anything about a person falling?"

"I knew that guy fell in the stairwell not long after we left. I believe he died."

"He did." I envisioned his hot-pink shirt as he lay crumbled on the bottom of the stairwell. "His name was Jonathan Mill." I said a quick prayer for Jonathan.

"You knew him?" Randy asked.

"We met."

The executive chef swept into the atrium, the tall white hat announcing his presence. He aimed toward the area where the news people went.

Should I speak to him now? Courtesy said I should. And maybe I could learn more about Tetter.

"Mr. Sandkeep," I called, making him pause. "Thank you. I really appreciate the gift." I forced a smile but couldn't muster a real one.

He stared at me and glanced at Randy beside me. The chef's brows knotted. Before I could take steps toward him, he gave me a brief nod and moved on.

Randy peered in my face. "Oh, well, I guess you're not telling what that's all about." He shoved up to his feet. "I didn't have breakfast, and I'm starving. You want to come up and eat?"

"Not now."

"Okay. See you later."

He ambled away. I might rush after him and tell him it was Tetter who fell. But something kept me in place.

He would know soon enough. And maybe it was best if he didn't discover the truth yet. Her husband should be the first to know what happened to her.

Besides, I wasn't certain of her fate.

The door that the camera crew entered opened again. Men and women wearing jackets sporting large letters of a popular national news station carried in more equipment. One man had his camera rolling as he stepped inside. He'd most likely started by taking exterior pictures and then some inside. And then he and the others would go above, probably getting pictures of all of the passengers waiting around the library.

An ache jabbed in my chest. It squeezed my lungs and pushed heat up to my eyes. Tears struck my cheeks. Hot, angry tears. My friend Tetter had a major problem, and I'd come aboard to help her solve it, but now she was…

"Cealie." Gil stepped toward me, arms open wide.

I ran and welcomed them around me.

He held me tight, his breath brushing against my hair as he whispered, "You know she's dead."

NINETEEN

I LET MY tears heat Gil's chest and trembled inside the strength of his arms.

He gripped me as if I might slip away. I needed him to hold my quivering body in place. Silently, I cried.

"There's a TV camera," he said, shifting me to his side and gripping me there. He leaned his face down against my head, possibly to hide it from being filmed.

I noted the sound of heavy footsteps and wheeled luggage. More newscasters.

"Let's get out of here. This way." Gil turned me toward the nearest door to go outside. Neither of us glanced at the TV crew on the opposite side of the atrium. We pushed onto the cold outer deck. I gazed at mountains, refusing to look at icebergs.

"That's on the starboard side near the land," the naturalist was announcing, "where you can see the pod of whales."

I lowered my eyes from the mountaintop to the water in front of them. Tails that seemed minuscule flipped atop the water. Small waterspouts could have been fountains turned on beneath the ocean's surface.

"This is good," I said. "Whales. Living things in the water, instead of death."

Gil stood behind me, arm wrapped around me keeping me snug against his chest. "Most things in the water live." A quiet moment ensued. "Some don't."

A young couple walked near, smiled, and moved on. Farther down the deck, a few passengers peered toward the whales, the smarter ones using binoculars. Many voices were excited. Maybe a whale leapt from the water.

"What could have happened to her?" I asked.

Gil took breaths before he answered. "What do you think?"

"She fell. She had been drinking a lot last night and was hungover and leaned against the rail…or over the rail…and then the ship swayed, maybe hit a huge wave. Nobody saw her, and she dropped overboard." Like vomit during a bad case of virus, words kept flying out of my mouth. "She used to be a good swimmer. But she landed on that hard iceberg, and it knocked her out. She lay on that frigid ice too long…" My mental images slowed. I did not want to think of how cold and frightened she must have been. I turned toward Gil, snuggling my chilly face against him.

He pulled me in tighter. "I don't think she suffered."

Nodding, I wanted to believe those words.

"Cealie, I don't believe she fell."

I held my breath, staring at pale blue threads in Gil's V-neck sweater.

He rubbed my upper back. "Somebody shoved her overboard."

I lifted my head to look at him.

Voices sounded as people stepped outside to the deck.

Gil pulled my face in against his chest. "More cameramen," he said. "As soon as they're through filming out here, we'll go inside."

"Gil," I said, gripping him, "who would do such a thing?"

His breath felt extra warm trapped near his chest. "I don't know. Who do you think would do it?"

"Me?" I worked my head back from his grip and peered up at him. "Why would I have any idea of who might…" I couldn't even think the rest, much less say the words.

A flash of light snagged my attention. A man wearing

heavy dark gear was filming us. I didn't care anymore, at least if he didn't tape our words.

I pinned my attention on Gil. "How could I know that? My God, everybody loved that girl. She was so bubbly and sweet." Of course Tetter's personality on this trip had been the opposite of the girl I'd known in high school. "She changed," I admitted.

"Don't we all?" He turned toward the door, and we returned inside.

The warmer air and lack of icy scenes helped me relax. Until I spied more men and women with the official gear of their news stations.

"Let's go to my cabin." Gil held my hand and we hurried to the interior bank of elevators, not the glass ones the news crews could film. We kept quiet while waiting and then when we joined others on the ride. Passengers chattered about reporters and people who'd fallen during this trip.

"And I'm sure she was dead," a slim woman in a sweat suit said.

"Maybe not," a woman behind me chimed in.

"Oh, I think so. Did you see? It looked like blood on her head," a man said.

I tightened my fingers around Gil's, fighting to withhold sobs and shouts at these people.

"We're here," Gil said.

I walked with my eyes ahead, not glancing aside as I heard the door opening to a cabin we passed. Gil and I remained mute until he unlocked his door.

"This is pretty," I said, stepping into the suite that made my stateroom a closet by comparison and momentarily diverted my sad thoughts. A recessed walnut-brown ceiling trimmed with a wide strip of white and thinner strips of darker cherry brought out the numerous recessed lights. I spied a separate sitting room with extra chairs and a love seat and dining area that led to his balcony. The pictures portrayed outdoor scenes, and a tranquil foam-green quilted spread topped his queen-size bed. This was probably the first time I had ever been in a bedroom with Gil when I knew for certain sex would not take place.

"Sit down here." He drew a cushioned chair from his desk. I sat and accepted the ship's binder he gave me. He snagged a small tab and opened the binder to that page.

"Room service," I read, and glanced at him.

"Your stomach's been howling," he noted. "Let's get some lunch sent up. I want this." He pointed to the club sandwich and fruit bowl.

"Can we share?"

"No, get your own. You need strength for everything that's happening."

He yanked the phone from a desk and placed our order, also asking for two raspberry iced teas. He hung up and stepped toward me. "Now can we have sex?"

Stunned, I chuckled.

"Ah, good." He trailed a finger across my cheek. "I knew I could get a smile."

"You always can, even in the midst of a tragic situation." I recalled something I'd wanted to ask. "Why were you in the library when security started questioning people? What did you know about Tetter?"

"The things you told me. And that I'd met her."

I stared into his gray eyes. They remained sincere.

"I don't think I told you much about her. And do you think everybody she met or talked to needed to report it to security?"

"That depends. Babe, I also mentioned the male classmate with all of you."

"What did you tell security?" I stood, his betrayal sinking

a stake into my heart. "Did you tell them everything I told you? I could do that myself if I wanted to."

He grabbed my hands. "No. I examined every photograph they took on this ship that has you in it. In most of the ones with all of your classmates, you're between Randy and Tetter. And he's glaring at you. In one picture he managed to stand beside Tetter. He's gazing at her and appears overjoyed."

"That's it?"

"Yes. I only told them what I saw."

I swallowed, satisfied. "And how did you know she was dead?"

"Uncle Errol. I texted him and asked about her condition. I knew you'd especially want to know."

"Thank you."

"He said he'll tell me more later. Since she'd been kept so cold out there, he worked on her much longer than usual before determining she was gone."

"And the morgue?" I said, worrying about it not staying cold enough.

"Electricians repaired it right away, before they started to work on the outside camera system that also developed problems. Uncle Errol was also going to have to inform the Coast Guard and the nearest quarantine station."

"Oh, maybe she was ill."

"I don't think so. They also needed to notify the sheriff's office in the ship's home port, and when the ship docks, an autopsy will be performed."

I shoved my palm against his lips, making him stop. I could not think of anyone cutting Tetter open. Queasiness snaked around in my stomach.

Pounding came from Gil's door. "Room service," a woman called.

The thought of food and the scent of bacon on the sandwich

and sliced ripe cantaloupe made my stomach skip. I rushed to a trash can, fearing I'd heave.

Gil handed her a large tip and signed her paper, and she gave me a wide smile and big hello, which I tried to return but could not. Once she went out, Gil gently shoved me back on the chair. The food trays sat in front of me.

"Eat. You need to. You'll have to help Tetter."

His words made no sense, but I complied. He sweetened our tea. We ate our sandwiches and fruit, not slowing to speak. What more was there to say? I didn't wonder how I could still try to help my friend, as he suggested, until we'd finished our meal, and Gil drew back the covers of his large bed.

"You need to rest. Your ankle still has some swelling, so you have to keep it up awhile. Then you'll be able to move faster."

Like a lamb, I heeded instructions. I noticed an ache in my leg that I hadn't before. I climbed into bed, and he drew up the covers.

Gil kissed my lips and turned off the lights. "I'll be back later." His footsteps fell across carpet. The door hissed open and clicked shut.

My head sank deeper into the exquisitely soft pillow. I was ready to nap. And then when I awoke, I would take care of Tetter's problem.

But how?

My befuddled brain kept me tossing around in Gil's bed. No way could I rest.

How could I relax? My good buddy Tetter was dead.

I sat up, angry at the bright sunlight beyond the sheers at his window and the balcony door. The sun shouldn't shine today.

I stepped out to the large balcony and shivered from cold. Too weary to return inside and grab Gil's robe, I plopped on a plastic chair. I propped my feet on another one and peered at pure blue water and gorgeous mountains. "Damn you," I said to nature's beauty.

A crackle let me know someone was making announcements. At least we didn't hear them in our cabins while we were trying to sleep.

"So in the water near the ship right now, you can see otters playing," the naturalist said.

"Crap!" I shouted, wishing whoever was telling about those cutesy things would stop.

That wasn't going to happen. He continued to talk about all of the beauty passengers could see.

Right, and what about my dead friend?

"Oh, that's true. Y'all saw her, too," I said into the wind, aware that neither the man describing the pretty things nor the passengers he spoke to could hear.

I stormed back inside Gil's stateroom, slamming the door. My friend died. I needed to find out why.

Anguish squeezed my scalp and pressed my elbows against my torso. My main purpose for coming on this trip was to help my buddy with some major difficulty in her life.

I had failed.

The other event that enticed me to Alaska was getting to spend time with my son. I'd also failed in that.

I stood in place, shutting my eyes. I often failed in things I hoped to achieve, but I reminded myself that I wasn't a failure. Some events in life I couldn't control. But some I could.

I opened my eyes.

Most pressing was Tetter's death. Like Gil, I also believed someone murdered her. And I hadn't even discovered her trouble.

Now I must.

Jane had shared a room with her. Jane must know more than she'd told me.

I went outside Gil's door and grabbed the ship's newsletter from the wall bracket that held many. He hadn't removed any of them to see what events were offered.

I took only the one for today and skimmed it as I walked down the hall. Recalling Gil had fed me what he called a late lunch, I figured it was early to mid-afternoon. The ship offered high tea about now. Jane would not be at a tea, and I wasn't hungry. There was a game show in one of the bars. I couldn't imagine her wanting to play a game at this time. On the Lido Deck, a talented crew member would be carving an ice sculpture, chipping away at a massive block of ice to create a pair of swans or some such lovely creatures. Many passengers would watch this carving, which I imagined meant we were not sailing near many other sights the naturalist would mention.

I had watched ice carvings on ships and enjoyed them but would not today. Today my friend died. She died on ice. I didn't want to see any more of it than I needed to.

Where would Jane be? In her room? I doubted it. I imagined that after going through an inquisition with security members in the library, she didn't want to be cooped up in a room any more than I did.

I located a wall phone, charged the call to my room, and called hers. As I suspected, no answer. I also dialed her cell. She again didn't answer. I did not leave a message asking her to call me, since I wouldn't be staying in this spot.

Jane would desire to run now.

Her jog had been cut short this morning. Now she'd especially want to get her endorphins flowing.

I'd seen her walk up the open stairwell from the Lido Deck this morning to reach wherever she planned to jog. Imagining a jogging track was on the next deck above, I opened my tri-folded map showing the ship's plan to check.

Eek, the jogging track was way up on deck 15. And I would have to walk up three flights of outdoor stairs.

With relief, I saw an elevator could take me up to the sports deck, which meant I would need to walk up only one flight. Promising myself I'd begin that exercise routine soon, I made my way to the elevator. Riding with others, I heard two of them whisper that I was one of the dead woman's friends.

Struggling, I kept my chin up and mouth shut. Once we stopped, I stepped off and trudged upstairs toward the uppermost smallest deck. Gripping the rail, I could feel the ship rock.

I reached the top deck and peered at people lolling on decks below. We rocked on a massive sea. Brisk, blood-chilling air lashed against me. I felt like I was on a balcony. Fear pinched the rear of my neck and squeezed my back muscles as though trying to hide them inside my spine.

Was this what happened to Tetter? Panic. And then she dropped over the side?

Struggling for clear thoughts, I spied Jane. She was running, the only person on this deck besides me.

She jogged toward the opposite edge of the oval track. I tried to call her, but my throat released only trapped air. The ship shifted. I envisioned myself tipping into frigid brine. Spreading my feet, I bent my knees for balance and tightened my grip on the handrail.

Jane pumped her arms, looking much younger than I felt, eye-catching in her slenderizing jogging suit and confident air. Her running shoes pounded the outdoor carpet. She peered back, seeming to sense she wasn't alone. Her face registered concern. Then recognition. She dashed toward me.

"You changed your mind and want to run?" She jogged in place.

"If I tried, I'd surely slip out there." I shifted my gaze from the water so I wouldn't swoon.

"Do you think that's what happened to her?"

"She wasn't here when you came up this morning?"

Jane shook her head. "Tetter was already down there." Her gaze trailed toward the water we sailed through. "Cealie, I've never heard of anyone falling off a ship unless they leaned way out or tried some dangerous stunt. I can't imagine her doing either of those things."

"Did you find out anything from the security staff that questioned us?"

"All I knew is they can ask about a lot of things." She pursed her lips. "And that they bag all of her possessions. They're doing that in my room right now. They have the room sealed off."

"How horrible." I grasped her hand. "Then you know she died."

Averting her eyes and retaining her pace, Jane nodded. "Since she was my roommate, they told me." She sucked in air and met my gaze. "I separated her things and set them in the middle of the room so they could find everything that's hers. They'll give her possessions to her family."

"Oh my gosh, her family. Do they know about her yet?"

She stared at her running shoes, still lifting and hitting the outdoor turf track, and shrugged. "The chief purser was going to contact them and make arrangements for them to get her in a port."

"I can't believe this is all happening."

"I can't, either." Her lips pressed together.

"Did she ever tell you what was really troubling her?" I asked, and Jane shook her head. "We'll have to try to figure out what happened."

"Yes. But first I've got to get rid of some of these jitters. I need to run."

I experienced the strange sudden sensation that since I was blocking her, she would run over me if I didn't get out of her way. I stepped aside and backed away from the track. "Let's talk later."

She took off in a hurry right where I'd been standing. I watched Jane dashing away, arms pumping, legs pounding, and could not envision myself doing that ever again.

There was a time, I reminded myself, gripping the handrail and inching backward down the stairs, trying not to think of balconies and falls. There had been a time when I could run like that. Keeping my eyes on each step, I tried to recall running after I'd finished high school. Yes, during my college phys ed classes. I was down on a lower deck. I dashed to the elevators and hopped in the first one that opened its door.

Where to now? How could I get information?

I pulled the ship's newsletter from my purse, glanced at the large watch on a woman who joined me two decks down, and saw that high tea would be taking place in the Pacific dining room.

I didn't need tea or food, but the dining room could hold people who had answers to some of my questions. The executive chef might be in there and explain why he sent me champagne. Gil could be there, snacking. He'd tell me what troubles he was having with that chef and why they were together on the outer deck. Mainly I wanted to know whether he'd gotten anymore information from the doctor. I headed for the dining room to find out.

TWENTY

CAMERAMEN AND REPORTERS swarmed the deck. I peered straight ahead as I walked toward the mid-ship Pacific dining room.

Enthusiastic crowds gathered around camera crews made me notice the library and the guard still outside it. The security staff probably hadn't finished questioning all the people I'd seen in there. In fact, they might have summoned more passengers for their inquisition. Who saw her last? they might be asking.

I also wanted the answer.

Why and how had Tetter gone overboard?

Did anyone actually know?

"There she is," a woman said, pointing at me.

Many in the gathering commented and snapped my picture. My stomach churned. I turned away. A bright light came at me, a bearded man gripping its source, a TV camera on his shoulder.

"Stop," I said, thrusting my hands in front of my face.

"You knew the deceased?" a well-dressed attractive woman with the cameraman asked, the camera getting her face with mine.

I opened my mouth to scream that my good friend had died. My peripheral vision let me see more people with cameras approaching.

"You went to school with her?" a woman with a microphone asked me.

"How did you know that?"

She smiled. "A lot of people on this ship met members of your group. Others saw all of you together. So you were here for a mini class reunion, and one of your classmates fell overboard."

My chin tightened and quivered.

"I am so sorry about your loss," the reporter said, but I knew the cameraman was getting a closer shot of my face. "And you are…?"

"Wanting my friend back." I bumped against the cameraman's arm as I dashed away. I darted off amid the swell of comments from passengers watching and reporters who surely made annoying comments into their mikes.

I slowed as I neared the room where they'd questioned me. The same security guard stood at the door. He eyed me, and I gave him a curt nod as I passed. Relieved that I didn't get stopped, I yanked open a door to the Pacific dining room.

It seemed identical to our dining room, the same chandeliers and glitter and colors and crystal on tables. The chief difference was that now reporters scattered everywhere.

I was ready to do like a crayfish and back from trouble. My glance through the room, however, let me spy Gil. He stood and spoke to a reporter while being filmed by a cameraman.

I imagined quills springing up on my back. Then I would bend over and fling them at him.

What was he telling the world—he knew a woman who was friends with the person who fell off the ship?

The executive chef did not like Gil or Cajun food. Was Gil trying to call attention to his own chef and his dishes?

Okay, Cealie, Gil is not the kind of man who would do that. I believed what I told myself, believed it with all my heart, yet the ornery, judgmental part of my nature took hold. I needed to rid myself of that negative part of me, but meanwhile, there it was.

More annoyance built. Not long ago, Gil had put me to

bed, saying I needed to rest. He had something to do. Is this what he'd intended? Get coverage on television?

He wouldn't do that, but I could not make the nasty part of my mind stop that line of thinking.

I studied the room once more. A tall white cap was rising. Executive Chef Andrew Sandkeep stepped away from a table where he had sat. With my aunt.

Before he could escape the room or the area near her table, I rushed to him.

"Chef Sandkeep," I called, and he turned. So did Sue. I pretended not to notice her, and I spoke to him as he watched me, thick eyebrows wrinkled, giving me a curious expression.

"Yes?" he said.

I couldn't tell whether he knew me or not. If I told him my name, Sue would realize we were almost strangers. For some unfathomable reason, I wanted her to believe otherwise. I also hoped Gil was seeing us and wondering why I wasn't still in his bed.

I stepped closer to the chef and took hold of his soft hand. "I really want to thank you for the champagne. It was so kind of you to send the bottle to my room."

Skin at the outer edges of his eyes crinkled. Would he laugh and say he had no idea who I was?

After a long moment, he lowered his head. Lifting my hand, he kissed it. "I hoped you would enjoy it."

"I'm sure I will." My peripheral vision let me spy Sue watching from her table. I wanted to ask the chef questions but did not want her to hear the replies.

I tugged on the chef's hand to get him farther from her. Nearby dining room stewards glanced at him and smiled, seeming to make extra effort at their tables. Our maître d' gave the executive chef a nod and straightened in a stance of attention. He appeared to snap his heels together.

Surely the man I stood with commanded respect from a large number of people.

"They admire you," I said. "Or maybe fear your reprisal?"

He awarded me a generous smile. "Every one of us shares mutual esteem."

"How admirable." I considered asking if he sent many people champagne but thought that an inappropriate question. I'd seen a number of bottles awarded to passengers as prizes on cruises. But I had done nothing to win a prize.

"You seem confused," he said, watching my face.

"Well, I am." I swung my gaze toward Gil. He was gone. So was the reporter. "Mr. Sandkeep," I continued, returning my attention to the man before me.

"Please call me Andrew."

"All right. And I believe you know my name is Cealie."

"I do."

"Okay, Andrew, why did you send me champagne and that note? I don't even know you. And you don't know me."

He chuckled. "Maybe I know much more than you think."

My face relaxed. "Maybe you sent it as a peace offering for Gil and me."

"Or anyone else you might want to share some bubbly with." One edge of his lips cocked up. His gaze held on to mine.

Was he suggesting I share the liquor with him?

Our maître d' waved to call him.

"If you will excuse me." Andrew Sandkeep snagged my hand and kissed it. "I am wanted elsewhere."

"Sure, go ahead. And again, thank you."

Warmth remained on my hand where his lips pressed. Once more I looked for Gil. He wasn't around. If he'd seen me with the chef, annoyance could have sent him away. He didn't like this chef and had declared that the chef didn't like him. He usually had good instincts about people. Possibly this time he was wrong.

I wasn't certain of my own feelings about Chef Sandkeep.

"Cealie, come here." Sue waved from her small table.

"How are you?" I sat beside her.

"Too full. I need to get them to take all of this food away."

"Wait a minute," I said, noting the sweet mint and cinnamon scents of flaky scones piled on a platter. Chocolate coatings and drizzles of strawberries made the pastries extra tempting. I set a cinnamon roll and one flaky chocolate dessert on a napkin.

A waiter slid a saucer in front of me. "Coffee? Or cold or hot tea?"

"Coffee, please."

Sue watched me eat a goodie. "I'll wait before sending them away. Maybe you'll make all of them disappear."

I swallowed the final bite of chocolate. "That's rude."

"I was never known for my tact in school, was I? Or in our family, either."

Calling up a vision of Sue as Stu, I recalled the smart-mouthed boy who often told people things that offended them. The insulted person gave an angry retort, and he would snort and say he'd been just kidding, and why did they take things so seriously. No one ever appeared to think he was funny.

Many in our class displayed antagonism toward him.

In fact, I realized, hands shaking, if a fortune-teller had predicted that someone would kill a person from our class on this trip, I would have guessed the victim would be Sue.

Someone from our class would *kill* a person?

My mouth zapped dry. Tetter did not fall off the ship. I was certain someone pushed her.

"Good grief, Cealie, you can eat more of these sweets. Don't look so damned morose." Sue shoved the platter in front of me.

"Who do you think killed her?" I said.

"Tetter?"

I nodded, leaning toward her.

"I guess you think I did." Sue narrowed her eyes. "Damn, you decided I killed Jonathan Mill and now I knocked off Tetter. How did I ever stay out of prison?"

"I don't believe you killed those people."

"Of course you do." She shoved back from the table and stood. Even when angry, she was a gorgeous woman. "And I guess you and our classmates and our extended family all wonder if I had every part of my body altered with the surgery."

The kind part of my nature told me to shake my head and say *Absolutely not.* But there was that wicked part, which took over much more often than I wanted. I waited, not saying a thing.

"Well, you can all keep wondering." She snapped up her purse and stomped away.

People at nearby tables stared at me. They probably heard Sue's last statement about altered body parts and found that a curious subject.

Face heated with shame, I left the table. I did not need to know about Sue's body and certainly didn't believe she had anything to do with the death of our shipmate.

I stopped in mid-step. Two people from this ship died since we embarked.

I'd had contact with both of them—Jonathan, briefly when he and Sue flirted during our drill on the Lido Deck before we left shore. I knew Tetter much better—or had known her well in school…maybe.

Maybe not, I considered, walking on. Tetter had been the most popular, friends-with-everyone girl in our high school. As such, I knew her, and she knew me.

But had we really known each other?

I paused at a bench near a large window and gazed out at
the water, trying to recall any instances of really being close
to her. We'd seen each other in groups at recess. She was
normally the center of attention, cheering up everyone who
seemed sad. In the halls we all called out her name when we
saw her, and she gave a bubbly yell back at us. Having Tetter
know you was a thrill.

Had she known me?

She knew my name and where I lived but had never come
to my house, even when I'd invited her to my birthday parties.
Those parties felt less sparkly because she never attended.
Her absence made me feel I wasn't special enough for Tetter
to come. I now watched the water roll, smelled fresh coffee,
and heard a little girl and a woman talking as they walked
behind me. The realization struck—Tetter had never invited
me to her house.

Some of my classmates went there. Never me.

Anguish wrenched in my chest as though a large hand
reached inside and twisted, attempting to yank out my
heart.

*Good grief, Cealie, why don't you feel sorry for yourself?
Your friend and a man died, and you're the one feeling pain?*

My inner vision returned to locating the teenager I once
was—the girl who tried to act so self-assured—but wasn't.
I'd wanted to know who I was and where I wanted to go with
my life and had often pretended I knew both.

What I'd been instead was a girl ridden with angst and
uncertainty.

"Pretty, isn't it?"

"What?" I asked, shocked out of reverie.

Gil slipped an arm around my waist. Beside me, he stared
out the window.

I peered out there. Blue rolling water. White-tipped mountains. In the distance, a glacier that our ship would probably

stop to watch. Everyone would listen to it rumble and groan. Most likely while we remained near, it would calve with an explosive crash as a massive section of it shot off into the sea.

"I guess it's okay."

He eyed me, forehead wrinkled. "Just okay?"

I knew there was some reason I wasn't happy with Gil, but it wasn't important. "Have you gotten anymore information that you haven't told me?"

His wrinkles deepened. He gave his head a slight nod.

"I need to know. Tell me everything," I persisted.

He loosened his grip on my waist. "You know there's a brig on board. If they find that anyone caused her death, they'll lock up the person in that small padded room. It has a small round window so they can watch the prisoner."

"Okay, so do you know if anyone caused her death?" I watched his eyes, waiting to see if they'd flinch, more satisfied when they didn't.

"I wouldn't know that."

"All right. What else?"

His gaze shifted upward. "They need to find a funeral home that will accept the…Tetter. The chief purser and hotel director will let her family know what they locate."

I shut my eyes, imagining the anguish her family might feel. The pain was too great. Opening my eyes again, I nodded at Gil to continue.

"These are things my uncle told me would happen after Jonathan Mill died. I haven't really gotten to talk to him except for a second since Tetter fell."

"Tell me what you know."

"The manager of the photo department is in charge of taking all of the pictures, with and without clothes, from all angles."

"Stop!" I shoved a hand toward him and the other one

over my mouth, ready to gag. "Don't tell me the guy in charge of taking our pictures also snapped pictures of my friend naked?"

"You wanted to know."

"Not that."

"I'm sorry. Besides, we probably had a different photographer. After Jonathan fell, and I asked my uncle what happens on a ship when a person dies, those were some of the things he said. I'm not aware of any specifics about your classmate."

"Why were you giving an interview on TV? To get your name out there?" I was ashamed the minute I spewed the words and wished I could retrieve them.

He lowered his gaze. I'd hurt him. Why couldn't I rip all meanness out of myself?

"That reporter had seen me coming out of the library, so he knew I'd been questioned. He asked what I could tell him about Tetter. I only said she was a nice person."

I gripped his hand. "I'm sorry. I'm just... You know I can't be myself right now. Or maybe I can, and I'm really a horrible person."

"There's nothing horrible about my Cealie. Except that she lost a good friend." He squeezed my hand. "I'll see you later." Gil kissed my forehead and walked off.

I could have run after him and apologized. But I had already done that. I could have said how terrible I was. But he was right. I was riding an emotional roller coaster, full speed ahead toward a volcanic eruption. Until I learned what caused my classmate's death, I could not remain stable.

I ambled down the long hallway, glancing in bars to see if any of my classmates were inside. A few rowdy passengers gyrated on the dance floor, something I was not interested in doing anymore.

From the crowd ahead in the hallway, a familiar friendly face came into view. I smiled as Jane headed toward me.

She swung her index finger toward my face, her face pinched in a scowl. "You screwed my little brother?"

People around faced me, many appearing shocked. Others grinned. What high entertainment.

"Let's go somewhere private to talk." I gripped Jane's arm.

She jerked away as though I tried to share leprosy. "I don't need to go anywhere private with you. You seem to have spent lots of private time with my brother. Darn, Cealie, my naive little brother."

"But we only went out a few times."

"And did what?"

People sucked in closer, wanting to hear my sordid story. I flung a furious stare at them. They scattered like sprayed roaches.

"Jane," I said, aggravation building with my louder voice, "it's none of your business what I did on a date. I never asked what you did on dates."

"I never went out with your brother!"

"Who told you I dated Donald?"

She shoved her face closer to mine. Her breath smelled of spearmint. "You should have told me you were seeing him. Or putting out with him."

"You have absolutely no idea what we did when we went out. But Donald's the one who should have told you. He's your family."

"I guess he was embarrassed to tell us he dated you." Her face twisted with rage.

Her statement hurt. I chose to believe she only said it out of anger. "He wanted to get that new little blond in our class jealous. It's the only reason he asked me to go out a few times. And then he got her."

"Right. And I'll sell you that mountain." She flipped her hand toward the nearest large window, spun, and stomped away.

"Who told you?" I yelled.

She didn't turn back. "Ask the guy from our reunion."

Randy.

Why would he tell Jane I dated her brother?

TWENTY-ONE

I NEEDED TO FIND OUT why Randy told Jane about my few dates with her brother. Especially, why now.

Jane was my very best friend from school and on this ship, except for Gil. If they were both irritated with me, who would I do things with? I could accept her talking to me the way she did because I admired her so much, and I probably should have told her I went on those few dates with Donald.

I walked on, wondering who might help me discover what really happened to Tetter. *Had* someone killed her?

And had that person also killed Jonathan?

I quit moving. Of course security would have thought of the possible connection. I needed to speak to those in charge, to tell them more and insist they give me answers.

I headed toward the inquisition room and slowed, recalling all of the TV cameras and curious people. Now would not be the time to return to their location. Glancing out a large window, I noticed a heavy mist had rolled in. It probably kept more people than usual inside.

My ankle ached. Time to give it a rest so I could think better. I entered a bar with only one couple inside and stretched on a cushioned love seat against the wall. I shook my head at the bartender to let him know I didn't want anything.

"It's water," he said, carrying a glass to me. "You look like you could use it."

"Thanks. You're right."

I sipped my icy water, deciding to take a pain reliever for faster respite. The couple in the bar shared secret smiles and kisses. I glanced away, allowing their privacy. The TV on the wall was off.

"Would you mind turning your TV to the ship's channel?" I asked the bartender.

"Sure thing." He remoted the set.

Our cruise director appeared on the screen wearing a wide smile. "Here you can see the fun you experienced during the Captain's Party your first night aboard. And don't forget—all of your excitement and entertainment is being captured right here with our onboard cameras. You will be able to purchase a CD reminding you of your exciting cruise before you leave the ship."

These same scenes would be playing in staterooms and elsewhere on the ship, anywhere to get passengers' attention so they would search for themselves in scenes and want to purchase a reminder of their fun.

My time during this cruise was anything but fun, except for brief moments. I concentrated on the screen. Security members would be doing this, too, all of us looking for anything out of the ordinary that might relate to two dead passengers.

They would search for any scenes showing Jonathan or Tetter. By now they'd know of those victims' friends on the ship. Surely they'd found the photos of our group sharing our little class reunion. Tetter stood with all of us.

Would they notice Randy glaring at me in those pictures when I purposely shoved myself between him and her?

Of course they would. These people were trained to look for problems.

But they didn't know the relationship between all of the people in our group.

Did I?

I wasn't certain and didn't know what else to do now. I relaxed and put my legs up on the love seat.

Onscreen, waiters and waitresses served trays of complimentary hors d'oeuvres and offered colorful stemmed glasses of champagne and lime-green margaritas and pink daiquiris to seated guests in the massive theater. The camera panned the room, getting close-ups of people with smiling faces, wearing dressy casuals.

I searched for our group, also hoping I would see Gil. I missed him. I'd annoyed him—but before being any good with him, I had to know what caused my friend's death. He was so forgiving of all my faults.

Guests streamed into the theater…

"Your trip started soon after you boarded, and we made sure you were all safely aboard before we embarked, and that you knew how to protect yourself should any problem arise," a narrator's raised voice said, waking me. I noticed I'd dozed and was prone on the love seat in the bar. I set my feet down on the floor and sat up. The TV showed scenes from the first day. Maybe it was on its second go-round. Crew members were displaying the proper way to fasten life jackets, and they checked on guests who were having problems. Many passengers donned theirs quickly.

The man telling how safe those jackets would keep passengers sent my blood pressure pumping higher. How safe had those jackets kept Jonathan and Tetter?

"This safety drill took place in many stations before you left shore," the unseen narrator said as the camera jumped to a different place. One passenger snagged my attention. The bride in her strapless gown.

"Can I get you anything?" the bartender asked me from across the lounge.

"No thanks, but would you raise the volume?" Intent on the screen, I tried to hear background talking as the camera closed in on the bride and groom. He caressed her breast while bringing her life jacket strap around her and hooking it in front.

Motion from the side of the newlyweds grabbed my interest. It was me, walking away right after I'd congratulated them. I was looking for Sue then because she was no longer where she and I had stood.

"As soon as our all-clear is given, you will be able to return your jackets to your staterooms, and we will be on our way," our instructor onscreen said. I watched a stately couple holding hands and walking right behind her. My heartbeat sped. That woman was Sue. She gripped the hand of a man wearing a hot-pink shirt. Jonathan, the man who died later that day.

I swallowed, watching myself heading for Sue. She spied me and dropped Jonathan's hand. Immediately, she jabbed her finger downward as though toward another place, maybe his stateroom, where, I imagined, she was saying she would meet him. She didn't signal up toward the sports deck that held the spa where she'd insisted to us that she later went.

The camera jumped to a new scene, and I got to my feet. Sue had lied to us that evening. Now I had proof.

Or did I?

Knowing she pointed to Jonathan and downward, and later told us she'd gone up to the spa, when it probably wasn't open yet, didn't prove a thing.

But I could tell the security staff.

Did I want to?

Why? I asked myself, sagging back against the wall.

My friends and I never cared much for her, but that was no reason to start a witch hunt if no witches existed.

Gil had suggested Sue might have gone to Jonathan's room, and once they stripped down, ready for action, Jonathan might have teased her and put her down so badly, she wanted him dead.

Then why might she have killed Tetter?

No reason I could think of.

"I appreciate the water—and nap," I told the bartender and turned to leave a tip. I glanced at the TV.

"Have a good one," the bartender said.

"Here is the evening meal from your first day with us," a hidden announcer mentioned on television, showing a dining room. It was ours, I could tell, recognizing our maître d'. Sconces on walls, fresh flowers on beautifully appointed tables. Dining room staff members looked splendid in tuxes and were anxious to please. Most of the guests who gawked were most likely on their maiden voyage.

Our table was near the door on the left. The camera panned the area on the right, part of it blocked from ours by a dividing wall, as passengers entered. Many people speaking and dishes clattering prohibited my hearing any individual words. But I noticed something that I feared would have a major impact on some people's lives.

My breath slowed. I stepped closer to the bar. The bartender said nothing as I peered up, watching the scene unfold. First, the pink-and-orange paisley printed shirt snagged my attention, and then the chin-length cut of Tetter's white-blond hair. A table steward checked her sailing card and pointed beyond the ten-foot-square wooden partition at the dining room's entrance, certainly to show her where to locate our table. But she shook her head and showed him she was going in the opposite direction. She rushed ahead, her face brightening more than I'd seen it during this entire cruise, making her look like the Tetter I'd known in school.

A man stood near a wall. *Randy.*

He broke into a massive smile, not one of surprise at seeing her. A leer built in his eye.

More shocking was Tetter's response. She threw her hands out toward him. The camera panned her face as she ran a searing gaze over him. Her passionate smile widened.

"Wow, hot stuff going on there, huh?" the bartender told me with a grin.

I caught my breath, not believing what I watched. I could not take my eyes away from the set.

The scene cut to more passengers coming into the dining room. Another cut took us into a galley, where the unseen narrator said our food was prepared. I checked the scene for Gil's chef or the head man. Didn't see either one.

"And throughout your trip, all of these exquisite dishes prepared in the galleys will be served to you, our treasured passengers," the onscreen voice said.

The scene jumped back to our dining room.

"That's our executive chef," the bartender told me, pointing at the TV.

Andrew Sandkeep stood beside the stairwell, soon to be introduced to us that evening.

I entered the room behind a young elegant brunette. I looked frumpy beside her, I decided, watching myself follow her into the room. I met Jane and Tetter at our table and hugged them. Tetter appeared unhappy, as she would for most of the trip. Randy was not around.

Executive Chef Sandkeep stepped nearer, staring at us.

No, he was not staring at our entire group. The lecherous smile stamped across his face made confusion wrack my brain. My stomach twisted and knotted.

Like Randy, he aimed his leer at a woman.

That woman was me.

TWENTY-TWO

I WANDERED OUT OF THE BAR. What had those scenes of our first evening in the dining room meant? The television screen inside it had jumped to a new setting right after I witnessed the executive chef's reaction to me.

I stopped in my tracks and tapped the side of my head. "Oh, come on, Cealie," I said. The chef could not have actually thought I was hot! What an imagination I had.

But he had sent me champagne and a note with two fluted glasses.

I needed a replay of the chef's face when he looked toward our table. I could purchase a CD, but I knew they wouldn't complete or sell them until the trip was almost over and they had added scenes from many more events.

Would they add the scene that took place right after we ate that first dinner? I wondered, ambling on. That excitement we witnessed down that stairwell would really sell, a man lying dead. And if they showed Tetter across that iceberg, their sales would surely swell. But not their bookings.

I normally loved taking cruises, but our reunion was proving to be deadly. Now that the media swarmed this ship and told the world about the two people dying during one cruise, would anyone ever want to sail on it again?

The next possibility struck like a hardcover book full of thoughts slamming my forehead.

Suppose dead bodies *increased* their passenger list?

The idea seemed so strange I couldn't believe I'd actually considered it. But what if the possibility of people dying onboard actually enticed some folks, just like many visitors flocked to see and sleep in supposed haunted houses?

"Absurd," I said, shaking my head in case cobwebs had settled in there. I needed to find people I knew. I had to know what happened to Tetter.

Able to move better with my leg rested and no ache from my ankle, I walked with a quicker pace. I glanced in each store but did not know anyone. I moved through the smoky casino. Machines clanged. People at tables placed bids.

Randy sat in the same cove as before. He pressed the Play Max button. Two sevens stopped in a line on his machine.

"You won't win like that," I said at his side.

"I never do." Without glancing at me, he again pressed *Max*. Still no luck.

"You certainly had the hots for her."

"Who?"

"Tetter."

"Lots of people did." He pressed the button. His machine whirred, its sevens swirling one way and another as it went haywire.

"What do you mean—lots of people did?"

"You didn't really know her, did you?" He kept his eyes trained on the machine. "Damn, I win four, but bet six. Great winnings, huh?" He reached for the Max button.

I stopped his hand. "Tell me what I didn't know."

He shook his head, mouth pinched in a frown. "She was so exciting and sexy. All the boys thought so." He stared at me, eyes narrowed. "She still was."

I ran my mind through the possibilities of what he meant. "Randy?"

He jerked his hand away from mine. "Don't you get it? She was a player. Tetter ran around and jumped in the sack with every guy around."

I shook my head. "No way. No way would that sweet girl…"

He hopped up from his seat and pressed his face close to mine. "That sweet girl messed around with almost every boy at our school. Were all of you gals so clueless?"

"She might have been with one or two of you, but—"

"And even now—on this ship."

My face loosened like dough someone might mold but hadn't begun yet. I didn't know whether to sob or laugh in his face. Tetter? He was talking about her?

"But she was a grandma." I voiced the only sane words coming to mind.

Randy's laughter roared out.

I struggled with the urge to slap his face until every inch of it stung.

He grabbed my hands, moving closer. "Listen, it didn't matter what age your girl was. She was hot. She wanted sex most of the time. Yes, she was married and had kids and grandkids. And she liked sex. With lots of people. With me on this ship."

"But... No, she had a problem. She came on this cruise with a problem."

"She always had problems. She *was* a problem. She affected lots of us guys with our girlfriends when we were in high school and a bunch of us since then, too."

"I don't believe you."

"Would you believe she and I made out twice since we boarded this ship? I let her know I was serious about her. I've always wanted her."

I shook my head. Its shaking slowed as the chance of his words being true sank in. Lots of boys in school *had* liked Tetter. I recalled the smiles some of them gave her in the hall. They were different from the flirtatious looks guys gave many other girls.

"She was seeing some other guy on board, too." Randy

tightened his grip of my hands. "I don't know who, but that really pissed me off."

"But if you knew she liked other guys, why would it bother you if she was seeing another man on the ship?" I asked, trying to wrap my mind about what he told me while shoving emotions aside.

"I wanted her to leave her husband and come away with me. I told her that before we came on this cruise. She said she would give me her decision after we sailed."

I didn't want to believe his words. But Jane had said that after Tetter declined coming on this trip, she called to say she changed her mind, even though she still had a major dilemma. Had her difficulty been what Randy suggested? And he'd told Jane he heard we were having this reunion and wanted to come along. Had Tetter been the one to tell him we were coming?

"Did Tetter give you her decision?" I asked.

He stared toward the hallway where a crowd gathered. "No. She said she would decide before we finished this cruise."

"But she finished her cruise early," I uttered, not wanting to believe what he was telling me. "What do you think happened to her? Did she have a drinking problem? Could she have gotten drunk and fallen off the ship?"

"You've got to be kidding. And don't make yourself even think she could have jumped, either. Somebody threw her overboard."

My breath caught. "Who?"

He gave the top of my head a pat. "It wasn't me."

Shoulders slumped, Randy wandered off into the crowd.

What would I do with the information Randy gave me?

Talk to security?

No way. Not until I decided whether I believed him.

Share what he said with Gil?

Absolutely.

I located a phone on the wall and connected with Gil's cell. It wasn't in service. I rang his room. Nothing.

Possibly he'd be checking a galley, but if I barged into one, cooks would most likely scream bloody murder, especially considering there had been two unexplained deaths since we sailed. They might try to stop an intruder with their large sharp knives. Besides, Gil could be standing on the Lido Deck, peering out to sea, wondering what to do about me.

I shook my head. How could I think about myself when people died?

He would be working to sort out what happened to them, mainly my good friend Tetter.

I snagged an elevator up to the Lido Deck and stepped outside. The brisk damp cold made me shiver. I hurried along, my gaze skimming the faces of people, and I almost tripped over one of the new signs that stood everywhere warning passengers to hold on to railings and walk carefully. I moved through the turquoise-covered housing for one of the swimming pools.

My need to find Gil intensified. Heart pounding, I rushed through the sliding door into the buffet area, frantically searching for him in every seating area. Before reaching the pizza station at the ship's aft, I stopped. He would not be eating pizza.

I inhaled gulps of air, struggling to get rid of my panic. What was the crisis I needed to take care of so quickly?

I had to have someone I could talk to, who I could tell about everything Randy said to me about Tetter as she'd been in high school. And as she was now—before her fall. We needed to sort out the truth.

"Excuse me." A bearded man with a walking cane nudged against me.

"Sorry I was in your way," I said, noticing I stood in front of the ice cream machine. Exactly what I needed to get calmer.

I waited behind him, and once he was done, I fixed myself a cone, making the curly top as high as I could. I walked off from the dining area, momentarily satisfied to lick my velvety soft vanilla ice cream.

Where would I go next? To talk to Jane? Surely she wasn't really mad at me for going on a couple of dates with her brother.

But she'd mentioned something earlier. In my stateroom. She seemed to wish for all of the neatness and space I had.

After hearing that, maybe I should have invited Tetter to come and room with me.

No, I could not discuss what I'd heard with Jane. Neither Sue.

I finished my cone, watching a family frolicking in the pool while my thoughts ran around in a maze. I would find Gil. I'd relate everything Randy said and together, we would know what to do next.

His chef, Adam Hebert, might know where he was, but I didn't know where to find him. The only other person Gil knew well on this ship was his uncle. He might know where Gil was, or possibly Gil was visiting with him, trying to get more answers about my classmate.

I took an elevator down to the undecorated deck 3.

No security staff stood around. Probably most were still questioning people and guarding those rooms, trying to fend off the media and curious onlookers.

I stepped inside the medical center. A light was on, but no nurse sat at the counter. Everything appeared empty. The hall leading to the rear was lit.

"Hello," I called.

Tension gripped my shoulders. One of my friends lay back there, somewhere with no light or warmth.

I wanted… *What do you want, Cealie?* I asked myself, stepping toward the back. I knew I did not want my friend dead and did not want her to be alone, no matter what she did or whether she was the person I thought I'd known.

"May I help you?" Dr. Thurman sat at a desk, poring over papers. He stood as I walked in.

I inclined my head toward the papers. "I imagine you're filling those in for my friend who just died."

He nodded, the skin between his eyes creasing.

"I don't want to see her now, do I?" I asked, struggling against my fears but wanting to do what was right.

"No." The cold look he gave made me take a half step back.

I pointed toward the front office. "I didn't see nurses or anyone up there."

"They're going to dinner and for questioning by the security staff. If anyone has a medical problem, I'll be called."

It was time for me to go. I knew that. Yet I wasn't satisfied. My curious nature and desire to probe for the truth kept me in place. "Tetter was my classmate."

The drab expression in his eyes told me he wasn't interested.

"At Westside High School. Good old W.H.S. And she was my friend. But I just discovered she wasn't the person I thought she was."

A spark ignited in his eyes. "What did you learn?"

"She—" I pointed toward where I thought a rear room held her body. "I shouldn't be telling her personal business."

"It might help." A concerned expression swept over his face, and he stepped back. He held up a page he'd been writing on. "I'm working to gather all of the information I can to assist authorities and help her family and friends like you discover what caused her demise. Your information might help police put things together."

He appeared solemn. Concerned about my dead friend.

Too concerned about what I knew about her personal life.

The shiver of fear inching along my spine like the slowest caterpillar told me I should leave.

This man, Gil's uncle, was a killer.

TWENTY-THREE

"Doc," I said, "I don't really know much about Tetter. And I really came down here hoping I might find my boyfriend."

Dr. Thurman's dark eyebrows knotted.

"You know, your nephew Gil Thurman." I worked to force my voice even, although my pitch rose. "You remember he introduced us when you were sitting with him, and you received a message on your pager and had to hurry away." *Surely you won't hurt anyone who goes out with your nephew.* "We've dated each other for a long time," I said, trying not to whine. "In fact Gil loves me. And I love him."

"Love," he said, with the slightest nod, eyes going out of focus. "Love is good."

"Yes. So I was just searching for Gil and thought you might know where he is. But I see he's not here, so I'll just go find him."

"No!" The doctor's body shot forward as quickly as his word. He stood so close, we could have hugged, although I was certain neither of us had that intention.

"But he's probably looking for me, too," I said, the knot in my chest thickening, the walls squeezing in on me. "And you know Gil. He just doesn't give up." The smile I forced felt like it came out as a sneer.

"I don't know Gil much anymore. His father and I had a falling out when we were in our early thirties, and I moved out of state. I never kept up with him."

"But now you can." I jammed my lips into a smile. "Gil

is the nicest man you'll ever know. He's loveable and considerate. I don't know about his daddy, but Gil is the best."

"During our few exchanged emails, I've asked Gil to meet me sometime on a cruise and bring one of his chefs. I never thought he would decide to come on the same cruise as Tetter."

"That's funny, and another funny thing," I babbled, trying to keep my saliva from drying so I could still speak, "is that my aunt is on this ship, too. Well, actually she used to be my uncle. Aunt Sue used to be Uncle Stu—it's a kind of joke, you know. Oh, I think Gil told you about her. Anyway, Gil has an uncle on board, and I have an aunt, so besides my having a little class reunion, the four of us are sharing a family reunion, you and Gil and me and my aunt. Isn't that funny?"

His face snapped toward mine. "Do you always talk so much?"

"Mainly when I'm scared. I need to go. I have to get to a bathroom." That statement was half true.

"I loved her."

His blurted words seemed so out of place, I glanced aside to see if he'd spoken to someone else. But nobody else was with us in this cell-like space.

I eyed the doorway, too many steps behind me to run out before he could grab me. I needed to keep him talking. Fright pushed down on my shoulders. My lungs felt nearly empty. My only hope for safety was to have someone page him. If a call came through on a speaker, I would scream for help. At least then he might let me get away so he could hide or loosen a lifeboat and drop it into the sea and go away inside it.

I did a mental head slap. What did I think this man had done? Just because goose flesh popped up on my arms, I had no proof that he did anything wrong.

"I'll just go." I turned toward the door.

He grabbed my wrist, yanking me back. "I did love her."

"Okay." I kept my head nodding. "Love is a really nice thing."

"Nobody else knows," he said, face closer to mine, eyes intent. "Nobody has any clue how much Tetter meant to me."

"I'm so glad you're telling me. If you want me to share that information, I will. If not, I won't."

His head-shake and raised eyebrows told me I'd said the wrong thing.

Somewhere in the distance, a man made announcements. The faint sound of soft rock music trailed down from an upper deck.

"I have to tell someone," he said, expression so sincere, I nodded. "We met nine months ago when I was ashore."

"Ah, of course. The ship's crew gets to take a break between shifts."

"And she loved me." The insistence of his expression left no room to mention doubt. "But I wanted her. I wanted her all to myself."

"She was married," I said in a soft tone, although the words seemed to mean nothing to him.

"I thought this time she would commit to me." He inhaled, slowly exhaled. "But she showed me. She saw that Jonathan fellow and hopped in the sack with him."

"The Jonathan who—"

"His body is in that morgue." Dr. Thurman pointed to the rear.

I didn't dare move my eyes away from him.

He peered toward where dead bodies reclined as he continued to speak. "She told me he was so sweet. That was kind of her joke. She pointed him out to me and said he was diabetic. He was also extremely punctual. So I fixed a needle for her sweet guy and slipped it into my pocket. I easily discovered when and where he'd be eating."

I took a tiny step back.

He nailed me in place with his glare. "So I dressed like lots of other guys with a sweater over my shirt and a cap and glasses. I found her Jonathan outside the dining room." The doctor smiled. "A quick shot of potassium chloride jabbed into him stopped his heart. I nudged him to the stairwell, where he fell, and then quickly changed my clothes."

My mouth dried. Legs wobbled.

He gripped my wrist. "She still didn't believe me and said I could go straight to hell. I showed her. But then she said she slept with that guy from your class."

"Randy," I managed to squeeze out.

"I plan to kill him next."

My chest emptied of air.

"And I will," the doctor said, pulling me, making me walk with him. His hand that didn't hold me opened a slim drawer and dug inside it.

"Don't kill Randy," I managed to squeak.

"Oh, but I will. Maybe not on this trip. Maybe not until he disembarks, but he'll be gone. And no one will know why."

I'll know. The words filled my mouth. I clamped my teeth to keep them inside.

"We made mad love during this cruise," he said with a wide smile. "You and your group probably missed her at times. She was fantastic in bed."

"But then she died."

He peered aside as though seeing where she was. "She has a place in our morgue, too. A shame. I didn't plan for her to be discovered. Except by ravenous sea creatures."

Nausea swept up. "You?"

"I insisted she stay with me, but she swore that before the day was over, she would sleep with another member of our staff, probably our executive chef. He's my good friend. I couldn't let her exchange sexual favors with him."

The doctor glanced into the drawer. He removed a needle and a vial.

"No," I said, for some reason thinking I could straighten out facts. "That chef liked me. I barely met him, and he sent chilled champagne and glasses to my stateroom."

The doctor laughed. "So he thought you were the slut."

"What?"

A fiendish chuckle left his lips. "I'd told him I had a woman coming on board who jumped into bed with any man with the right part, and he wanted to bet he could get her first. He knew she would be with a group, like a small class reunion."

"So Chef Sandkeep found out about our planned reunion and decided the loose woman was *me?*" I shrieked.

He snorted with laughter.

"What did you do to Tetter?" I asked, fury building. "Did you give her a shot of that stuff you put in the needle for Jonathan?" And, I feared, it was the same stuff he was drawing into that needle for me. "Because if you did—and if you're even thinking of doing that again—the police will get you, you know."

"She screamed while we were in a stateroom close to yours."

Seconds passed before I realized what he was talking about. "I thought that was Tetter's voice, but I couldn't find her."

"She said I'd gotten too rough with her." He shook his head, his vision seeming to momentarily go inside. "She was going to get drunk and ran out of the room crying. I waited awhile and then hurried off the opposite way, again in disguise."

That must have been why the bartender in the ship's aft

didn't seem to want me to buy her any drinks. She'd probably run in there crying and then started tossing down liquor.

"Tetter was even easier to kill. I met her later in another
room and told her I loved her. She laughed. She said I was
only one of the many men she was making out with. I got
furious and just threw her out over the side since the outdoor
security cameras in that area weren't working. But I didn't
notice that tiny iceberg so close to the ship. I had no idea she'd
land on it." He let go of my wrist.

I rubbed it, still watching, trying to take in all he told me.
He lifted a needle. Aimed its tip at my chest.

"Don't do that." I could barely whisper. My tightened
throat snagged my words.

"It will be quick." He stepped closer.

I took a step back. "I'm not ready to go yet."

"Most people aren't."

"You'll get caught."

"I am a brilliant man. I can do things." He thrust his needle down at me.

I swerved to the side, letting out the most blood-curdling
scream I could muster. *"Nooo! Help me! Help!"*

He chuckled. "That would be easy to explain away. No
one is near us. And many people scream when they're about
to get shots." Dr. Thurman gripped my shoulder, his needle
aiming for it.

"Stop! Help! No!" I twisted around, determined not to
feel the slightest prick of that needle in any part of my body.

"Nobody cares if you love my nephew." His palm slid from
my shoulder down my arm. He lifted his deadly needle and
squeezed my fingers together, going for the top of my hand.

"I care!" I thrust my forehead against his in a major
head-butt.

He yanked his head back and glared. Gripping me tighter, he swung his needle toward my breast.

"Nooooo!" I yelled, crashing my head against his while forcing a fierce kick against his knee.

Sweat dripped from my scalp. No, it was blood dripping over my eye.

I saw nothing else.

TWENTY-FOUR

"CEALIE. CEALIE, SWEETHEART." Gil sat holding my hand, rubbing my arm.

"Wha…" I managed to force my eyelids apart. Tried to get Gil into focus. I lay on a soft surface.

"It's all right. Sleep now."

I slept.

"DID I KILL HIM?" I asked, waking again, searching Gil's face for the answer. "Did I kill your uncle?"

I was on the bed in his stateroom, much more awake than hours earlier when the medical staff took care of my busted forehead, and the security staff bombarded me with questions. More would come later. Many more questions than I wanted to think of, much less answer. But I knew many answers. I did not understand, could not understand. Yet it all happened.

Gil kept his pensive expression. "I don't know."

"But he had that stuff in the needle and was swinging it toward me, and I butted his head farther down and kicked his kneecap. What I did could have made his hand jerk down so that he stuck himself with it."

I recalled someone had told me he was dead. Meds in the needle had killed him.

Gil pushed hair away from my forehead. "Was that a bad thing?"

I tried to sort through my conscience. "Not if he was trying to kill me."

Gil nodded. "Everybody forgives you for not letting yourself be killed. My relatives all forgive you. So do I." He cocked his head and gave me the gentlest smile.

"I love you," I whispered, head throbbing.

"Smart woman." He pressed a soft kiss on my lips. "And I love you. You've always known that."

I savored his nearness. His love. I felt more grateful than ever that he'd been the one to find me alongside his uncle on the floor. Just as I had been searching for Gil, he had gone all through the ship looking for me.

I sighed, content that he'd found me. And I had found him.

"Relatives," I said, making him give me a curious look. "You mentioned your relatives. I miss Tommy so much. I wanted to see my son on this trip. And when I saw him with that man instead of his wife and children, I turned my back on him."

Gil kept his face level, giving no judgment.

"I need to see him. I want to call Tommy and apologize and tell him I need to spend time with him and his mate as soon as we dock. And soon after that I'll go and visit his wife and the kids."

Gil pressed a kiss on my cheek. "If you wouldn't mind company, I'll join you."

"Company would be great."

He gazed at me with a smile. "Are you hungry? I can order something. I heard there's this great Cajun food on the ship."

"Later. I'll want to see my classmates later, too."

"Jane begged me to tell you she's sorry she was so mean. She really didn't care if you dated her brother." He leaned to stare into my eyes. "Want to tell me about that?"

"Sure, and you'll tell me who you've taken so many cruises with."

He grinned. "My parents brought me several times when I was a kid, and once I started making money, I brought them. We all love to cruise, especially in this area."

I felt my tense face relaxing.

"Randy said he hopes you get better soon, and Sue asked me to apologize for her. She acted poorly because she wondered if you cared about her at all. She feared you might consider her a freak and wish she would have remained your uncle instead of becoming your aunt."

I let out a laugh and shook my head. "I twisted my ankle because I wanted to be like her with those spiked heels. I'll have to tell her to just be herself, and people will like her."

"And maybe counseling would be good for her. Anyway, they've all been asking about you. I said you were okay, but they couldn't see you now." He gently touched my face. "Now you're with me."

"I'm so happy I am."

"Stay with me, Cealie."

"In your room?"

"At my side." He gazed into my eyes. "Always."

During the time since I became a widow, I had been searching for myself. I'd tried to find the true Cealie and determine what she wanted from the rest of her life. I called to mind my mantra: *I am woman. I can do anything—alone.*

And now I knew. I was an independent woman who *could* go through life alone. But I didn't choose to. What I wanted from the rest of my life was to remain alongside this wonderful man.

I leaned my head against Gil's shoulder. "I'm here to stay."

* * * * *

SEAFOOD GUMBO LA BOB

First make a roux:
½ C. all-purpose flour
½ C. vegetable oil
In a heavy pot, stir together over a medium fire until golden brown.

Then add these:
1 large onion, chopped
½ bell pepper, chopped
2 stalks of celery, chopped
3 cloves of garlic, chopped
1 t. salt
1 t. pepper

Stir continuously over medium heat. You may have to add ½ C. water to prevent sticking or burning. After stirring for 5 or 10 minutes, add about 3 more cups of water.

You might add 3 or 4 crabs that have been halved. Cook mixture 15–20 minutes. Add ¾ C. water. Cook 15 minutes. Add 1 lb. shrimp and ½ lb. crabmeat. Cook 10 minutes and serve in bowls over cooked rice.

Scrumptious!

BOB'S SHRIMP ÉTOUFFÉE

3 lbs. chopped onions
⅓ stick of butter or margarine
⅓ C. vegetable oil
1 t. salt
1 t. black pepper
½ t. corn starch
1½ lbs. medium shrimp

In a heavy pot combine all ingredients except corn starch and shrimp. Cook over medium heat until onions caramelize. (About ½–⅔ hr.) Add shrimp and corn starch. Cook until shrimp are pink and look done, about 20 minutes. Eat in a plate over cooked rice.

So good it makes you want to slap your mamma! Enjoy!

REQUEST YOUR FREE BOOKS!

2 FREE NOVELS
PLUS 2 FREE GIFTS!

Your Partner in Crime

YES! Please send me 2 FREE novels from the Worldwide Library® series and my 2 FREE gifts (gifts are worth about $10). After receiving them, if I don't wish to receive any more books, I can return the shipping statement marked "cancel." If I don't cancel, I will receive 4 brand-new novels every month and be billed just $5.49 per book in the U.S. or $6.24 per book in Canada. That's a savings of at least 31% off the cover price. It's quite a bargain! Shipping and handling is just 50¢ per book in the U.S. and 75¢ per book in Canada.* I understand that accepting the 2 free books and gifts places me under no obligation to buy anything. I can always return a shipment and cancel at any time. Even if I never buy another book, the two free books and gifts are mine to keep forever.

414/424 WDN F4WY

Name	(PLEASE PRINT)	
Address		Apt. #
City	State/Prov.	Zip/Postal Code

Signature (if under 18, a parent or guardian must sign)

Mail to the Harlequin® Reader Service:
IN U.S.A.: P.O. Box 1867, Buffalo, NY 14240-1867
IN CANADA: P.O. Box 609, Fort Erie, Ontario L2A 5X3

Want to try two free books from another line?
Call 1-800-873-8635 or visit www.ReaderService.com.

* Terms and prices subject to change without notice. Prices do not include applicable taxes. Sales tax applicable in N.Y. Canadian residents will be charged applicable taxes. Offer not valid in Quebec. This offer is limited to one order per household. Not valid for current subscribers to the Worldwide Library series. All orders subject to credit approval. Credit or debit balances in a customer's account(s) may be offset by any other outstanding balance owed by or to the customer. Please allow 4 to 6 weeks for delivery. Offer available while quantities last.

Your Privacy—The Harlequin® Reader Service is committed to protecting your privacy. Our Privacy Policy is available online at www.ReaderService.com or upon request from the Harlequin Reader Service.

We make a portion of our mailing list available to reputable third parties that offer products we believe may interest you. If you prefer that we not exchange your name with third parties, or if you wish to clarify or modify your communication preferences, please visit us at www.ReaderService.com/consumerchoice or write to us at Harlequin Reader Service Preference Service, P.O. Box 9062, Buffalo, NY 14269. Include your complete name and address.

WWL13R

REQUEST YOUR FREE BOOKS!
2 FREE NOVELS PLUS 2 FREE GIFTS!

HARLEQUIN®

INTRIGUE®

BREATHTAKING ROMANTIC SUSPENSE

HIDIR13R